Paul hadn't been on the scene initially when the body was found quite by accident, but he knew it was very likely that *murder* had been added to an already-convoluted puzzle that he and Dorothy were trying to solve...

They grew quiet, looking into the room where the coroner attended his newest client. A long narrow crate stood open on the floor. Packing straw and more of the same colorful cloth spilled over the edges. The coroner crouched over the coffin-like crate. Although Paul could see into it from his vantage point, Dr. Davidson's frame blocked the view of the victim's face, as he lay within the confines of the container.

Jim stood a few feet from the coroner, whose assistant was carefully taking photographs from various angles.

The doctor seemed oblivious to others in the room, so intent was he on gathering evidence and information that would aid in determining the cause of death. He began to speak, as if to himself, and Paul had to strain to hear what he was saying. "The deceased appears to be young Asian male, late thirties—early forties, no visible sign of trauma. Body temp indicates he's been dead quite a while, rigor has come and gone." He straightened up, and turned to address Jim. "Sorry, Jim, I really don't have much at this point, but I'll know more once I can complete a more thorough exam."

When Dr. Davidson stood up, the victim's face became visible, and Paul gave an audible groan.

"You recognize him?" Dorothy asked.

Giving a big sigh, Paul admitted, sadly, that he did.

What do Geisha dolls, industrial espionage, and a mysterious silken fabric have in common?

Though it sounds like the lead-in to a bad joke, it's the riddle that Portland, Oregon, private investigator Dorothy Dennehy has to solve when she's hired by businessman Paul Webster. Paul's company has become entangled in the rivalry between a firm he's merging with and a no-holds-barred unsavory competitor. While Dorothy's background as a cop—combined with her expertise in using disguises—comes into play, Paul's skills as a former intelligence officer are also an asset as the two work together to save his company from ruin. Dodging murder and kidnapping attempts, Paul and Dorothy follow a trail of clues leading to a long-forgotten art-and-antiquities theft…and murder. But the discovery of a body, showing a lack of the expected decay, has everyone puzzled. Can Paul and Dorothy survive long enough to unravel the mystery, or will they become the devious killer's next victims?

KUDOS for *The Silk Shroud*

In *The Silk Shroud* by Jamie Tremain, Paul Webster is a Portland, Oregon, entrepreneur whose company is merging with a Japanese firm that has invented a miracle fabric and is embroiled in a fierce rivalry with a Chinese company trying to create a knock-off fabric. When strange things begin to happen, including Paul's acquisition of two geisha dolls, he hires PI Dorothy Dennehy to help him unravel the mystery. But as the two struggle to put the clues together, the stakes are upped with kidnapping and murder and the theft of priceless antiques. Now the two need answers—and fast—if they are going to survive the investigation. Told with a unique and refreshing voice, the story is a combination of an intriguing mystery and a sweet romance, a book mystery and romance fans alike will love. ~ *Taylor Jones, The Review Team of Taylor Jones and Regan Murphy*

The Silk Shroud by Jamie Tremain is the story of corporate greed, espionage, and corruption. When successful Oregon businessman, Paul Webster enters into negotiations for merging his firm with a Japanese company, weird things begin to happen. Suddenly, Paul becomes the not-so-pleased owner of two Japanese geisha dolls in silk kimonos. The dolls show up in mysterious circumstances, and then one of the dolls gets shredded while on the backseat of Paul's car. But when a Chinese company, a fierce competitor of the Japanese firm Paul is merging with, claims to be the owner of the dolls and demands their return, Paul realizes that he's missing something, and he hires a local private investigator, Dorothy Dennehy, to help him solve the mystery. But Paul and Dorothy soon discover that the problem is much bigger than just two strange dolls. Someone involved with one of the foreign companies is hiding a dark secret, and they will stop at nothing, including murder, to keep it from being exposed. A mystery skillfully merged with a romance, *The Silk Shroud* is charming, intriguing, and fast-paced. Hard to put down once you pick it up, it's got a little something for everyone. ~ *Regan Murphy, The Review Team of Taylor Jones and Regan Murphy*

ACKNOWLEDGEMENTS

We'd like to acknowledge the fact that many people contributed to *The Silk Shroud* becoming a reality. We'd like to thank our families, friends, and all our contacts within the writing community for never-ending encouragement. Special thanks to our Killer Author Writing Group, and to Black Opal Books for believing in us.

The Silk Shroud

Jamie Tremain

A Black Opal Books Publication

THE SILK SHROUD
Copyright © 2017 by Jamie Tremain
Cover Design by Jack Jackson
All cover art copyright © 2017
All Rights Reserved
Print ISBN: 978-1-626946-17-0

First Publication: FEBRUARY 2017

Published by Black Opal Books http://www.blackopalbooks.com

DEDICATION

Dedicated from Pam to Peter
~ whose love and support never wavered.

Dedicated from Liz to Bob
~ with thanks for his ongoing encouragement and belief
that The Silk Shroud *would be a success.*

Chapter 1

I *diot*!" Paul Webster swore at the speeding van that cut in front of him.

Before he had time to react, one of the rear doors opened and a garbage bag was tossed at him. He swerved his car to the side of the rain-soaked road, jamming on the brakes, as the bag bumped its way to the ditch behind him.

He glared at the disappearing van, wishing he'd noted the licence plate to report them for illegally dumping trash.

Then he took a second look at the bag and shifted into park.

He swore under his breath. "A hand? Blast it—I'm late for the meeting. I don't have time for this."

But he was already opening the door to step out of his car, despite the drizzling rain and his tight schedule. After all, he was only minutes away from his Portland office. More to the point, he couldn't dismiss what he'd seen. No way would his conscience let him drive on without investigating.

Probably a load of old clothes or trash.

Reaching for his phone, Paul sent a quick text to his assistant Catherine.

~ *Running late—hold the merger group till I get there.*

His imagination raced ahead. Would he find a body, or worse—a dismembered one? Spending time in the military had certainly exposed him to bodies, but this wasn't something he had expected. Today, of all days, he didn't need to be late for a crucial meeting.

Paul eyed the green trash bag, lying so still. He surveyed his surroundings. Without thinking, he grabbed a small branch lying nearby, wishing he had a pair of disposable gloves and praying he wouldn't find a child's body inside.

The first gentle prod yielded to softness. A little more force and he met with resistance. He was rewarded with a small tear in the plastic, now slick with rain. Needing to see more, he enlarged the hole. Instinctively, he held his breath and prepared to start breathing through his mouth.

"What the—"

It was a body all right, but not human. Glossy jet-black hair showed through the opening, and was clearly the crowning glory of an oversized doll. Stooping down for a closer look, he marveled at the exquisite detail of the fully dressed, life-like creation. Its appearance reminded him of a geisha, with its vibrant colorful kimono and ghostly face. Tucked into the waistband of the garment lay a bamboo fan, folded at the ready, and, by her side, a proportionately sized parasol. Her tiny feet wore fitted white socks and wooden sandals.

Thinking it might make a special gift, once cleaned, Paul carefully picked up the doll. It was about three feet tall. Although the head was porcelain, the suppleness of the body felt real. The eyes spoke to him of an age-old sadness.

He thought Kimi a good name for the doll, reminding him of a girl he'd met once in Japan. This made him smile as he laid her carefully on the back seat of his car, wiping rain drops from her face. He grabbed a travel blanket and draped it over top of her.

Thankful it wasn't a real body, his mind switched gears. His expectations for the upcoming merger were now in jeopardy. Being late was not an option for this group.

Thoughts of apology ran through his mind as he arrived at his office building. He noticed a silver sedan close behind, but didn't pay much attention as he swiped his security pass to gain entrance to the underground parking.

Paying top dollar for rent in the building allowed for some extra perks.

He tossed his keys to the valet and exchanged the usual comments about the weather with him on his way to the elevator.

The doors slid together and he groaned as he realized he'd left his laptop and business notes in the car. He pounded the button to return to the parking level.

Could anything else work against me this morning? he wondered, urging the elevator to hurry.

His car was already parked in its designated stall. He strode toward it and stopped. Two men approached his car. Owning a late model Audi, Paul knew car theft was a possibility.

Concerns about the pending meeting were pushed to the side.

He didn't think they'd spotted him. Curious as to their intent, he crouched behind another vehicle. He didn't question what sixth sense made him cautious. Those instincts had saved his life on more than one occasion.

From his position, he observed the pair draw closer

toward his car, and he eased out the breath he'd been holding.

The respite was brief. He watched in disbelief as they used a remote, not unlike his own, to unlock his car. Pulling out the doll, they seemed to give her a cursory look before putting her back. Outnumbered, he kept silent, containing his anger at the violation of his vehicle. His fists clenched, he wanted to confront them, but he also needed to see where this was headed. Another car approached and the two men casually walked away from his vehicle. They crossed the parking level to a silver car, got in, and headed toward the exit. The license plate was too far away to read. Once the car was out of sight, Paul straightened up.

Where the hell did they get a duplicate of my remote?

Grabbing his laptop and notes, he considered taking the doll with him, but as he slammed the door shut, he decided to leave it in the car

His eyes traveled upward, seeking security cameras. "Big help you've been," he muttered, shaking his head.

Security and I'll be talking once the meeting's over.

Needing to calm down, he let out a huge breath and rocked back and forth on his heels—a trick he'd picked up in the service to regain control. Calmer, he turned toward the elevators. He had to focus on the meeting by putting all other distractions aside. The upcoming merger, and all its implications for his company, deserved his undivided attention. He was anxious, and excited, to present a new idea to the group.

Entering through the double glass doors to Paul J. Webster & Associates, he greeted the receptionist on duty, picked up some messages, and hurried toward his office. Plush carpeting absorbed his heavy footfalls. Catherine St. Ives's anxious face greeted him.

"Catherine, sorry for the delay. How are our guests?"

"They left, about fifteen minutes ago, said they'd be in touch later. They refused to accept any excuses. I'm sorry. I did try to keep them here."

He pursed his lips, "Of course—just the way this day has gone. Not your fault, I had one delay after another getting here. I'll talk with them."

"What on earth happened?"

His response was abrupt. "I just saw my car broken into, but I'll have to save the details for later. Right now I need to call Yashito while you inform security I'll be right down to see them."

Her eyes grew wide. "*Broken into*? Where was security while all this was going on?"

"Good question. No alarm went off. They must have had a pass."

Her hand went to the phone. "I'll tell them fifteen minutes?"

"Make it ten."

He strode into his office, left a message of apology for Akiro Yashito, and expressed a desire to meet as soon as convenient.

Then it was time to deal with security.

He'd calmed down by the time he arrived at the security office. It was not Paul's nature to stay angry. But he made sure the man knew that he wasn't pleased when he greeted Don Franks, the burly security chief who could easily moonlight as a nightclub bouncer.

"Mr. Webster, your office told us what happened in the garage, and I'm going to personally review the security tapes and file a report with the police. Your car appears undamaged."

"Damn good thing it wasn't. My car's not the only one here that would attract thieves." Paul's voice rose. "How can an unauthorized vehicle get into the structure?

What good is a security pass if anyone can get in?"

Franks rubbed the back of his neck. "That's a problem we're working on, sir."

"For what we pay, I certainly hope the problem is corrected."

Franks' face tightened. "Security issues will be fixed by the end of the week, if a vehicle's not locked—"

Paul fixed the man with an icy stare. "It was locked. That's the problem. Somehow they had a copy of my remote."

"Not amateurs then." Franks turned to his desk and handed Paul some papers. "These need to be completed, even if nothing was taken. It'll be part of the police report. You'll get a copy." He scratched his chin. "So they must have been after something inside. Thieves that have those gadgets usually want the car. Unless they were spooked and scared off before they could steal it."

Paul didn't comment about his car's contents. If something showed up on the tape and he was questioned, he'd deal with it then. For now, he was done. "I'll have these back to you by tomorrow so you can get your report off to the police."

Still annoyed, he left the office and headed for his car. He gave a quick glance into the back seat, where the doll lay, covered with the blanket. A quick call to Catherine let her know he'd be at home if she needed him.

Turning onto his street, Paul felt the day's tension leave in anticipation of arriving home. The rain had stopped, and he took time to enjoy the newly washed green leaves of trees as they contrasted with the darker tones of rain soaked trunks. Many homes on the street attested to the green thumbs of their owners. Spring flowers were blooming, just waiting for lengthening days and warmer temperatures to bring them to full maturity.

His home was his refuge, where he'd moved after the

divorce from Sheila two years earlier. She'd kept the house they'd built when their marriage was in its first phase of happiness. The marriage lasted only five years, with no children. The more he worked building his business, the more estranged they became. It hadn't helped that her patience with his past and all its baggage finally ran out. During those years it had been easier for him to build his business than deal with his history.

But he was happy now in his own space and took pride in his garden, where he liked to entertain on weekends. Mountaineering and squash kept him in shape.

In his driveway, he shut off the engine and got out. Opening the door to the back seat and pulling the blanket off the doll, he went rigid with shock. Kimi's beautiful kimono had been slashed and the torso from neck to navel had been sliced cleanly open. Stuffing was everywhere.

∾∾∾

Private Investigator Dorothy Dennehy tried to relax on the small deck of her floating office, the *Private Aye*. The houseboat lay sandwiched between two luxury catamarans. It was the perfect spot to conduct the less than exciting business end of Dennehy Security and Investigations. Since she generally met clients off-site, very few knew the exact location of her home office, and she liked it that way. No point bringing trouble home.

She raised her coffee cup, taking a break from dealing with accounts and balancing the books. Staring ruefully at a spreadsheet on her laptop she bemoaned the fact that income didn't quite equal the number of completed investigations. She frowned as she scanned the numbers, reached for a bowl of chocolate covered almonds without looking, and popped a couple in her mouth.

Methinks it's time we hired a proper bookkeeper. I've got better things to do than this.

She closed the laptop, stretched her arms, and rocked her head from side to side in an effort to loosen tension knots that threatened to grow into a headache. Forgetting about work, she focused on relaxing by taking in her surroundings.

The deck had recently been painted in pale blue, its woodwork trim stained teak, and the only shot of color came from pots of geraniums. A sigh of contentment escaped her lips as she stared out over the Willamette River, feeling the gentle lap of water on the hull. She turned her face toward the sun and enjoyed its early morning warmth. A peaceful moment before promised rains arrived.

Placing her empty cup back on the table, she was reminded of what else she needed to work on this morning. The *Portland Tribune*'s business section yesterday announced the upcoming merger of Paul J. Webster and Associates with Yashito Design and Textiles from Japan. She'd only given it a cursory glance at the time and, fortunately, hadn't discarded the paper before her cousin's call.

Lucas Dennehy was a coroner's assistant. He and Dorothy were close friends as well as cousins, and he'd been instrumental in helping her establish Dennehy Security and Investigations, supplying contacts and referrals.

Last night he called with another lead. Paul Webster, a casual friend from the squash court, was apparently looking for a private investigator. Lucas hadn't provided much detail, but said to expect a call before noon.

She glanced at her watch, still a little time to do some research before the call came. Opening up the laptop, she Googled Paul J. Webster, first gaining information on his business.

Paul J. Webster and Associates had been established for several years and was prominent in the Portland business arena. Primarily financing companies in the bio-technology field, the company also backed innovative business ventures. Progressive thinkers open to new ideas kept them fresh and a jump or two ahead of their competitors. The latest news of the merger with a textile company from Japan seemed to fit their profile. The company occupied the top floors of a downtown Portland office tower and was financially sound, according to the post. Google led to some archived news items where Paul Webster received various awards and accolades from both business and volunteer organizations.

She followed a link on his name.

He was divorced, early forties, had built his company from the ground up, and was highly respected amongst his peers. Photographs showed a tall, handsome man, graciously accepting applause in one setting and then, in complete contrast, decked out in mountaineering gear with a small group of rugged-looking men, victoriously holding fists in the air.

Another link led to a small article touching on a distinguished military career, ending with an Honorable Discharge.

She made some notes and opened a file, in case he did call and she decided to work with him.

Her phone rang.

"Dorothy Dennehy."

"Ms. Dennehy, my name's Paul Webster. I need some private investigation services and your name was highly recommended."

His confident, warm voice had a rich timbre.

"Yes, Mr. Webster, I've been expecting your call. Lucas let me know you might be in touch. How can I help you?"

"Well it's not the usual cheating wife or ugly disagreement with a neighbor kind of problem."

Dorothy laughed. "I've had my share of those. What've you got? Is it personal or business related?"

"I'm not sure yet. In fact, it might concern both, and it involves geisha dolls."

"Did you say geisha dolls?"

Now it was his turn to laugh. "Probably why the police don't take it seriously either."

Dorothy made notes as she spoke. "I can't say I've investigated any type of doll before, so I'm more than a little curious. Can we meet to discuss this in person?"

"Perfect. Its nearly noon. Can we meet over lunch?"

Dorothy put a book over the bowl of almonds. "You name the place, I'll be there."

"Do you know VQ?"

"I do, it's a favorite. They have a great Caesar salad."

"Excellent. Shall we say twelve thirty?"

"See you."

❡❡❡

"Great job on the McCready case. It's all yours to wrap up. Hand in your report and expenses soon as you can." Dorothy smiled at her right hand man, Holden Bartholomew. "Thanks for the ride. I could've biked over, but wearing this outfit, it might've been tricky."

"Must say, boss, this is a pretty fancy place you're having lunch at. Meeting a new client? Or something more personal?"

"A potential new client, a referral from Lucas. Someone with doll troubles."

HB raised an eyebrow. "Dolls, eh?"

"Not *that* kind of doll, real dolls, but not the Barbie

type either. It could be interesting. I'll give you more details if we take the case. You could be back on the clock
before the end of the day."

"Suits me. Call if you want to be picked up, especially if this rain continues."

HB dropped her in front of the restaurant and drove
off. She strode through the doors of VQ. As her eyes ad-
justed to the difference in lighting, she noticed the patio
was closed to the elements with a sliding glass wall. At
the moment, a sparkling sun shower rained on umbrellas
of deserted tables and dripped onto the lush foliage of the
restaurant's patio oasis.

Glad I brought an umbrella.

The hostess greeted her, and Dorothy informed her
she was meeting someone.

"Yes, he's arrived already. This way."

Dorothy followed the hostess and recognized Paul
Webster as he sat engrossed in the menu. She wasn't surprised to see he was impeccably groomed, not a dark hair
out of place. Tall, dark, and handsome to the point of a
cliché, his Armani suit completed the picture.

Paul glanced up as the hostess neared. Behind her
followed a confident, tall redhead. She appeared to be in
her late thirties and wore her long hair casually pulled
back.

As she neared his table, he noticed the freckles scattered over her fair skin.

He rose and extended a hand in greeting. "Ms.
Dennehy, thanks for coming."

She noted he was over six foot, and his deep brown
eyes were set in a face resting on a strong jaw line, already sporting a five o'clock shadow. She didn't miss the
appraising look from those eyes either.

Retracting her hand from a firm handshake, she said,
"I'm always glad to follow up on a referral from Lucas,

and I have to admit the geisha doll angle has intrigued me."

He smiled. "Let's order first, shall we? And then we can discuss my 'girls.' Would you care for a drink?"

"Just a Perrier, please," she said to the server who stood nearby. "And I'll have the Caesar salad."

"A pale ale, and the trout for me."

She looked around the room. "I haven't been here for a while." Gentle background music was piped into the dining room and tantalizing aromas drifted by as tables filled with hungry patrons.

"Hasn't changed much. As to my situation—"

"Do you mind if I take notes?"

"Go ahead."

Dorothy reached into her bag and laid a notepad on the table.

"You come highly recommended," he said. "Not just from Lucas either. I made a few online enquiries."

"Ah yes. The Internet—so much information available. The trick is discerning fact from fiction, or worse."

He swallowed some ale. "If anyone had told me a week ago that I'd need the services of a private investigator, I'd have laughed. I'm not laughing now." He glanced at his cell phone. "Sorry, waiting for a call."

He was all business and Dorothy gave him marks for that. Too often, new male clients didn't take her seriously. Maybe with him she could bypass the stage of having to prove herself. "Mr. Webster, I've also done a little background checking."

He held up a hand. "Please, it's Paul."

She nodded. "Dorothy." Putting her fork down, she said, "Even though you and Lucas are well acquainted, I've learned people don't always give me the whole truth, so I make it a point to arrive prepared."

"I'll do my best to be upfront with you."

"I read about your upcoming merger with a Japanese textile firm in the *Trib*. Do these dolls have any connection—you did say geisha, correct?"

He leaned back in his chair. "I don't believe in coincidence."

She flipped open her note pad. "All right then, I'll listen—you talk. Tell me what's been happening."

Paul summarized what had happened since his drive to work on the day of the merger meeting, up to when he found the gutted doll in his car. Dorothy kept her interruptions to a minimum until he was done.

"Can you describe these two who broke into your car?"

"Asian descent, good quality suits. Not more than thirty years old. One was slightly taller, maybe five eight? Clean cut. For all appearances, they could've been doing business in the building. They soon made tracks when another car drove in. They were silent, but worked in unison. It was eerie. Once they were out of sight, I checked the back seat. Nothing was disturbed so I grabbed my laptop and headed back to my office."

"Unfortunately, it's not a lot to go on, but it's a start. Any idea when they began tailing you?"

He frowned. "Wish I could be more specific, but I was focused on making it to the office. They could've been watching when I picked up the doll, or waiting for me to arrive at work. Sorry."

"No problem. Now, you said you left that day a little earlier than usual. Went straight home?"

"That's right. I wanted a better look at the doll. Those two must have returned. There was nothing neat about the damage. Something must have been hidden in the body, and they just tore through that outfit and slashed into the torso to find it."

"What'd you do next?"

"Didn't feel like carting all that loose stuffing through the house, so I locked the car and went indoors." He paused and glanced at his watch. "Sorry, I have a meeting at two-thirty so I'll have to try and wrap this up."

"Not a problem. We can meet again if we don't cover everything this time."

"As I was saying, I went inside, thinking I'd grab a beer, and see if this doll was connected somehow to the Yashito merger. Never got to the beer. Sitting in my living room was another doll."

Dorothy's head snapped up. "A second doll? That's no coincidence."

"Agreed. At first, I thought they were identical, but compared side by side there were noticeable differences in their outfits.

"You didn't notice any evidence of a break-in?"

"I do have a security system." He hesitated, and a sheepish look crossed his face. "But, maybe I didn't set it that day."

She smiled. "They work much better activated."

"Point taken."

"Was anything in your home disturbed or vandalized?"

"Nothing seemed disturbed. But finding the second doll inside my house pissed me off. Breaking into my car was one thing, and now this? So I called the police. Not much help there. They suggested the whole thing might be a prank. Said car thieves can acquire universal remotes if they have the right connections. My break-in obviously wasn't worth the time of day to them. Didn't impress me much."

Dorothy stopped writing. "I spent a few years on the force and have to admit a call such as yours wouldn't rate high priority."

Paul winced. "Sorry, no offense meant."

She waved her hand. "None taken. I've certainly heard complaints worse than that. Did you notice any unusual cars on your street?"

"No."

He fell silent and Dorothy took the time to more closely observe him. His jaw was set, and she sensed he was the type who liked to have all the answers. From what she was hearing, these recent events were probably more than just annoying to him. Her curiosity piqued, she was leaning toward taking on the investigation.

"I'd certainly like to have a look at these dolls. You still have them at your house?"

"I've hidden them. You're willing to look into this?"

She smiled as she closed her note pad. "Let's just say I'll give you my decision once I see them, how's that?"

"Fair enough. What time's good for you? I'm usually home around five-thirty."

"Five-thirty's good. In the meantime, I'll see what I can turn up on Yashito and make a few other enquiries."

She reached into her bag for her wallet, but Paul stopped her. "I've got it."

She handed him a business card. "My cell number is here if you need it. Otherwise we'll continue this discussion later."

Leaving the restaurant, she glanced at the heavy skies and was grateful to see HB parked across the street.

∂∾∂

Paul returned to his office, relieved that Dorothy hadn't outright turned him down. He knew the circumstances sounded very offbeat, and he had no real proof any of it was connected to his business. But Yashito seemed distant now, and Paul needed to coax them back on track. He'd do whatever it took to secure this deal, especially as he had new ideas to present. Pushing those thoughts aside, he prepared for his meeting and hoped it would wrap up on time. He didn't want to be late and keep Dorothy waiting.

Catherine handed him a note as he came through the door. She was smiling from ear to ear. "Yashito's ready to talk again."

Paul read the message with relief. They were still interested in the merger. He had one more chance to pull this off. "This evening?" he said as he continued reading. "They're sending a car to pick me up at seven thirty. It's not dead yet."

"Good luck."

Later, as he turned into his driveway, his thoughts circled back to events of the past days. Geisha dolls and unexpected meetings had not been on his agenda at the beginning of the week. He was glad Lucas had recommended a private security firm to look into these concerns.

Unlocking the door to his house, he speculated on the meeting with Yashito. While he would have preferred to keep business at his office, he was willing to do whatever it took to keep the merger on track.

Tossing his keys on the table inside the door, he started toward the living room, but stopped dead in his tracks. In the doorway, between the living and dining rooms, stood his newly acquainted private investigator.

Leaning against the door frame, with arms crossed and a smile on her face, Dorothy nodded. "Hello again."

Paul quickly recovered from his surprise at seeing her in his house and tried not to stare at what he saw.

She'd changed into jeans and a light green tee. Her long hair was pulled back under a ball cap. She looked like she worked out. Tucked under one arm was a file folder.

"Do you always startle your clients by breaking into their homes?" He was irked but admired her spunk.

Her smile grew wider. "As a means of proving a security system is inadequate, it's pretty effective."

"You've proved your point."

"What you've got now isn't much of a deterrent to a determined intruder. But I think we could beef up the existing system. I'll make sure it won't let you out of the house unless it's set. How's that?"

"Sold." He eyed the folder she carried. "Contract to sign?"

"Possibly. But before we get down to that piece of business, I'd like to have a look at the dolls. You've hidden them well. I had a quick look around and couldn't find them, so I'm curious—where did you hide them?"

"You're standing pretty close to them right now."

Paul followed her eyes as she took in the room. He refrained from saying "colder...colder," as her gaze wandered away from the hiding spot.

"In this room?" she asked.

He nodded, pleased to be outsmarting her.

"I give up. Show me."

He pointed to the largest segment of the sectional sofa. He moved over to it, grabbed the back rest, and pulled the sofa forward and to the floor so that its underneath was exposed. Duct tape covered a long section and Paul carefully began removing it. As the coarse frame-covering cloth was pulled back, the two dolls were revealed packed tightly together in the confined space.

"Well done, Paul. You show potential for this business."

He gave her a mock bow. "Would you like to see them?"

"Please."

As he reached for the first doll, he said, "I nicknamed them. This," he said standing up straight with one of the dolls, "is Kimi. Unfortunately, she's been damaged, and you can't really appreciate the craftsmanship that I first saw."

"What a shame," Dorothy said as he laid the doll carefully on an upright portion of the sectional. She turned her attention back to the remaining doll as it was removed from its hiding place.

He held out a beautifully outfitted geisha doll, still in perfect condition. "This is her sister, Yoko."

"It's stunning! I've never seen anything like this." She gingerly stroked a fold of the costume. "The detailing on this fabric is amazing. Must be silk, I'd think."

As she leaned closer for a better look, Paul caught the slightest hint of a very inviting fragrance. "There has to be a story behind them, and a good reason someone would destroy one."

As Dorothy examined Kimi, she nodded in agreement. "And in a hurry, too."

Paul watched expectantly as Dorothy chewed on her lower lip and kept glancing between the two dolls.

She faced him. "It looks like DSI has a new client. If you still want my help, that is."

"You bet I do. Especially since I've had a last minute request to meet with Yashito this evening. Looks like the interest is still there."

"You must be relieved. Let me make a call."

She reached for her cell phone and tapped in some numbers. "Lucas. I might have some work for you if you're interested."

Paul listened as Dorothy explained to her cousin that she wanted to bring some samples for him to examine.

"Great...First thing tomorrow if that's okay...See you then."

"So Lucas can make use of the coroner's facilities to

help you out? That's a good set up," Paul said as the call ended.

"It's a long story, but let's just say that, because of help I've provided in the past, the coroner owes me a few favors. I just have to be careful not to wear out my welcome. Now then, I'd like to gather some samples. Can you pass me that bag over there?"

He admired her take charge attitude and handed over the bag, watching as she took out small plastic bags, scissors, and a marking pen. She quickly took samples of the fabric, hair, and even scraped some of Kimi's "skin." With tweezers, she extracted a small amount of the stuffing for another bag. Marking the bags and sealing them, she tucked them away into the carrier. When she looked up from her task, Paul smiled at her.

"What?"

"Oh nothing, really. You just made me think back to my days in the military when I had to gather evidence. So much can depend on the fine details and, if evidence is mishandled, it can blow a case right out of the water."

"No kidding. So do you approve of my methods?"

"I give you passing marks."

"I'm much relieved," she joked back. "This should be enough for Lucas to make a start. If you're free, you're more than welcome to tag along tomorrow when I drop these off."

"I'd like that, thanks. How about a cup of coffee while we go over the contract?"

"Sounds good. What time's your session with Yashito?"

"Seven thirty—they're sending a car for me. Guess they want to make sure I'll be there this time." He inclined his head in the dolls' direction. "Somehow these have to be connected to Yashito."

"By the end of the meeting you should have some

answers. But I agree, geisha dolls and a Japanese company? Can't be a coincidence."

Over coffee, Dorothy outlined details of the contract and the fees her company would charge. Paul didn't begrudge the potential small fortune he could end up paying—he just wanted answers and the sooner the better.

"You mentioned earlier you'd do some more digging on Yashito. Is it too soon to ask if you've found out anything?"

"We're working on it, and I'll email you anything I find out. But let me guess, you'd really like this before your meeting."

"I know, it's very short notice, but you probably have resources not available to me, and if there's anything not kosher, I'd sure like to know about it beforehand."

Her smart phone at the ready, she sent a quick text message to HB. "If anyone can dig up new info, it's my top agent. So leave it to us."

"Excellent."

"I'd like to drop off these samples early tomorrow. Is eight-thirty okay?" Dorothy finished the last of her coffee.

"My morning's clear. Shall I meet you there?"

"Perfect," she agreed as she gathered her things, "I'll see you then. Oh, and don't forget to set the alarm when I leave. I'll have a new system installed within forty-eight hours."

"I don't suppose I need to be here to let anyone in?"

"No." She laughed. "You don't. I'll be waiting to hear all about the meeting when we hook up tomorrow."

She leaned over to pick up her car keys. Their eyes met briefly, and Paul felt a charge of excitement. He'd be glad to see her tomorrow. "Pleasure working with you.

I'll be sure to give you all the details. See you in the morning."

As the door closed behind her, Paul reached up and set his alarm system.

Chapter 2

Only a short time remained before his appointment
with Akiro Yashito, and Paul finished showering
in record time. Choosing a pale gray suit and
matching tie, Paul wondered if he should shave.

He ran a hand over the stubble on his jaw. He'd have
to shave, even though he'd much prefer to wait till morning.

After a recent excursion to Japan, he and his mountaineering group had crossed Mount Fuji off their list of
conquered peaks. During the trip, he'd been approached
by Mr. Yashito, head of Yashito Design and Textiles—
the company he was now anxious to merge with his own.
Enjoying the euphoria of climbing one of the most beautiful sights on Earth, Paul had been reluctant to discuss
business. But when he returned to Oregon, the Yashito
company was waiting to talk.

He made a quick last minute check of his email and
was gratified to see a note from Dorothy. HB hadn't been
able to find anything out of the ordinary, but cautioned
he'd only had a short time to search.

Paul was grateful to be given a chance to make
amends for the missed meeting earlier. Still disconcerted
over the appearance of the dolls, he wondered if any con-

nection between them and the merger would be cleared up. Were they the reason for this new meeting, or was Paul J Webster and Associates to be shown the door. Paul was acutely aware that the missed meeting was a huge business faux pas.

I just need a chance to sell this new proposition to them.

Paul's company had, for many years, been primarily a financial backer for research firms, often underwriting start-up costs for promising newcomers. His business sense rarely led him astray and had brought him to pursue this new direction for his firm. Previous financial undertakings in the bio-technology research field had given him great success. Because this alliance had little to do with research, it had been a hard fought sell to his board of directors. He'd put a lot on the line to bring about this merger into a business area new to his team.

The doorbell rang. Opening the door, he looked up into the expressionless face of a tall and imposing chauffeur. Silent, the man merely glanced toward the waiting car, and turned on his heels leaving Paul to follow.

With no other passengers, Paul's attempt at light conversation was met with stony silence. "Can you tell me where we're headed?"

"We will arrive in ten minutes," was the curt reply.

Cheery soul, thought Paul, dismissing him from his mind. He sat back and tried to anticipate what this meeting would bring. He worried they'd want to back out, or change conditions of the offer.

No longer content with merely backing research, Paul felt a more hands-on approach was necessary. Ultimately his vision for Paul J. Webster and Associates saw the company as a leading-edge player in diversified fields.

Partnering with a proven industry leader such as

Yashito meant Paul was that much closer to realizing his goal.

A large and stately gray stucco building came into view. Many older homes in this area had suffered renovations over the past decade and resurfaced as elite businesses or day spas. With no visible advertising, Paul assumed this was still someone's private residence. The driveway was flanked by meticulously manicured lawns and flower beds.

The driver opened Paul's door, and, as before, gave no verbal instructions, but pointed ahead to the main doors. The door opened, and he was led inside by a member of the house staff.

The foyer was large and Paul was surprised to see such an abundance of greenery. Loving his own garden, he could appreciate the care and expense involved, as his eyes were drawn from plants to small trees and an array of delicate orchids. A barely discernible sound of trickling water had him searching for a fountain.

He had no time to linger in this peaceful oasis as he was led to a tastefully appointed formal living area, where several business men were quietly talking. Upon noticing Paul's arrival, the conversation ceased.

A slender, middle-aged Asian man moved forward and bowed. "Welcome to my home here in America, Mr. Webster. Please make yourself comfortable."

"Mr. Yashito," Paul said, returning the bow.

"My associates," said Akira Yashito. It was the only introduction Paul received for four older men who quietly acknowledged him. Yashito nodded toward the fifth member of the group who stood off to one side. "My assistant, Henry Yamada. He is my liaison here in America and you will primarily deal with him, should we proceed with our arrangement."

Paul guessed the pleasant-looking man to be in his

mid-thirties. His casual, but alert, appearance said he was more at ease than his older colleagues. As he spoke, Paul guessed that Henry Yamada was well educated and possibly American born. The man was doing his best to make Paul feel comfortable. His manner was the perfect blend of relaxed American society and Japanese formality.

"Please, Paul, we have tea and other refreshments, but if you have other preferences, I'm happy to provide them."

"Thank you. Tea will be fine."

Henry poured jasmine scented green tea into a delicate porcelain cup and passed it to Paul.

Taking a sip, he wondered who would start the ball rolling. He decided not to offer up anything yet but to see how Japanese etiquette played out.

He didn't have long to wait.

"Paul," began Akiro Yashito, "I am sorry our meeting earlier this week did not take place at the appointed time."

Paul felt the displeasure directed at him. It had been an obvious error on his part, but would it prove fatal to the merger? He mentally formulated an apology, but before he could speak, Yashito continued.

"The events which led to the canceled meeting have proven beneficial for my company." Yashito paused, but with no reaction from Paul he continued. "I believe on your way to our meeting, you were delayed due to an incident, which you felt inclined to investigate." Not a question, but a statement of fact.

Paul struggled to make the connection. His curiosity about what was going on and what these people knew was growing into a sense of personal violation. He cautioned himself to tread cautiously. If he wasn't careful, he'd lose the edge and excitement he wanted to share with his future partners. He placed the fragile cup back on its matching saucer and, in a carefully measured tone, responded, "It seems you're privy to information I'm not aware of. An explanation is in order."

Yashito glanced silently toward Yamada, who responded, "By way of explanation, I would say that you were meant to find the dolls. The reasons should become clear in due course." He paused as if waiting for Paul's reaction.

"We may both be full of surprises this evening," Paul said, not rising to whatever bait they dangled in front of him.

Henry Yamada allowed a small grin to cross his face, which was in contrast to the deepening frown creasing Akiro Yashito's visage.

The older man focused on Paul. "I'm not sure I understand. We, Yashito Textiles, intended the dolls as a ploy to test your commitment to us. It may have been unorthodox, but we wanted to gauge your curiosity level. And now you say you have a surprise for us? I sense our paths are about to cross. Ah, which may perhaps be an omen of our merger?"

Paul's mind began to connect the dots. The merger was built upon an exquisite fabric designed and manufactured by Yashito Design and Textile in Japan. They'd approached Webster and Associates to help them bring their award-winning product to North America. Already a proven best-seller in Japan, Yashito sought the backing and expertise of an American company to promote and market a textile based on a design heavily influenced by ancient Japanese culture.

"A good omen, I hope," said Paul. "It's about the fabric isn't it? The dolls were wearing it."

"Indeed, you are correct. However, we had hoped you would have made the connection before our meeting this evening. This has given us pause to reconsider the merger. We gave you time, but eventually we were the ones who summoned you. As you Americans like to say, there is more here than meets the eye."

"So the merger falls apart, even though you're the ones who changed the dynamics by throwing these dolls in my way?" Paul couldn't mistake the undertone of discontent and had to salvage this. "We're still talking about the fabric, I assume? Before coming here, I made arrangements to have samples from each doll tested. Is there something specific I need to look for—"

Henry Yamada clasped his hands together. "Mr. Yashito, with respect, perhaps we have not allowed Paul and his associates enough time to investigate. He has begun the process."

"How long, Paul, before you expect results?"

"I should have feedback within forty-eight hours." Paul was about to make excuses for the time but decided to leave it. "In the meantime, if you are willing to wait, I have something for all of you to consider. Something I believe will seal our merger beyond a doubt."

"You may explain," Yashito responded.

As Paul released an inward sigh of relief, he reached for his briefcase and passed copies of a colorful brochure to all in the room. "As we've discussed before, my firm and I are enthusiastic about partnering with you and bringing the textile designs you've perfected to the North American market." He opened the pamphlet. "One of my senior managers, Laura Innes, brought this to my attention, thinking this might be an excellent opportunity for you—well, actually, for us."

The pamphlet advertised an upcoming exhibit to be held later in the year at the Portland Metropolitan Exposition Center focusing on all things Asian—fashion, art, food, home furnishings, and more. The exhibit was to run for five weeks.

Henry nodded his head as he scanned the information.

I think he gets it, thought Paul. "I made enquiries and there is one display space available, which would be ideal to highlight your product and introduce our newly merged company. An excellent preview and opportunity for us to network and promote what we want to offer to the public." He paused then threw in the closer. "The organizers have allowed me until noon tomorrow to book the space, or it will be gone to someone else. What do you think?"

"Do we have enough product, and time, to offer a worthwhile display?" asked Yashito.

Henry jumped in. "We can make this work. We are all aware the textile industry we're part of can be considered a creative art form. With some thought, we can present a dynamic vision of what the finished textile would look like, as we combine technical aspects of different properties. Such as fibre yarn and extensive dyes." His voice rose with excitement. "We could move from clothing textiles to bed and bath accessories and home décor."

Paul agreed. "We're on the same page. With our combined computer design team and visionary ideas, we can take your fabric designs to many levels. Your commitment to being environmentally sound in your manufacturing, and having awards for reducing carbon footprints, is a natural selling point for this area. I see it as a win-win situation for us."

The room fell silent, waiting on a response from Yashito. His stone face gave no clue to his thoughts as he studied the paper in his hand. After a few more moments, he raised his head. Briefly glancing at his colleagues, he turned to Paul. "Yes, I am most interested in this proposal, but seek your indulgence for my colleagues and I to discuss in private."

"Of course. But keep in mind the deadline tomorrow to reserve space at the Expo Center."

"Do not be concerned, Paul. You will have our decision by the time you return home. Oh, it appears my assistant has more to say."

"I do. Before you leave, there's something we'd like you to look at."

One of the silent members of the group opened a briefcase and handed Paul two small swatches of silk-like material which appeared similar in texture to the samples Dorothy had taken from the dolls earlier.

Henry explained. "As you already surmised, the fabric we've produced is connected to the dolls you now have in your possession.

Glancing at the men congregated around the room, Paul said, "All right, I see the connection. But those dolls, exquisite as they are, were they necessary?"

"Paul, if I may ask for your patience a little longer, I will explain." Henry stood and turned to face Mr. Yashito and colleagues with a short bow. The bow was returned and Henry turned to Paul with a smile. "Yashito Design and Textiles apologizes for going about this venture in such an unconventional way." Henry paused. "May we continue?"

Paul nodded his head in agreement, but decided to wait and hear everything Henry had to say before asking more questions.

"While our two firms were in merger negotiations, we became aware of an unwelcome competitor for our design. In your hands you have two pieces of fabric. Please examine them and tell me what you think."

Paul placed the swatches side by side, examined them, held them up to the light, and paid attention to the texture of each. When he was done, he knew what Henry was after. "Obviously, one sample is a knock off of the original." He held up one sample. "This is your fabric, I believe. And, therefore, the other is a counterfeit. From your competitor?"

Henry smiled. "Yes."

"And do you know who this competitor is? Are they a viable threat to undermining our investment?"

A fit of coughing interrupted Henry before he could continue. Reaching for a handkerchief, he apologised. "Our biggest competitor is China. America and India are not far behind. China has all the resources in place, but we know our product to be superior."

Small nods of approval greeted Yamada's evaluation.

"And yes, we discovered a specific threat to profits."

Paul digested this for a moment, trying to predict how this might affect future plans. "How serious of a threat, and how concerned should we be?"

Henry seemed to find it difficult to keep his expression as unreadable as the rest of the room's occupants, and Paul picked up on an undercurrent of excitement in the young man. The color in his face had heightened and a sheen of perspiration appeared across his forehead. "We are confident the fabric we have produced is far superior. Our production techniques, which you have seen the specs for, cannot be easily duplicated. Any imitation would not stand up to scrutiny." The passion in his voice confirmed his belief in Yashito.

As if sensing he was too animated, he toned down the rest of his sales pitch.

Paul held up a hand. "I agree. What I've seen so far is of excellent quality. Our research backs you up as well. If I hadn't believed in it, and your company, we'd have never progressed to merger talks."

"But even though it is a superior textile, our vision is to produce affordable designs without relinquishing market share," Henry continued. "The concern is that our competitor, Jinan Import and Export, will undercut us with an inferior product and ultimately tarnish a reputation we've worked hard to establish."

Paul took a long moment to absorb what he'd just heard, then addressed the group. "Gentlemen, should you decide to proceed, and be part of the upcoming exhibit, we need an action plan to counter any inroads your competitor threatens. And I may know just the person who can assist us."

All eyes turned toward their potential business partner.

"The dolls which recently came into my possession were not by accident. You've now explained that. However, were you also responsible for breaking into my car, not once, but twice?"

One of the silent businessmen cleared his throat. He looked toward Mr. Yashito with a questioning dip of his head and, once receiving approval, began, "Mr. Webster, you must know we did our homework on you and your firm. We sought not only a sound and credible American company to merge with, but one whose owner meets our standards of integrity, honor, business acumen, and—curiosity."

Paul raised an eyebrow, but didn't interrupt.

"We have mentioned our competitors and believe they may be in this city seeking a similar foothold with their knock-off version. We were able to arrange for one of our employees to begin working with them. It was he who originally came into possession of these dolls, and so we arranged for the first to be dropped, literally, in your path, and the other placed in your home."

"So these are not technically *your* dolls?"

"Correct. The Jinan Import and Export firm legitimately purchased our fabric, but with the intention of copying it. They dressed the geisha dolls in samples of each. This would allow them to show a visual comparison to their potential buyers, thereby opening up the market to an inferior, but almost identical, product."

Paul tapped a finger against his pursed lips. "This puts an urgency on moving fast and ensuring Yashito's product is the only one available in the market as a legitimate fabric."

"Agreed," Henry said. "As you can imagine, we must not be found to be in possession of these dolls. It was not on our orders for this man to obtain them, but he felt it would help our cause. No doubt, our competitors are eager to retrieve them. I apologise for the intrusion into your car, but again, the men were working on our behalf, and we needed to be sure you actually did pick up the doll from the road—"

Paul cleared his throat, interrupting. "What good did it do to tear it apart, destroying its beautiful garment and gutting it?"

Yamada and Yashito locked eyes, and Henry shook his head. "Torn apart? I don't understand. We're not responsible for such an action. My men were only to make sure you had the dolls." He looked away for a moment.

"I have to think our competitors are closer than we thought, and they're the ones responsible," Yashito said. "I wonder why they just didn't take them back into their possession when they had the chance."

"Perhaps," Henry said, "they are waiting to see how we will handle confirmation of their intention to undercut us. We think you'll be contacted by representatives of our competition, who may be less agreeable than we are. If this causes you concern enough to back out of the deal, we will understand."

Glancing at an ornate mantle clock, Paul was ready to wrap up this little get together. "Gentlemen, we all have a lot to consider, but the ball is in your court. If you decide to proceed and be part of the exhibit, let me know as soon as possible. Then, as a new business entity, we'll work together to counter any possible threat from *our* competitor."

Mr. Yashito rose, followed in unison by the others. Paul did likewise.

In silence, the house servant once again appeared, providing Paul his cue to leave. She led him back the way he'd come and opened the door. The chauffeur and car were waiting to return him home.

Chapter 3

Dorothy arrived at the medical examiner's building the next morning, where Paul stood waiting. Together they entered the facility.

Eager to hear about his meeting the previous evening, she plunged right in. "And how did things turn out last night? Is there a connection with the dolls?"

He recounted the meeting. "But when they heard what had happened to Kimi, they seemed genuinely shocked. I'm confident they weren't behind it. They also made mention of business competition from the Chinese. I mentioned knowing someone who might be able to help investigate the threat. Hope you don't mind"

"No problem. What else?"

"They showed me two samples of beautiful fabric. At first glance, they seemed alike, but I soon saw the difference. One is definitely inferior. A knock off version. So now I'm curious to see if Lucas has reached the same conclusion."

"I imagine the fashion world can be pretty competitive. A profitable, high-image product seems to be a magnet for knock offs. Think Rolex, or Gucci. If this competitor is a threat, it falls under the umbrella of this

enter to win

Name: _____

Phone: _____

Your City & Prov: _____

Are you   18-24 ☐   25-49 ☐   50 +☐

Do you have a Mary Kay Beauty Consultant?

_____

☐ Yes, I love her!
☐ I used to, but I don't anymore
☐ No, I do not

thanks!

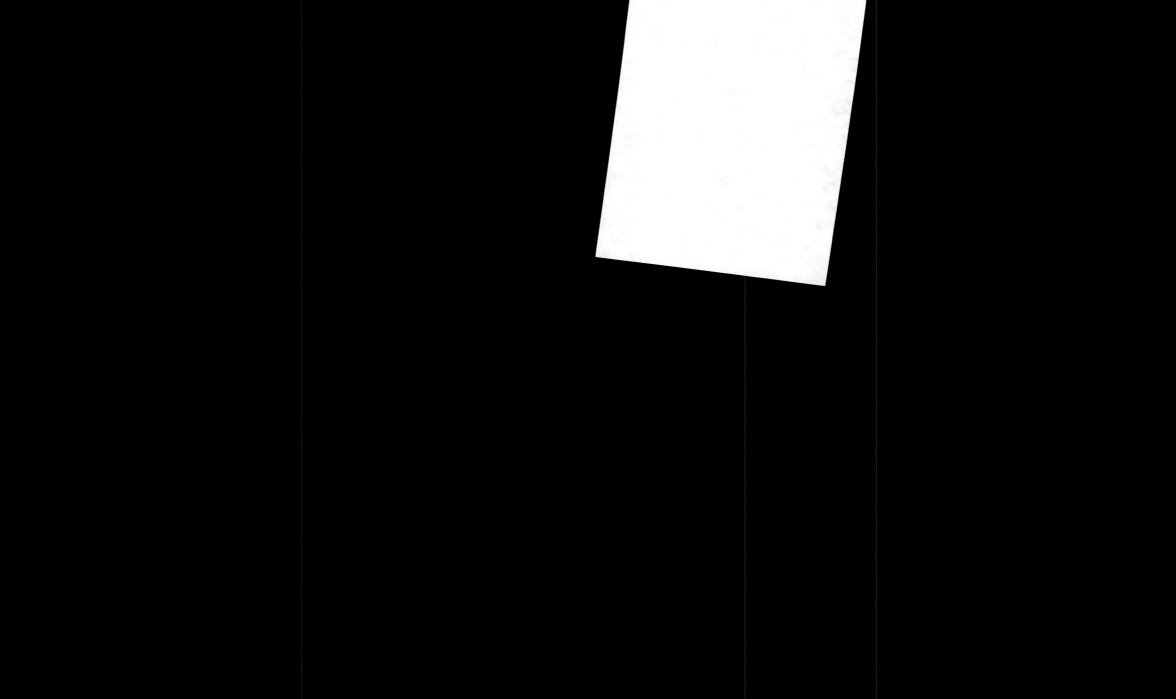

investigation." She wasn't fazed by the new information. "So how did you leave things?"

"True to their word, I had their answer by the time I got home. They have agreed to participate in the cultural exhibit at the Expo Centre."

"Good news for you."

"Yes, and it means the merger is back on track, but also more work ahead to be ready for the exhibit."

"Well, we'll have to see how Lucas can help us."

Paul had never been to Lucas's place of employment, meeting him only on the squash court. Dorothy, having been there on several occasions, took the lead and seemed to know exactly where she was going while they talked.

"Here we are," she announced stopping by a door sporting the name *Elijah Murphy, MD*. "Lucas is his assistant," she explained, opening the door.

A lone occupant sat behind a wooden desk, engrossed in his computer. Behind him were two doors, and his position implied no one would dare enter either of those doors without his permission. Framed newspaper clippings, attesting to the career of Elijah Murphy, adorned one wall, and a tired-looking philodendron occupied a lonely corner. One window allowed natural light to soften the room's austere feel.

The serious young man glanced up as they approached. His face broke into a smile as he greeted Dorothy.

"Good morning, Ms. Dennehy. Here to see Lucas?"

"We are. This is a client of mine, Paul Webster. Lucas is expecting us. I have some presents for him," Dorothy said, patting the small metal box she'd brought with her.

"I'll let him know you're here." He placed a call and, a moment later, one of the doors opened.

A tall, fit man strode out to meet them. With Dorothy's coloring and sandy blond hair, there was no mistaking the family connection. An engaging smile matched his light-hearted welcome. "You did say bright and early, didn't you? Come on back with me."

"So I finally get to see where you work," Paul said, following his friend and Dorothy down a short hallway.

"Sorry, no bodies here this morning. Hope you're not disappointed, Dorothy."

"I can live with the letdown, cuz." She laughed. "You've got to stop treating this place like a second home, you know."

"Guess I do spend a good chunk of time here, don't I?"

"Except when I'm not beating you on the squash court," Paul said.

"I'll be in better form next week. *If* you're still up for the challenge, *old man.*"

"Enough of the *old man,* I always enjoy an opportunity to beat you."

"Boys, boys. Back to business now. Paul learned last night there might be a Chinese connection to these geisha dolls we need you to check over. There may be more involved than we originally thought."

"Well, this seems to be taking on a real international flair, and that could tie in with what I'd heard about a Chinese manufacturer," Lucas said. "Not sure of the all the details, something to do with a new fabric impacting the fashion industry."

Paul chuckled. "You seem to know an awful lot about the fashion industry, Lucas. New hobby of yours?"

Dorothy smiled at the easy banter between the two.

"Yeah, well, it's my new girlfriend, you know. Spending time with her means watching The Style Channel and listening to what she's interested in."

"All in the name of love, right? But look, the time

hasn't been wasted, the in-depth knowledge you've gained of the fashion world may come in handy today."

Lucas laughed. "In-depth, huh? If you say so. I'm just waiting to see if she's equally interested in watching football with me."

"If she's serious about you, she will," Dorothy said.

"Yeah, well, maybe. We'll see. You know, my boss might be of help. He stays up to date on world events and not always the big news stories. He's always talking about information he's come across that I hadn't heard about. Let me see if he can spare us a few minutes. He'd like this story of yours."

He went off in search of Dr. Murphy.

Dorothy retrieved a small tape recorder from her bag. "Easier than taking a lot of notes."

Paul sighed. "This case could be more complicated than I first thought. You still game?"

"Nothing I like better than a challenge. It's all good so far."

Lucas returned to introduce Elijah Murphy, a tall lanky man, reminding Paul of a befuddled university professor. His lab coat hung open and pockets drooped under the weight of pens and unseen items.

"Just call me Murph. Glad to meet you both. The boy here says you've an interest in fashion design, and geisha dolls?"

Lucas rolled his eyes.

Paul nodded. "Thanks for agreeing to see us, Murph. Lucas thought you may have information or heard some news lately on a new fabric coming out of China. Anything ring a bell?"

"Hmmm. Well now, I don't rightly know just what kind of information I might have that may or may not be of any help to you," Murph said and then stopped as if waiting for instructions to proceed with more. "And you have yourself a private investigator on it as well?"

Dorothy nodded. "He does, and I've brought samples for Lucas to run tests on—when he has a moment."

"Any information you might have, even if it seems inconsequential might be of great help," Paul said. "Lucas mentioned there may be some new fabric the Chinese are onto that would have repercussions for me and my business partners."

"Yes, that's right."

"And?" Paul was becoming frustrated with having to have to pull bits of information from this man, piece by piece. He saw Dorothy smiling. "Does that mean you know something about it?"

"Why, yes, I do, as a matter of fact." Pausing, Murph seemed to be slowly preparing what he would say next, reinforcing Paul's initial assessment of him.

Lucas sent a glance of commiseration Paul's way. "Um, Murph? Paul has a busy schedule so if you could just give him some quick facts, then he can be on his way, you know?"

"Ah, well, it seems a certain Chinese company has become quite adept at producing excellent counterfeit textiles to undercut legitimate companies. They're continuing to perfect their production to the point of being indistinguishable from the original."

Murph removed his glasses and began to polish them. Paul suppressed a sigh of frustration as Murph perched the newly cleaned glasses atop his head.

"I don't suppose you have any samples of this fabric?" Dorothy asked.

"Wish I did. But you can be sure the criminals are closely safeguarding it, for obvious reasons. But, say now, the boy mentioned geisha dolls. What's the angle with them?"

Dorothy provided the ME with as much information

she felt necessary about Paul and the dolls. She opened the small metal carrying case and handed over the samples taken earlier from them. "These might be connected to the fabric you were talking about," she said, pointing out samples of brightly colored fabric. "We'll be interested to know what you think."

"I'll let the boy have a look first and he can consult with me if he needs my input. Only way to learn, hands on, I always say."

"We should go. We've taken you away from your work long enough," Dorothy said, closing up the case and putting her tape recorder away. "You know where to reach me. Lucas, I'll be waiting to hear."

Leaving the building, Paul squinted against the spring sunshine. "Nice day, no rain for a change."

Dorothy turned her face to the sun in agreement. "It does feel good, doesn't it?"

Paul felt a twinge of disappointment they'd be going their separate ways as he contemplated returning to the office.

"I'll be in touch if I hear back from Lucas. In the meantime, try not to pick up any more dolls today." She laughed. Turning away from Paul, she made her way across the street.

Paul found himself smiling as he admired the view of her retreating back.

ↄↄↄ

Once back at the office, he soon became immersed in email and phone calls. He discussed office details with Catherine and brought her up to date with the Yashito meeting the night before. He didn't mention Dorothy. Throughout the day, his mind wandered to the dolls and back to Dorothy, and he wondered if Lucas had any success with the samples. He decided to call a meeting for tomorrow and get everyone up to speed. "Catherine, I'm setting up a management meeting tomorrow. Follow up with them and help clear their schedules if need be."

She came to the door of his office, notepad in hand. "Do you want the usual coffee and pastries?"

"Thanks, yes."

She handed him a phone message just received. "Check this out. Someone sounds very full of themselves and seems to think you'll jump at her command."

He glanced at the note then leaned back, more than ready for a diversion. "Do tell."

"Her name's Alanna Scolfield. I've vaguely heard of her. Big PR hotshot in the fashion industry. Has write-ups in Vogue and other magazines. Reputation of a barracuda in some circles. From what I've gathered."

He chuckled. "Wonder what she wants with me?"

"She insisted you call right away and mentioned her new partners were a company from Beijing called Jinan Import and Export. Sounded like you should know exactly what she was talking about and that they're anxious to meet with you."

"Jinan Import and Export! Well, that *is* interesting. Our Japanese friends identified this company as a potential competitor. None too ethical either."

Further conversation was halted when his phone rang.

"Lucas, what have you got for me?"

"Buddy. Some interesting stuff going on here. I've got Murph and Dorothy on the line as well. Have to say getting my cousin involved was an excellent idea."

"Go ahead."

"Do you want the good news, or the bad, first?" Lucas asked.

"Just cut to the chase."

"Right. Well then, the two samples of fabric appear quite similar but, under scrutiny, there are definitely big differences. One is, according to Murph, extremely high quality. The weave and blend of various materials is superb. The dying process has to be second to none. We've identified bamboo, cotton, and, to a lesser degree, silk."

"I smell a 'but' coming," Paul said.

"But, there's also another component we've not yet been able to determine. Murph's going to be doing some research. Right, Murph?"

With a throat clearing cough, the older man joined the conversation. "The boy's right. Real curious to know what else is in the blend. Sure don't like being stumped, but no, not about to give up yet."

"Good to know. And, what's the bad news?"

"Paul," Dorothy said. "Yashito's competitors appear to be less than ethical. A whole lot less. Looks like, in order to compete with Yashito, they're willing to produce an inferior and potentially deadly, counterfeit."

"Deadly? Kind of harsh isn't it?"

"No, your friend is correct," Murph said. "As a means for the Chinese to mimic the Yashito design, with a quicker production time, they've used dyes which would never be allowed here in the States. Yes, I fear their production workers have been put at a severe health risk. And, I'm not so sure the risk wouldn't be still viable if this fabric were to get wet."

"You mean, someone's health could be compromised wearing it?"

"Bang on," Lucas said. "Nasty potential, all in the name of making a quick buck."

"Yashito should be told as soon as possible," Dorothy said. "Murph, can you email Paul and me a report, summarizing what you've found so far?"

"I can get it to you within the hour," Lucas countered. "Murph, I think, would prefer researching the fabric."

Paul chuckled to himself. *In other words, we'll get the report faster if Lucas sends it.* "Perfect. Appreciate it, Lucas."

"No problem, but after that I'm going to have to move on to other things. Murph will be in touch with any additional finds, but, man, I'm swamped with cases right now and will have the coroner and sheriff breathing down my neck if I fall any farther behind. In Murph's younger days, so he tells me, he was quite the detective and had a good nose for digging to the bottom of things. Any objections?"

"Fine by me. Dorothy?"

"Gentlemen, however you want to run your testing is good with me. I just want to see the results. We all need to be careful with whatever information we learn. No need to be paranoid, but choose carefully anyone to whom you want to share this information. 'Loose lips sink ships.'"

They ended the call with Murph promising to keep Dorothy apprised of any further developments. Paul asked Dorothy to stay on the line and relayed the call from Alanna Scolfield.

"I think you have your Chinese connection right there," she said.

"Any suggestions on how I should handle this?"

There was a brief hesitation before she responded. "If you want to meet me at my office this evening, we'll come up with a plan, and you can call her from there. I'll do some checking on her in the meantime."

She gave him directions to her houseboat and settled on seven o'clock for a meeting. Paul had no problem agreeing.

e∙e∙e

Dorothy enjoyed the best of both worlds. Working from a location she considered her home afforded her the luxury of enjoying the river's peace and tranquility under most circumstances. When trying to solve a problem, personal or business, she could be found quietly sitting on the houseboat's private deck, drinking in the view of the river and its coastline. To an observer, she might appear totally relaxed, but it was often far from the truth. Aside from her father and employees, not many had been on board, as she valued her privacy. Inviting Paul to meet her there had surprised, and excited, her.

This case intrigued her, as did he. Perhaps that was why she'd invited him to her sanctuary.

She smiled to herself. It'd been a few years since she'd been interested in any man.

All in good time, girl, she chided herself. *Business first.*

His love for mountaineering was well documented and was where most of his friends could be found.

Paul arrived on time, in casual attire. She'd been watching for him and waved from the dock at his approach. She smiled in admiration at her jeans-clad visitor. Attractive in a business suit, dressed down was even better. She put a brake on where those thoughts were headed.

Get a grip, girl, this is a client.

As he stood on the dock, he pointed a finger to the name plate, "*Private Aye*? Perfect name for your place, most appropriate. Pretty fancy neighbors, too," he said, glancing toward a striking double-hulled yacht beside her home. "Permission to come aboard?"

Dorothy glanced behind her and scanned the dock. When she saw one of her investigator's car tucked behind a truck, she turned back to Paul. "Welcome aboard, Paul."

He ducked his head to enter.

"Let me give you the grand tour." Dorothy was disconcerted to realize she felt a little nervous in his presence as she showed him a very sophisticated set up. The main cabin consisted of a comfortable living space with a couch that doubled as a bed, a compact kitchen, and dining area. A small corridor, flanked on either side by a toilet and shower, led to another room.

The flick of a light switch revealed a technology driven nerve center, with equipment hidden away behind cleverly disguised cupboards.

Her nervousness abated as she confidently showed him the latest in GPS tracking systems and a bank of switches and small screens allowing her to pinpoint the whereabouts of her operatives at any time.

"Close your mouth, Paul. You're drooling."

"Quite the setup, Ms. PI."

She just smiled, tilted her head to one side, and pointed to one of the couches. "Make yourself comfy. There's some beer—that pale ale you like—in the fridge, so help yourself. I'll be right back. I'm waiting on a report from HB."

"Can I pour you one as well?"

Flashing him a smile, she directed him to a small wine rack. "My poison is red wine."

She closed the door of the office and Paul opened the fridge.

He knew his way around a corkscrew and soon had their drinks on the table.

Dorothy joined him in the small living quarters, where he seemed quite at home. Raising her wine glass, she proposed a toast. "Here's to the beginning of a successful investigation and new friendship."

"Cheers to that," he returned. "I'm impressed you remembered the brew I like."

"Attention to detail is what investigating is all about. Now before you give Alanna Scolfield a call, let me tell you what HB has found out about the fashion diva."

"HB?"

"Stands for Holden Bartholomew. My best operative. You'll meet him later."

"I can see why he prefers HB."

She laid out some cheese and crackers.

"This'll hit the spot, thanks. You've got an amazing set up here, and I'm really impressed. Lucas referred me to the right person."

"Thanks, I like it."

There was an easy silence between them, and the sound of water lapping against the hull was peaceful. Dorothy was tempted to talk about anything but business, but her self-discipline took over. "All right, let me tell you what we've found out."

"Shoot."

"After I tell you about Alanna Scolfield, you can call her and see what she wants. HB's sent me her CV and it's quite impressive. Hard working ballbreaker is how he put it, but she has the credentials to back it up. She's been in PR for many years, mainly in the rag trade but her recent involvement with a company out of Beijing is really what we're interested in. It was all over the fashion news. Does the name Jinan Import and Export mean anything?"

"The name came up during my meeting last night as the competitor doing the knock offs, and Catherine said this afternoon that they and Alanna Scolfield's company are in some kind of partnership."

Dorothy spoke her thoughts aloud. "If Jinan is involved with a counterfeit fabric, it doesn't shed a good light on her. We need to know how this involves you."

"There's one way to find out. Guess it's time to make the call."

"In my office. I'll record it. Okay?"

"Lead on, you're the boss."

They moved into Dorothy's small office and sat side by side at the console. She handed him the phone. "Let's see what the woman's game is. She apparently likes to be in control, so perhaps you should play a little hard to get."

The call took no more than a minute, and Paul felt like he'd been steamrollered. He never got a word in edgewise, and all Dorothy picked up from the conversation was his agreement to see her tomorrow afternoon at three o'clock. When he hung up, they burst out laughing.

"I can't wait to meet the woman behind such a sugar-coated voice," he said.

They listened to the recorded conversation, and Dorothy then heard the instructions from Ms. Scolfield. In no uncertain terms, she needed to discuss his recent acquisition of geisha dolls. It was indeed a command performance. His presence was required at her home on Colbert Street tomorrow at three o'clock.

"So now we know why. I wonder about the real reason for these dolls," he said.

"What if I pick you up from work and drive you there? I can see what the place looks like and I'll wait for you—just in case you need rescuing from Ms. Scolfield." Dorothy beamed at his chagrined look.

"The rescuing won't be necessary, but I'll take you up on the ride." He finished his beer and glanced at his watch. "I'm glad the call is done and appreciate the information you've gathered. See you tomorrow."

"All part of the service."

She walked him back to the dock, where he said goodnight. She watched as he returned to his car, noting her team member was still on duty, keeping a watchful eye on her houseboat.

Chapter 9

During the brief meeting with his associates, Paul informed them of the pending changes regarding the upcoming exhibit with Yashito. He delegated to his most trusted staff the chore of cost comparisons, logistics, and demographics, coupled with a need for urgency in preparing their reports.

He refrained from telling Patricia Barry, his closest colleague and confidant, anything about the dolls or his private investigator.

He preferred to hold off telling them more until after the meeting with Alanna Scolfield. Mid-afternoon, he made his way down to the street. He'd only been waiting a few minutes when Dorothy pulled up in front of his office building.

"Looking for a ride?" she called out from her open window.

"You bet," he said, hopping in.

"Ready for this meeting?"

"As ready as I'll ever be. Thanks for the ride. I'm not keeping you from anything, am I?"

"No problem. I wouldn't have offered if I didn't have the time. And just so you know, HB's keeping an eye on your home. Don't want any other unwelcome visitors and, until the new alarm system is in place, let's not take any chances."

"Good to know. I look forward to meeting him."

"I'd be lost without him. In other words, I've put the best of my people on your case."

"I'm impressed."

Signalling a turn, Dorothy drove down a street represented by wealth and privilege. Gates and stone walls surrounded large estates, providing privacy.

She slowed the car, watching for the address. "Here we are." She pulled to a stop at the mouth of a large driveway blocked by a wrought iron gate. Beyond the gate could be seen a massive three-story home. The gate was flanked by a high stone wall where an intercom was visible.

"Fort Knox," Paul commented as he opened the door. "I hope you won't have long to wait."

"I'll park up the street," she said waving her phone. "I've some calls to make." She drove off.

Paul noticed a security camera above the intercom and before he could push a button, the gate swung open.

Walking up the driveway, he had the eerie feeling of being watched. He admired the manicured lawns and luscious plantings on either side of him. Two black Daimlers sat parked in the driveway, with chauffeurs resting, but alert, in the front seats. They glanced at Paul as he passed.

The house was immense and light spilled from ground floor windows. Just as he reached the front door, it slowly opened.

How melodramatic. Will there be organ music, too? The thought put a smile on his face and helped him relax. An elderly gentleman ushered him into a grand vestibule.

Entering, he heard faint strains of classical music, much to his liking.

At the foot of a Scarlett O'Hara staircase stood a striking woman with regal bearing. "Welcome to my home, Mr. Webster," Alanna Scolfield said with a throaty voice and outstretched hand. She didn't move but waited until her guest made his way to her.

A steely handshake accompanied a soul-piercing stare, held longer than necessary. Paul had to admire her sense of the dramatic.

When does the movie director shout "Cut," he thought with an inward chuckle.

"Your punctuality is appreciated, Mr. Webster. I'll do my best to ensure you are not wasting your time."

Paul gave a slight nod, deciding, as before, to watch and listen. Alanna interrupted his thoughts as she took his arm. She spoke to the butler who had ushered him in. "Johnson, we are not to be disturbed until Victor Lau arrives," Alanna said in the condescending tone reserved for servants in period dramas. "I'll ring if we need anything."

He'd been hovering in the background and now, at her command, silently departed.

Standing closer to her while she spoke to Johnson, Paul had more time to observe Alanna Scolfield. In her spiked heels, she was eye to eye with Paul. He pegged her age to be approaching fifty, and while he didn't consider her particularly beautiful, she'd gotten his attention. She exuded an overdose of confidence and self-assurance. It was no wonder she knew her way around the fashion world.

He now better understood Lucas's assessment of her ambitions and intelligence. No doubt, she'd built her business through sheer hard work and a lot of guts, developing a resolute persona along the way.

She opened a door into a room which could rival anything in Versailles. While it was stunningly decorated,

Paul noticed a lack of warmth which he'd felt when at the Yashito home.

Sitting before a marble fireplace were three men nursing drinks. At his entrance, they stood immediately.

"Let me introduce you to my business partners," Alanna said. "Larry Chung, Lee Chiu, and Eric Kiang, who represent Jinan Import and Export in Beijing."

Introductions complete, Alanna offered her guests canapés arranged on the coffee table. Paul resisted over-eating. He'd skipped lunch to meet with his board members.

Before any discussions got underway, he determined to assert some control. "Unfortunately, Ms. Scolfield, I've another commitment this afternoon so I won't be able to stay long. You didn't give me much notice."

His aim was not to appear as a pushover.

Alanna offered a saccharin smile and made sure her eyes found his. "But, of course, perfectly understandable. We'll keep that in mind. And, please, call me Alanna."

Paul smirked to himself as he recognized the beginnings of a concerted effort by Alanna to flirt with him. Two could play that game. "I appreciate that—Alanna."

He became aware of the presence of another man now entering the room. Immediately Alanna's attention was focused elsewhere. "Victor, my dear, you've managed to arrive in time! Splendid. Please say hello to Paul Webster."

Paul observed an impeccably dressed businessman and estimated him to be in his mid-sixties. The tight smile on his face did not quite meet his cold flinty eyes. His sallow complexion combined with the gray suit made Paul think of an eel.

A curt nod in his direction preceded a clipped, "Mr. Webster."

Sizing him up, Paul sensed that beneath the cold exterior lay a hot temper.

Ignoring others in the room, Victor turned to glare at Alanna and spewed his frustration. "Incompetent fools in customs, questioning my papers. Someone will pay," he threatened.

Alanna quickly explained that Lau had flown in from Vancouver, British Columbia, en route from Beijing, and had come straight to her home from the airport. His private jet stood on standby. "And Victor is, of course, the owner of Jinan Import and Export," she said laying her manicured hand elegantly on his arm.

Paul was more interested in the change which had come over the others in the room upon Lau's arrival, like children anticipating a parent's displeasure. Nothing about this new arrival impressed him in the least.

Shaking off Alanna's hand, Lau spoke brusquely to Paul. "Mr. Webster, I believe you have something of ours." Obviously the niceties were over. "We want them back."

"I wasn't told to bring anything with me. If you're referring to a couple of collectible dolls, I don't know who they belong to. What reason would I have for handing them over to you?"

"Reasons are not necessary. I will arrange to have my property picked up." Lau snapped his fingers at Lee Chiu.

If Lau's intention was to raise Paul's ire, he'd certainly succeeded. Maintaining his composure, Paul said, "With all due respect, Mr. Lau, how do I know you are the rightful owner of these items?"

Lau merely gave a dismissive shake of his head, where a vein pulsed in his temple

"I do *not* appreciate being jerked around," Paul continued in a more demanding tone.

Ignoring Paul, Lau turned abruptly to Eric Kiang and began conversing animatedly in Mandarin.

Quickly, Eric Kiang brought the conversation to an end and, with apology, addressed Paul. "Please Mr. Webster, we've no wish to upset you, we only want what belongs to us. We know you're a smart, an astute, businessman. We've been seeking the expertise of a company such as yours in order to gain a presence in America. You see we have a product we've created in Jinan which we think you might be interested in."

Paul folded his arms. "Go on, I'm listening."

"Yes, so perhaps we can resolve this situation to our mutual financial satisfaction."

Now we're getting somewhere, thought Paul. He took the time to make eye contact with each man and gave the appearance of weighing matters in his mind. But his course of action had already been set. Waiting a moment or two more for effect, he shook his head. "Please do not insult my intelligence by trying to tell me the dolls are not somehow related to this 'offer,' or assume I conduct business dealings in this manner." He turned on the hostess. "And just where do you fit in with all this?"

"Gentlemen, let's take this one step at a time. Paul's already told us he has another commitment, and Victor, you've just returned from a long trip. Perhaps a more agreeable time to meet would be helpful." Her carefully practiced smile was equally divided between Victor and Paul.

Lau's expression was unreadable, so Paul took the lead. "I'm certainly open to hearing more. But until such time, I feel no obligation to return *your property*."

"We'll meet again, the sooner the better," Lau growled with an intimidating gaze.

"Contact my assistant, Catherine St. Ives, and we'll set something up. Good day, gentlemen, Alanna."

Paul rose with his parting words and made his way to the front entrance.

Alanna was on his heels, and, before he could reach the door, she touched his elbow. "I do hope we'll meet again soon. My home's always open to you or, if you prefer, there's my office." As her hand pulled back from his elbow, she managed to offer him her business card. "My private line, don't hesitate to call, any time."

Paul offered what he hoped was a respectable smile at her veiled invitation, but made no comment as he left. Walking down the drive to the street, he had to make a conscious effort to shed the tension he'd felt since the moment he'd arrived. Glancing to his left, he was relieved to see the outline of Dorothy's car, and his step became lighter as he made his way toward her.

With a sigh of exhaustion, he slid into the front seat. "Home, James!"

She put the car in gear and accelerated. The more distance from Alanna's house, the more relaxed he grew.

Dorothy concentrated on driving, but, without taking her eyes off the road, she asked, "Well, how did it go?"

"I'm still trying to make sense of it." He paused and wrinkled his nose. "Her perfume is clinging to me." He gave a laugh. "Maybe what I really need is something to eat."

"Hungry clients don't tell me anything. So relax. I know a good place. Unless you prefer I take you back to your office to pick up your car."

"Lead on. The car can wait."

They drove for a short while and came to a stop outside a busy, well-lit diner.

"It's not fancy, but the food, and service, are top notch. With luck, we'll get a booth."

Settling in with a meal and coffee, Paul relaxed and let the tension drain away. He was ready to recount his visit to the Scolfield home. "Where to begin? Let's see, when I arrived at Alanna's lair, I found she already had company. Three business men, I assume from China, and we'd no sooner been introduced when a fourth arrived. She was all over him like glue on a stamp."

"Hang on. Let me make some notes." From her handbag she grabbed a pen and her notebook. "Does he have a name?"

"Victor Lau."

"The owner of Jinan Import and Export," Dorothy confirmed reading from her notes.

"Bull's-eye," Paul agreed. "The others there apparently work for him. He was quite insistent that I return the dolls, but wouldn't give me a reason. So I threw it back in his court and asked for proof he was the rightful owner of the dolls and why, exactly, should I return them."

"Good."

He continued to fill in the rest of the visit's details while she added to her notes. Lines of concentration creased her face. She laid the pen aside next to her empty coffee cup and reached for her phone. As she scrolled through screens, her head began to nod up and down and her eyes were bright when she looked up at him.

"Found something interesting?" he asked.

"Oh, I think so. I wonder just who is the rightful owner of these dolls. Because—" She paused and tapped her phone with a finger. "—I've received confirmation there's a prominent, and wealthy, Chinese family here in Portland, who are steadily accumulating an impressive art collection. You'll never guess one of the items they collect."

Paul tilted his head. "And that would be?"

"Oversized, lifelike dolls."

Chapter 5

Paul inhaled deeply and kept his eyes on his investigator. "And here I thought the day couldn't have any more surprises. So there are others out there like the two I have. Doesn't look like this is a one-off then. This family—do you think they're involved somehow?"

"Not quite so fast," Dorothy cautioned. "I need to review all this information before I go making any guesses. The sooner, the better."

He smiled. "As in, right now? I can take a hint. I'll grab a taxi and head home."

"No need for that. Hang on one sec."

He made eye contact before asking, "Can we meet up tomorrow?"

She nodded. "I'm sure there'll be more to go over by then." Picking up her cell phone, she punched in some numbers. "Hi, Dad, do you have anyone available to give my client a lift home? Sorry for the short notice but I'll fill you in tomorrow." She provided directions. "Ten minutes? That's great, thanks."

Paul gave her a quizzical look as he listened to her phone call. "Dad?"

"That needs an explanation, doesn't it?" She returned

his look with a grin. "I'd moved to this area because Lucas was here, and I needed a fresh start. My father had already retired from the force and had opened his own successful pub in Boston. When an opportunity here came up, he purchased a restaurant back at the Marina. Maxwell's Bar and Grill. It's named after him. It was basically an old warehouse someone had thrown a tavern in, but he upgraded the bar and expanded to a restaurant. He added living quarters upstairs. I divide my time between there and the *Aye*." She shrugged. "Anyway, not long after, I brought my dad in as an unofficial partner in my business. He's just the muscle I need at times, and he does try not to be over protective of me." She looked out the diner's window. "Here's your ride, and looks like it's Glenn. He'll get you home. Sorry to eat and run, but I'm on the clock to put this information together for you."

Paul laughed, even as a yawn threatened. "Got it. Don't pay the driver, just add it to my bill."

As they left the diner, she said, "We'll definitely meet up tomorrow. I'd like you to meet my unofficial partner at some point as well, and we can go over a plan of action. It's been a pleasure, Paul. I think we'll work well together."

"I agree. I'll wait to hear from you."

She walked him to the waiting car and introduced Glenn. With a hand on the door of her own car, she watched for a moment as they drove away, and then she too left.

A few minutes later, Glenn pulled into Paul's driveway, and pointed to the presence of HB parked up the street. "He'll be here for the rest of the night. Oh and I'll be picking you up in the morning."

"That's good to know, thanks for the update, and the ride," Paul said. "But I can call for a taxi in the morning."

"Not a problem, all part—"

Paul laughed. "Of the service. Got it."

He said goodnight and walked to his door. As he entered and reset the alarm, he knew it'd been a long day.

But he smiled to himself realizing how much he'd enjoyed the time spent with Dorothy.

Thoughts of her punctuated his dreams—where she chased drug-dealing dolls riding on dragons that looked like Victor Lau.

The next morning, Glenn arrived as promised. After Paul remembered to set his house alarm, they set off for the office downtown.

Catherine handed him a freshly brewed cup of his favourite java. Paul stifled a yawn. "I'm expecting a call from a representative of Jinan Import and Export. They want to set up a meeting between their number one, Victor Lau, and me. Anytime is good, as long as it's not before the management meeting."

"Got it." She looked at him a little more closely. "You seem tired. How did the meeting go?"

Paul gratefully sipped at his coffee. "I've a great deal of information to digest and, having said that, I need to prepare an outline of events and information for the meeting. I'd like you to attend as well to record minutes."

"Of course. I've pulled the file on the information we put together for Yashito Design," she said, handing him the folder.

He thanked her and entered his office. Mug in hand, he stood for a minute at the window and enjoyed the activity of traffic and pedestrians below as another work day began. The sun hadn't yet made an appearance, still hidden behind clouds. The coffee was beginning to chase away the cobwebs and he was ready to plan the day.

Sitting down to his well-organized desk, he glanced at one wall, covered with memories of his mountain climbing—among them were photos of Mt. Fuji, Table

Mountain, Ben Nevis, and closer to home, Mount Rainier. Some had been more challenging than others, but he recalled each with satisfaction. Finalizing the merger between his firm and Yashito was proving just as challenging.

Logging onto his computer he started on notes of an outline for the upcoming meeting with his team. After responding to emails, it was time to head over to the conference room. Already in attendance were two of his management team—Holly Westland and Laura Innis.

Laura Innis fit the role of a conservative and senior associate. Reading glasses were perched atop her head, and her calm, relaxed manner underscored her years of experience. Paul admired her negotiating skills, which were often in high demand as his business had grown.

"Good morning ladies," he said, greeting them and, as they responded, the rest filed in.

Taking the seat closest to Paul was Patricia Barry, often referred to by many as Paul's right hand person. Confident, but approachable, she'd been with Paul since the day his company had been founded. He valued her intuitive thinking and keen business insight.

Then there was Archie. Archibald James was a colorful character, proud of his Scottish background. His ever-present bow tie and suspenders often sported a tartan theme. A weathered face, thick gray hair, and lively moustache left no doubt he was nearing retirement. His normally scowling countenance relaxed in contentment when he could enjoy his pipe. Archie's analytical bent was often sought by Paul when considering new investment risks.

Catherine followed behind Archie.

Once everyone was settled, Paul brought the meeting to order. "Good morning. I appreciate you being here on such short notice. We've some new challenges regarding the merger to talk about, which you'll see on the agenda."

Some raised eyebrows met that comment, but they all waited for him to continue.

"First let me assure you that the merger is now finalized."

Applause greeted the announcement and the group was eager to hear more.

"I met with our Yashito counterparts and brought them back on line. After missing the earlier meeting, I had some back pedalling to do and, thanks to Laura, I was also armed with an enticing offer for them."

Eyes turned to Laura.

"I'll hand over the details to her in a minute. First things first, though. If you refer to the agenda, you'll see that a serious financial and marketing concern has arisen."

He went on to provide details about Yashito's competition and the threat a serious counterfeit product could produce.

Around the table, faces grew serious.

Archie scratched his chin. "These knock off products can impact the bottom line. Will it still be worth our resources to continue?"

"Now Archie, have you ever known me to back down from a little challenge," Paul asked with a smile.

"Aye, a little challenge, no. But this could prove financially irresponsible for all of us."

"I'm not taking this lightly, believe me. But I do believe we've had enough advance warning of this threat that we can develop an action plan to minimize the risk."

"Go on," Patricia encouraged.

"Not only did I meet with members from Yashito, but I was also invited to the home of Alanna Scolfield. She owns Scolfield Inc., a very influential public relations company here in town, focusing primarily on the fashion industry. She's backing another textile group, from China. Ironically, they're looking to make use of our business expertise to underwrite and market this product as well. However, no dollar figure was mentioned. The company owner, Victor Lau, is to contact me to set up an appointment." Paul paused to review reactions around the table. "But it gets better."

"Really?" Archie asked, with a raised eyebrow and sceptical eye.

Paul motioned to Laura Innes. "Fill them in on the proposal you gave me."

Attention shifted and interest grew as they heard her proposition for Webster/Yashito to participate in the upcoming Asian exhibit. She concluded by turning to Paul. "And now, you need to tell us, what did Yashito think of this?"

"They're in. Henry Yamada saw the potential right away and any reservations Akiro Yashito had were dispelled. Laura, I do believe your suggestion is actually what brought the merger to a successful conclusion."

Accolades poured over her.

"Glad it helped, Paul."

Archie appeared lost in thought as he absent mindedly tapped the stem of his unlit pipe on the table. "So with a nice red bow on top of the merger, what about this business with Jinan Import and Export? Is that something to be explored in another capacity perhaps?

"In other words, Archie, is there a way we can make this profitable for us as well?"

Small chuckles erupted around the table.

Paul raised a hand. "Business is business, after all, and I'm supposed to meet with Mr. Lau later today. I'll be open to a viable enterprise as long as it's ethical, but of course will bring any proposals back to the table before any decisions are made."

All were in agreement, and the meeting ended. However Laura was taking her time gathering her paperwork and seemed to be hanging back from the rest. Waiting until all were out of earshot, she leaned in closer to Paul. "I need to discuss something with you, in regards to Alanna Scolfield. It may or may not be important."

"Sure, Laura, what is it?"

"Alanna Scolfield happens to be one of my closest friends, and I'm concerned about a possible conflict of interest here."

Paul blinked at this unexpected revelation. "Don't you think you can look at this matter in a purely objective business sense?" he asked, but, at the same time, he wondered what implications might arise.

"I'd like to think I can but, even though Alanna is a close friend, I'm well aware she can be a formidable business foe and won't take losing lightly if you decide not to pursue working with them."

"Laura, I respect your honesty, and I value your contributions to this company, so I'll leave it up to you. Right now, I don't see a conflict, especially as you've been upfront. But if you feel uncomfortable and wish to abstain from any input, I certainly understand."

"Thanks, Paul, let me go and think on it for a while, and I'll let you know my decision when we meet back here."

As she turned to leave the room, Catherine hurried up to Paul. "Victor Lau just called. He can meet with you, here, in half an hour. Shall I call him back to confirm?" Paul took a deep breath but, before he could reply, she continued. "You've also had a call from a Dorothy Dennehy, and I've a number where you can reach her."

That piece of information finally brought a smile to Paul's face, which didn't go unnoticed by his assistant.

"Call Victor Lau," he ordered, "and ask him for an

hour instead of thirty minutes, and then I'll return this other call. Thanks."

With a lightness to his step, he returned to his office, closed the door, and dialled Dorothy's number.

Chapter 6

The sound of her voice and her cheery greeting made Paul's smile even broader.

"Paul, I've put together some information for you to read before your meeting with Victor Lau. Glenn will deliver a package to you, personally, in about ten minutes. Let your receptionist know he's been instructed to hand it directly to you."

"Great work, Dorothy. I'll look forward to reviewing it."

"He'll wait until you've read it and, if you have questions, relay them to him. You may be in for a busy day so I'll be in touch later. Call if you need me."

"Understood. Anything else?"

"As a matter of fact, there is. Dad's making his famous seafood specialty tonight and you're invited for dinner. Can we meet at the *Aye* about six-thirty?"

"Yes of course. Dinner sounds great," Paul agreed.

"Wonderful, I'm glad you'll be able to meet my dad. And now I'd better get to work. Talk to you later."

He said goodbye reluctantly. He would have preferred to continue the conversation, but needed to stay focused. Calling reception, he wasn't surprised to learn a visitor, with a package, was waiting to see him.

Paul hurried to reception and spotted Glenn. A large bulky envelope rested on his lap. As Paul approached, he rose and stood as if at attention.

"Hi, Glenn, package for me?"

"Yes, sir, it is."

Taking hold of the delivery, Paul showed him the waiting area. "Please relax and have a seat. If you don't mind waiting, I need to have a quick look through this material before I send you on your way. Help yourself to coffee on the side table."

"Thanks, a coffee would be great," Glenn said.

Paul returned to his office and set about reading the material.

Within minutes, he realized he'd need to concentrate on these documents. He called his assistant and, when she entered his office, her eyes were drawn to the opened envelope and scattered pages spread across the desk.

Gathering up one pile of documents, he handed them to her, "I need these copied and distributed to be read before our next meeting. I'll get through this as fast as possible and let you have anything else I'll need copied."

"I'll get right on this."

Always professional, she moved out of his office and prepared to call the associates.

Paul made good use of his speed reading skills, learned many years ago, and scribbled some notes for Dorothy as he finished up.

Returning to where Glenn sat sipping a coffee and reading a magazine, Paul thanked him for waiting, and sent him off to deliver the notes to Dorothy.

After reading more than he needed to know about Victor Lau, Paul was anxious to get the meeting over with. He stood at his office window, staring aimlessly at the traffic below, reflecting on what he'd learned.

Catherine announced Lau's arrival with two other

guests. Paul decided to let them wait a few minutes.

"Good morning gentlemen," Paul said in welcome, as he came out of his office to greet them.

"Good morning," said Victor Lau in an equally neutral tone of voice.

So far so good, thought Paul as he escorted them into his office and closed the door.

Eric Kiang accompanied Lau. A third man Paul hadn't seen before made up the trio. Although not a large man, he possessed a demeanor of intimidation and his eyes threw a menacing glance around the room.

Paul assessed this person as someone he wouldn't like to meet in a dark alley and pegged him as a bodyguard. Lau made no effort to introduce him.

"Gentlemen, please have a seat."

"Mr. Webster, we are here to discuss the return of merchandise in your possession which belongs to me. Last night you asked for proof these dolls do in fact belong to me. I have brought that proof with me." Again, there seemed to be no small talk where Lau and company were concerned. He handed a file over to Paul.

Paul opened it and saw photographs of his two "girls," along with a detailed description. A brief write up indicated a company in Portland had negotiated with Victor Lau a selling price in the thousands for each for these dolls. They were to be added to the private collection of Dominic Qu, owner of Bamboo Fine Imports. The sale would be final upon receipt of said dolls, but a substantial deposit had already been paid. Signatures of both parties involved were at the end of the page.

"These dolls were stolen while under shipment to Bamboo Fine Imports. I demand they be returned." Victor Lau was all about getting his point across in no uncertain terms.

Paul refused to be intimidated and was in no hurry to

agree to the return. He leaned back in his chair, folding his hands across his stomach. "Very interesting. It's quite a sum of money to be paid for a couple of dolls. Surely their worth goes beyond what the eye sees?"

"What do you mean?" A dog's snarl would have had more warmth than Lau's voice.

"It's just that I can't help but wonder about the true value of these dolls. A competitor of yours, Yashito Design and Textile, also has information regarding these creations, specifically in the fabric they're wearing." There was no noticeable change in Lau's expression, so Paul decided to drop the bombshell. "But I want to know, who's responsible for tearing apart one of the dolls while it was still in my car?"

"The doll has been damaged?" Eric Kiang exclaimed.

A riveting glance from Lau silenced any further outburst. He then turned his attention back to Paul.

"Explain," Lau demanded.

"At some point while the doll was in my car, the hair was undone and the body was slashed, stuffing scattered all over the place. You might not realize your full selling price on Kimi."

"Kimi?" Lau asked with raised eyebrows.

Paul leaned forward. "A nickname for the doll," he said dismissively.

"This is unacceptable. And Yashito knows about them as well?"

Paul wasn't certain, but perhaps the overbearing Mr. Lau was a little shaken by this news. "Let's be upfront. You and I both know what the fabric represents." The Asian man's countenance remained wooden, so Paul continued. "Let me just say that I've been in negotiations with Yashito to partner and merge with them. We have now signed an agreement to merge and promote Yashito Textile and Design."

"That is now not a concern of mine because it seems any chance of our companies working together is impossible," Lau finally responded through terse lips. "However, I insist on return of the dolls immediately."

Paul had already made up his mind about dealing with the nefarious Victor Lau after reading the material on Jinan. And not all of it had to do with textiles.

"On that point, we agree. Webster and Yashito would never consider dealing with a company which intends to offer a counterfeit product to ours." Paul was going out on a limb, and perhaps treading dangerously. "As such, I feel no obligation to return either of the dolls to you until I have some more answers .Perhaps they should be turned over to the authorities to be further investigated. I'm also considering consulting my legal department as to the interpretation of who is the rightful owner."

Lau's eyes narrowed ever so slightly. "Mr. Webster, a word of advice. Be very careful before you make me an enemy."

Paul sat up straighter in his chair. "And I advise you, sir, I don't take kindly to threats."

And with those final words, he rose, indicating he was done. He opened the door for them, but didn't see them out. He continued to review detailed notes provided by Dorothy. Jinan Import and Export had approached another company in Seattle, Washington, six months ago, for financial backing or partnership, but no deal had been finalized. Shortly after the deal fell through, two of their top executives had taken unexpected early retirement. Coincidence?

The local doll collector—Dominic Qu and his wife, Lily—owned Bamboo Fine Imports in Portland, which specialized in the import of unique Asian objects and artefacts. Some of which ended up in their own private collection, valued in the millions. Dorothy's digging had revealed some recent financial investment into Bamboo Imports by Jinan Import and Export, an interesting note, in light of his recent meeting with its owner.

Yashito Design and Textile was an older, well-established company, and all its dealings appeared above board. Jinan Import and Export, on the other hand, offered limited public information about its history, being established only five years ago.

Alanna's involvement with Victor Lau began about two months ago, when they were searching for financial backing, or partnership in the Portland area, and approached her public relations firm.

For the second time that day, Paul and his associates assembled. All had read the information provided by Dorothy, and Paul filled them in on the dolls, and how they came to be in his possession. He didn't mention that Kimi had been damaged, or that Victor Lau was insistent on their return.

Breathing a sigh of relief, he was gratified his associates agreed with his assessment to be no part of either Victor Lau or his company, Jinan Import and Exports.

Within minutes, Paul was speaking to the representative of Yashito. The conversation ended with the promise of a meeting to finalize the legal documentation.

Returning one or two more phone calls, Paul ended his business day, said goodnight to Catherine, and headed home. Reaching for his cell phone, he dialled Dorothy to bring her up to speed on the day's events.

"Can we discuss the day when we meet this evening?" she asked. Without waiting for a reply, she continued on in a very businesslike tone. "I have more information, as I am sure you do, that's better relayed face to

face. I'm looking forward to dinner and we'll meet as arranged."

Dorothy cut the connection, and Paul sat looking at
the receiver, feeling disappointed at the brevity of the
conversation. Not for the first time, he thought how nice
it would be if he'd met her under non-business circumstances.

Arriving home earlier than usual, Paul made himself
a drink. After looking in on the "girls," still nestled safely
inside the sofa, he wandered down by the water's edge
which was his favorite spot to relax. A pragmatist, he re-
viewed the order in which all had happened since he first
set eyes on the bundle by the side of the road. Once he'd
sorted everything in his mind to his satisfaction, he returned to the house.

Not long after, he answered the door to find Glenn,
with apologies for disturbing him.

He'd come to pick him up on Dorothy's instructions.

"She doesn't want you followed, and we've noticed a
car driving past your house several times today. It means
a slight change in your meeting arrangements."

"Come on in. Do you still have someone watching
the house?" Paul asked, standing aside to let Glenn pass.

"Yes, HB will be here all night, and no, you won't be
able to see him. He's positioned in a vacant house three
doors away."

Paul digested this information and appreciated the
thoroughness of Dorothy's operation.

Glenn glanced at his watch, "It's almost six now.
We'd need to leave soon to get you to the boss lady by
six thirty or so. Not too sure how much of a detour we
may have to make if we're followed."

"Of course, make yourself at home and I'll be with
you shortly."

Moments later, Paul returned. With his hair still

damp and, pulling on a lightweight jacket, he was ready
to leave.

Deliberately, he set the alarm system Dorothy had
managed to penetrate. He'd be glad when the upgrade
was installed. They left the house and sped off into the
evening light.

Glenn grunted as he glanced in the rear view mirror.
"Hold on to your hat. We've got company."

They picked up speed traveling away from the house.

Paul made no comment, but double checked the security of his seat belt.

"The car we've been watching all day is not far behind us, and we need to lose it. The boss prefers to keep
her business location unknown. I may have to take you
straight to Max's instead of the boat. That okay with
you?"

"I leave it in your capable hands."

Glenn talked quietly into his Bluetooth ear piece
while driving as if participating in the Grand Prix. Paul's
heart was certainly beating a little harder, but he enjoyed
the ride. After driving about ten minutes, he wondered if
they were still being tailed.

"They're a few hundred yards behind us," Glenn
said, as if reading his mind, "but I should be able to shake
them in a minute. Hold on!"

He swerved the car fully around in the direction
they'd been coming from, passed the tailing vehicle, and
quickly entered a narrow alleyway. Paul could see it
would exit just ahead.

Glancing in his rear view mirror, Glenn smiled.
"There they go, right on cue."

Off they went again, but slower, until they came to a
large warehouse. Glenn opened the doors remotely and
when they were inside Paul noticed a souped-up
Volkswagen Cabriolet. They pulled up alongside.

"Time to switch chariots, Paul."

"This is Maggie, our hero," Glenn said, patting the
hood of the Volkswagen. "I can't tell you how many
times she's come to our rescue. I've just had a word with
Dorothy, and she says I can drop you at the houseboat,
everything's clear."

The VW sped back the way they'd come and it
wasn't long before they were at the marina. Paul jumped
out of the car and Glenn shouted after him. "I'll be on
call if you need me. Have a good evening."

With a short wave, Paul turned and boarded the *Aye*.
"Hello!" he called out, "Anyone home?"

"I'll be right there, Paul, one sec," came the reply. A
moment later, Dorothy slid open the door and greeted
him with a smile as she stepped outside to join him. "Sorry, but we need to get a move on. Dad's had dinner waiting for a few minutes."

"I might have been a lot later if Glenn hadn't been
able to lose the tail. And how was your day?"

They continued talking as they made their way along
the waterfront boardwalk toward the marina and Maxwell's.

Paul grimaced. "I meant to tell you, I hadn't realized
how close this marina is to my home on the river as
well."

She only smiled as if that was no news to her at all.

Paul now had a chance to enjoy Dorothy's company
before the rest of the evening began.

Freed of its baseball cap, her flowing red hair cas-
caded over her shoulders. "Was the information I provided helpful to your associates?"

"Yes, thanks, you were quite thorough and gave me
the ammo to show Lau the door."

"I'm glad the outcome went your way and, from
what I've learned of the two companies, I'd prefer to deal

with Yashito myself. Lau and company are definitely a crowd I'd not want to mess with."

They neared a large two-story structure, obviously the renovated warehouse Dorothy had mentioned earlier. A busy parking lot attested to the popularity of Max-well's Bar and Grill.

Dorothy led Paul down one side of the building to a flight of stairs ascending to the residence above. Halfway up the stairs, the tantalizing aroma of garlic and spices wafted on the evening breeze and enveloped them the moment she opened the door.

"Hi, Dad, we're here. Sorry we're late."

The door opened up on a large, practical kitchen. Standing at the stove was a bear of a man.

Max Dennehy stood an easy six foot four and sported a harsh brush cut. But when he turned to greet his daughter, the warmth in his face let Paul know where Dorothy got her friendliness from. "Darlin', about time you got here. Business slowed you I expect," he said in a deep bass voice, returning the kiss on the cheek which his daughter gave him. Wiping his large hands on the apron about his waist, he extended one to Paul in greeting. "Max Dennehy, and you must be Paul? Glad to meet you, son."

"My pleasure, Mr. Dennehy."

"It's Max to any friend of Dorothy's. Have a seat, dinner's all ready. Oh and say hello to Houdini."

At Max's glance, Paul's eyes drifted downward to a hefty cat, sauntering into the room. A brilliantly marked tabby, with amazing green eyes, he gave Paul the once over, and then, in apparent approval, entwined himself around Paul's ankles. At the contact, he realized this was one solid kitty.

Reaching down to scratch the feline around its ears, Paul remarked on the name, "Houdini?"

Dorothy laughed. "That's what Dad named him. About a year before he retired, there was a drug bust. When the perps were cleared out of the premises, Dad's partner, Joe, found a scared little kitten cowering in a corner. He went to reach for it, but the thing spat and hissed so bad, Joe actually backed off." She and Max chuckled at the remembrance. "He radioed for the humane society to come and get it. Well, about half an hour later, when Joe and Dad had finished up at the scene, they went back to their squad car, and when they opened the door, there was the little fella curled up on the front seat sound asleep, in Dad's hat. On the spot he was named Houdini and when Dad moved him off the seat, there was no hissing or spitting at him, so they made friends and have been ever since. He's living the good life, as you can see."

"Okay, okay, enough of this mushy sentimental stuff, let's eat," came the chef's command.

Paul was more than willing to comply. A garden salad and warm biscuits accompanied hearty seafood chowder.

"Delicious meal, Max. One of the best I've had in a long time," Paul said.

"Dad learned to be a good cook out of necessity. My mother died when I was a baby, and while we had relatives nearby—Lucas and his family—Dad pretty much did it all."

"And you never remarried?" Paul realized that, just as with Dorothy, he felt very comfortable in Max's presence and didn't feel awkward asking the question.

"No, Paul, when you've had the love of your life, even briefly, why bother trying to recreate it with someone else. And besides, I don't think any woman would measure up in Dorothy's eyes, would they, love?"

"Probably not, Dad, but it would be nice for you to

have a companion. I mean Houdini's great and all, but—"

"Ah well, what's meant to be will be, and now let's change the subject, shall we?" He patted her hand across the table and turned his attention to Paul.

Paul cleared his throat. "Dorothy tells me that you lend a hand with her investigations," he prompted, agreeing to the change of subject. "So I'm assuming she's probably filled you in on what's been happening?"

"Yes, son, she's told me all that's necessary. I'm quite intrigued by these dolls of yours too. I believe she and I have a suggestion about them. Dorothy?"

"Dad's right. I know you've said you're going to hand them over to Victor Lau, but I'd like you to stall on that a little longer. I've a couple of tests I'd like to have run on them myself and will try to have it done within forty-eight hours. For your protection, we've agreed Dad will hide them here for safekeeping, if that's agreeable?"

"That's fine with me, but if my house is being watched, it might be tricky to get them here." Paul noticed the glance between father and daughter. He was pretty sure they already had that angle covered.

"Not to worry, Paul. I'll be driving you back home a little later, and there will be no effort to lose any tail that might be about. Oh, you were told about the home I have secured on your street?" He nodded. "So while I drive you home," she continued, "Dad here will be taking his canoe out for an evening paddle, and voila, when he comes back home, he'll have a couple of overnight guests with him."

"Good plan. I did set the security alarm, but, as you've already enjoyed pointing out, I'm sure that won't be a problem for him, will it?"

"Not at all son, not at all." There was the same sparkle in his eyes that Dorothy had shown at different times. "And speaking of which, I think I'd best get a head start on you two. It should take me about half an hour to paddle up to Paul's property and it's nicely dark now."

"We'll start on the cleanup, Dad."

"No you won't. You know I'm a night owl, and I'll need that to do when I get back. So just relax for a few minutes. I'll give you a call when I've returned. I know you'd worry about me otherwise, wouldn't you, darlin'?"

"Thanks, Dad, and thanks again for the meal, it was great, as always."

"Well, someone has to see that my little girl eats. Right then. I'm off. Hope to see you again soon, Paul."

"I'd like that, Max, thanks."

As the door closed to the darkness outside, Paul again thanked Dorothy for all her work. She put a finger to his lips, "Enough shop talk for one day. Come with me."

She took his hand and led him out to a balcony overlooking the water. Stars glowed in the evening sky and the sounds of chatting diners below in the restaurant wafted up toward them. A spring-like breeze blew in from over the water, and they stood at the railing, enjoying the peacefulness of it all.

She moved a little closer and released his hand. Paul laid his arm over her shoulder, and she leaned into him. Then she tensed and retreated.

Neither felt the need to speak, and Paul was quite happy to enjoy the silence with her. Soon she glanced at her watch and announced they had better be on their way.

The drive, this time, was more leisurely, but too soon for his liking, they turned into his driveway. She turned off the ignition and looked at Paul. "I've enjoyed this evening with you, and glad it wasn't all strictly business."

"Me too, and I'd like to get to know your dad better."

She just smiled. "Goodnight. I'll be in touch tomorrow."

As she reached for the ignition switch, Paul's hand covered hers, and in the dim light their eyes made contact. Without another word they drew together and their lips met. Slowly they pulled apart.

"Sorry, Dorothy, I—I—"

"Shh, Paul, it's all right."

As she smiled at him, Paul felt his heart give a leap, and a foolish grin threatened to overtake his face.

"But I'd best be on my way, for both our sakes."

He quietly left the car. She watched as he walked to the front door and waited till he was safely inside before driving away.

The evening had given them both a lot to think about, and sleep might not be easy for either of them.

Chapter 7

The transfer of the "girls" went without a hitch. HB had slipped from the back of the surveillance home three doors away and, keeping close to the water's edge, made his way to the rear of Paul's home. Taking note of a parked car that had been in front of Paul's home for a couple of hours, he quietly entered through Paul's back door, after disengaging the alarm.

Dorothy had informed him where the dolls were hidden, and he'd had no trouble finding them aided by moonlight streaming through the windows. He quickly unfolded two large trash bags brought with him and put a doll into each. Leaving the house, he carried them out into the garden and silently made his way to the water's edge.

Crouching down, dolls by his side, he waited for Max to paddle up the river. They'd been in touch by cell, and HB knew he wasn't far away. It was a cool, but pleasant, evening and the moon helped him spot Max as he approached. His canoe nosed gently to the shore.

No words were spoken as HB handed the dolls to Max for safekeeping. With a tap on the end of the canoe, he was off again for the return journey.

As Max slipped away into the darkness, HB returned

to the surveillance house. Moments later, Paul had arrived at his own front door.

Entering the darkened dwelling, he soon realized the alarm system wasn't activated. He moved toward the living room and, with mixed feelings, saw the sofa had been emptied of the dolls.

While he felt confident their absence meant Max now had them, he also knew there was the possibility Lau had retrieved them first.

So much had happened over the past few days. He shook his head, playing the events back in his mind, and realized he felt relief that the dolls were out of his keeping.

Putting his living room back in order, he noticed a light flashing on his answering machine. A call from Victor Lau, pushing for a meeting as soon as possible.

Restless, Paul wandered down to the river's edge, pushing thoughts of Victor Lau and mysterious dolls from his mind, preferring to dwell on Dorothy. He stood and gazed out at the water, drawing a sense of calm from the quiet evening.

Feeling more at peace, he turned and followed the familiar path back to the house. Preparing to turn in for the night, he paused by a window and looked out at the dark street.

He saw a car a few houses away and could see the glow from at least one cigarette.

He chuckled to himself and spoke under his breath, "Enjoy the quiet, boys, the dolls have left the premises, and your boss isn't going to be happy you allowed that on your watch."

Satisfied, he decided to wind down with some television.

℘℘℘

Dorothy was still very much at work on his behalf. After taking him home, she'd called Murph to say she was now in possession of Kimi and Yoko and had suggestions for more tests to run. She agreed to bring them to his office first thing in the morning.

Then it was back to reviewing the information gathered regarding Bamboo Fine Imports, and their apparent connection to Jinan Import and Export. From experience, Dorothy knew that "importing and exporting" were often covers for dealing in contraband. Creativity ran rampant among such firms, and their connections overseas, to avoid detection by the authorities. Knowing that someone was up to no good was one thing—proving it, much more difficult.

Dorothy loved a challenge. Putting together pieces, doing research, or calling in favors—it was all part of the path she had chosen. Defeating criminal behavior motivated her to go above and beyond. Sometimes she felt it was as basic as good winning over bad. And if there was physical action required, she didn't hesitate to take part.

But it could also be tiring. Stifling a yawn, Dorothy continued adding to her notes and compiled a list of people to contact. When another yawn overtook her, she realized she needed some rest. The hour was late. Grabbing a pillow and blanket she stretched out on one of the couches.

She loved being on the water and found the evening sounds so comforting. The peace and serenity it provided compensated for the makeshift bed.

With her cell phone in hand, she dialled HB. "Just checking to see if all's right with the world?"

"Everything's quiet," came the response. "He was outside for a bit, but appears to have settled for the night. Still have watchers, though."

"About what I expected. Your backup should be

there shortly, and then you can go home. I'll be in touch tomorrow."

"Sounds good, you get some sleep yourself, boss lady."

Dorothy lay back with her arms behind her head, reflecting on the day's progress, glad to know Paul's home was under HB's watchful eye. That led in turn, to thoughts about Paul himself. She had to admit there was a strong attraction. She'd closed herself off from romantic entanglements for several years while healing from her past. Was it time to let someone in? She vowed to herself to take it slow. This was, after all, a business arrangement first and foremost. To let personal feelings come into play might hinder her ability to provide the professional services for which she'd been hired. Still, as she drifted off to sleep, the memory of the brief kiss between them gave her reason to smile.

Saturday was overcast. The promise of more rain hung heavy in the air. Dorothy worked in her office, finalizing other cases, and marked them as closed with a satisfied smile. Now she could put all her attention to working on Paul's geisha girls.

In addition to handing the dolls over to Murph, Saturday also meant time to catch up on housekeeping chores. Phoning her dad, she asked about bringing laundry over.

"Of course, you can darlin'. I won't be in your way. I have to go into town to stock up on supplies."

"Thanks, Dad—and your guests are still comfortable?"

"No complaints from them. Whenever you want to take them, let me know and I'll be sure they're ready."

"That's great. I'll be taking them to Murph this morning." She had no real business reason to contact Paul, but couldn't resist the urge to touch base. "I'll be away till Monday morning—anything I need to know about?"

"No, all's good here. But thanks for checking. I've got paperwork to catch up on and maybe some gardening. Seems some of my plants have been trampled and need a little TLC."

She laughed. "Aha—so the plot thickens does it?"

"You might say that. I'm glad you called, though."

"All part of the service. I'll be in touch Monday."

She disconnected the call and started on chores, feeling content after talking with Paul.

❦❦❦

Monday morning, Paul arrived at his office, ready to face the day. Meetings with the legal department to finalize merger arrangements were set up. He knew he'd have to contact Victor Lau at some point. He'd stall long enough to allow Dorothy time to gather results from Murph. What he was not expecting was a message from Alanna Scolfield, asking him to call at his earliest opportunity.

Best deal with this first, he thought as he settled to make the call.

"Paul! How wonderful to hear from you. I so enjoyed meeting you the other night. In fact, I'm planning an intimate cocktail party for Tuesday evening and would be pleased if you'd come. Please say yes."

Paul wondered if his mental *"No!"* would resound through the receiver, but he had to consider any potential implications. "Thank you, Alanna, I enjoyed meeting you as well. I already have an engagement that evening but I may be able to postpone it. I'll let you know."

He didn't want to make this easy for her.

"Oh. Well, of course, darling. I'm sure an attractive

man such as you has most of his evenings booked," she purred. "Are your business dealings with Victor going well? He's on track to making a business name for himself in the Northwest. Aligning yourself with him would be a smart move."

Again Paul's thoughts ran ahead of his reply. *That's what you think.* But out loud he answered, "I'm sure you can understand that whatever we discuss is restricted to the parties involved. Means my lips are sealed."

"Of course. Well, I'll let you go for now, but please try to make it Tuesday. Talk soon."

"I'll be in touch. Goodbye."

He'd run this invitation by Dorothy and see if she thought there would be any benefit to him accepting. Of course, a lot could happen between now and then.

The morning progressed and, just before lunch, Dorothy called. "Hi, Paul. How are you this morning?"

Delighted to hear her voice and glad of the interruption to his work day, he answered, "I'm doing great. Weekend went well?"

"Glad to hear that. Yes, good weekend, thanks. I've updates. Can you meet me for a bite to eat?"

"Sounds great, sure. Where'd you like to hook up?"

"How about I pick you up and we decide then?"

"It's a plan, see you at noon."

The morning passed and he was pleased when the noon hour arrived. Exiting the main lobby door, he saw her right away, parked just up the street, and walked toward her. Opening the door, she gave him such a warm smile he was lost for words.

"I made a last minute decision—the weather is too perfect to be inside. Trust me?" she asked.

"I'm in your capable hands once again. What did you decide?"

"Take a look in back and see if that gives you a

clue." She seemed to enjoy being in a playful mood.

Paul stretched his neck and saw a picnic basket and blanket. "I see I'm in your debt in the food department."

"If it bothers you, I'll just add it to the bill," she teased, a smile playing at the corner of her mouth.

"I'd rather reciprocate with dinner."

"I'm sure we can work something out. Gardening all done?

"Most of it and all the new plants are in for the summer."

Dorothy expertly maneuvred the peppy vehicle amidst the midday traffic. Paul eased off his jacket and rolled up his sleeves. Folding his tie into a pocket, he was now ready for a picnic.

He stole a sideways glance and, with her hair pulled up in a ponytail, she looked more like young college student than a successful private investigator.

Driving through unfamiliar streets, dodging pedicars, Paul took in the scenery with a questioning look. "Are you going to tell me where I'm being hijacked to? Not that I mind a surprise. I thought I knew Portland pretty well but can't say I've been in this part of town."

"How about Washington Park, to start. Ever been there? There's one particular nature trail that's so peaceful I thought we'd picnic there. If we have time, there's another place I have in mind, too."

"Great. I've been to the Rose Gardens with my ex but never really explored the whole park."

"You're in for a surprise then, it's my favorite part of the city, next to the *Private Aye*. When I started my business, Lucas introduced me around. Then I began venturing out and explored the city and surrounding areas. I visited clubs and restaurants and made myself familiar with the pockets of diverse people who live in Portland."

"That's the best way to familiarize yourself to a city. Bet you made good contacts, too."

She nodded in agreement. "I found it's helped me in my line of work. I also joined a ski-club. Helps build the network as well. I know you mountain climb. Have you ever done any downhill skiing?"

Paul guessed that there wasn't much she didn't know about him.

He laughed. "Only a little, but how about you? Done any climbing?"

"My husband was into extreme sports and we did travel to lots of events, but although I like a challenge, climbing's never been one of them. Maybe I should give that a try sometime."

Leaving unfamiliar neighborhoods behind, the drive soon became more familiar to Paul as they neared the park.

Turning into the park entrance, Dorothy sighed. "What's new with Victor Lau? I'd rather talk about him before we eat so as not to spoil my digestion."

While he recounted Lau's call and the invite from the indomitable Ms. Alanna, they pulled into a quiet spot, ideal for a picnic.

"Bring the basket and follow me." Dorothy headed through some brush to a small clearing, cool in the shade of giant trees.

Paul obliged and was grateful to see a couple of tables basking in a shaft of sunlight. He was pleasantly surprised to see a magnificent view of Mount Hood through the trees.

"Pass the blanket. Looks like the ground's too damp for it, but I think it'll make a good table cloth."

Dorothy spread the blanket and unpacked the picnic basket. They sat in companionable silence, enjoying cold meats, delicious cheese, and fresh bread. Sharing a bottle of red wine, they relaxed and enjoyed the breathtaking view. Small talk turned to business as the food disappeared.

"So what should I do about my big date with Alanna—do I go?"

She began packing the basket with leftovers and appeared to consider his question. "Definitely I think you need to go. You can be my eyes and ears. Is that okay with you?"

"Sure, I'll just need some Alanna repellent," he joked.

Finishing the clean up together, not much was said, yet Paul sensed there was definitely something changing between them.

He expressed his thanks to her for a wonderful lunch and choice of location but hesitated to say what he was really feeling. She sat relaxed beside him, arms wrapped around her knees, almost touching him. Fearing to spoil the sense of comfort between them, he resisted an urge to kiss her, and instead sighed. "This was a great idea," he said glancing toward Mt Hood. "I climbed there a few years ago when I first felt I was a qualified mountaineer. It was one of the biggest challenges of my life, and I remember it clearly. Brings back great memories. We should do this again."

Dorothy straightened her legs back under the picnic table. The sunlight streamed behind her and Paul caught his breath at the sight of her. "Dorothy—I—"

She held up a hand and took a breath. "No, please, let me speak first. I think we've both been caught unawares with feelings for each other. But you've hired me to work for you, and we have a business relationship first. For now, it's best to stay that way. Should it move on to something more…well, there are things I need to tell you. I'm not ready for that."

The sadness on her face touched his heart and he reached for her hand, caressing it briefly before she pulled away.

"Dorothy, I agree and I think if we just take it slow it'll work out. Whenever you feel ready to talk, I'm all yours." Realizing he might be venturing into dangerous territory, he deftly changed the subject. "I guess we need to make tracks."

He stood and gave his hand to steady her as she rose up from the table.

But as they stood, his resolution crumbled. He reached for her and a quick embrace. She didn't pull away. Soon but, with reluctance, he broke the hold. "You mentioned there was somewhere else you wanted to show me? I can manage a little more time away from the office."

She smiled. "Do you know about the Japanese gardens that are part of Washington Park? They're authentic and boast beautiful walkways, and a garden perfect for an evening of moon gazing. And now that I know Mt. Hood is significant to you, I'll have to show you another view, where it's especially spectacular. I thought, perhaps, as you're dealing with the Japanese in a business venture, you'd find it interesting to see something of their culture without going to Japan."

"You think of everything. I've visited Japan and climbed Mount Fuji. But more exposure to their culture couldn't hurt. Then what about the Chinese? Should I take a trip to Beijing and pick up a little culture to deal with Victor?" he teased.

"I think he's the one in need of culture." She laughed. "You could visit the Classical Chinese Garden right in the midst of Chinatown. It's styled after the Ming Dynasty period."

"Let's do the Japanese Gardens for now, and we can continue our business discussion."

Walking back to the car, Paul looked back and vowed he would return to this spot.

By the time they reached the Japanese Gardens, their discussion had turned to Alanna.

"She has a reputation of involvement with dubious ventures," Dorothy said. "Apparently she's not a good loser and woe to the person who crosses her."

Paul winced. "I don't want to be counted in that group."

Dorothy went on to reveal lab results. They weren't conclusive and Murph was waiting on further tests. "He likes to remind Lucas and me that 'this is not CSI you know.' But he had found something interesting when he examined Kimi's insides. Murph discovered the smallest chip of very high quality jade," Dorothy said.

"Hmmm, perhaps the Qu family are adding more than dolls to their collection. As much as I don't want to hand them over, maybe they do legally belong to him."

"Murph will be finished later today and will have the dolls ready for you to pick up whenever you like. Hopefully your man Lau won't realize they've undergone some testing."

Walking through the beautiful and serene Strolling Pond Garden, they admired the pagodas and stone lanterns. Gorgeous iris plants gently waved in front of a soothing waterfall. The afternoon had turned much warmer, and Paul was in no hurry to put his tie and jacket back on. Strolling across a bridge, it seemed natural that they reach for each other's hand in such a romantic setting.

Paul was reminded of his time in Japan and thought how wonderful it might be to see it again, only with Dorothy by his side. Mentally forcing himself off that track for now, he broke the spell. "I'm sorry, but I really must get back to the office. This has been a wonderful break."

"No problem, Paul. I'm glad you enjoyed lunch. I did too."

She dropped him off in front of his building and promised to be in contact before day's end. "Oh and one more thing," she said, reaching up to the car's visor.

Dislodging a piece of paper, she handed it to him. "This is the pass code for your new alarm system. After you use it the first time, you'll need to set your own code. There's paperwork at your house with more information on its use, but I think you'll find it's a much more secure system. I know I'll rest easier now that it's installed."

And without waiting for any comment, she drove off.

Chapter 8

Back at his desk, Paul called Murph to say he'd be at the coroner's office later that day to pick up the dolls.

"Great, but say, can you make it as late as possible? I'm still checking your dollies and a little more time would be a big help."

"Just be gentle with them, my friend," Paul said.

There were documents to sign regarding the merger and meetings to arrange. Then it was time to set up the one meeting he'd been putting off. He shuffled papers until he found the number he needed, and the call was placed.

"Hello, Paul Webster calling for Victor Lau." Before he had time to wonder how long he'd be kept waiting the voice snapped in his ear.

"I trust you are calling to arrange for the return of my merchandise?"

"Yes. Where can I drop them off? It'll be after five."

"Bring them to Colbert Street. I need to complete my business there."

"Understood, but I hope you realize as I mentioned earlier, one of the dolls has been quite badly damaged, and not by my hands."

There was a pause before Lau responded. "We will discuss that further when we meet this evening. Seven o'clock."

Paul felt he'd been backed into a corner and could think of no way to bow out of the meeting. He was in no hurry to return to Alanna's fortress. "Seven will be fine."

The call was terminated.

"Pleasure as always," Paul muttered to the receiver.

Finding this a good excuse to call Dorothy, he was disappointed to only reach her voice mail. While he left a message updating the evening ahead, he felt confident she'd ensure that one of her people would be nearby as backup. He closed off more files as the afternoon ended, and then he headed over to the coroner's office.

At the reception area, he asked to see Murph, confirming his appointment. A door opened and the doctor beckoned for Paul to follow.

"These girls of yours proved to be mighty interesting," Murph drawled, closing his office door behind them.

"Dorothy mentioned you found evidence of precious gems?"

"Ah yes, precious gems. If the fragment I found is any sign of bigger and better, well, my guess is that Miss Kimi was hiding a mighty fine sample in her tummy."

Murph turned to shuffle some papers on his desk, humming tunelessly under his breath. Paul waited for him to continue. And waited.

"I know it's here someplace."

"What are you looking for?" Paul asked, hoping to speed up the conversation and gain some useful information.

"Aha! Here it is." Murph held up a clear vial containing a minute dirt-like particle. Paul raised an eyebrow and hoped clarification was at hand.

Tapping softly at the vial with his index finger, Murph began to explain in his finicky way. "What we have here is a tiny fragment of jade, very high quality, not the stuff found in most trinket shops around these parts. I don't want to guess at the value, and have no idea how big the original piece was, but it might allow someone to retire in style. I'm thinking…" Murph paused, cocked his head to one side, and stared at the far wall.

Paul suppressed a sigh and gave him a moment. "Thinking what?"

"Oh, right. Yes, I'm thinking you might be on to a smuggling venture."

"That's more than a possibility," Paul commented, thinking about Lau. "Now, you mentioned earlier that you were also taking a look at her twin. Anything interesting there?"

The would-be investigator's eyes sparkled as he put a finger to his lips. "Follow me," he whispered theatrically.

Paul trailed after him into an adjoining room, where he saw Yoko lying on a table, apparently still in one piece. Next to her was a piece of equipment. Paul thought it resembled something from a dentist's office.

When Paul glanced at the equipment, Murph slowly removed his glasses and started to polish them, checking them against the light for smudges.

"And?" Paul prompted. "What did you discover. Something else to back up the smuggling theory?"

"See, the challenge I had was to examine this doll without causing any visible damage."

"Which, it seems, you accomplished. She doesn't look any different from when I last saw her."

The coroner smiled and looked pleased. "Exactly. Just as I'd examine a real corpse before cutting, I used an X-ray to see what might be inside."

"It worked?"

"Uh huh, it did."

"You found something."

Nodding, Murph turned to touch a switch on the X-ray viewing screen. As the fluorescent light flickered on behind the X-ray film, Paul asked, "What am I looking at?"

"See that circle?"

And, of course, once it was pointed out, Paul could see what appeared to be a CD.

"Oh, But crap, won't the X-ray destroy what's on that CD?"

"Not quite." Murph reached for a photo which had been upside down on the desk. "Took me quite a while, but I was able to carefully unstitch the main seam and retrieve this."

Paul studied the photograph. The object was about the size of a CD, but in fact it was a carving. "Looks like a round piece of marble with a hole in it."

Murph just smiled and Paul knew he was in for an education. "It may look like marble," Murph said, "but, in fact, it's an exquisite piece of jade."

"But I thought jade was green?"

"Not always. This beauty is what's known as a Neolithic jade bi disc. And, if it's as I suspect, worth quite a pretty penny on the black market. Jade bi discs come in various sizes, some are intricately carved and of different colors."

"Well can I see it, other than in a photo?"

"Um, that brings me to another point, something I didn't want to talk to you about over the phone."

Paul waited.

"I don't need to remind you that my salary is paid for out of the taxes of this city. Now if I were a private investigator, things would be different, yes indeed."

"How, and what things would be different?" asked Paul, trying not to let the exasperation he was feeling creep into his voice as he checked his watch.

"I was obligated to report this find to those who deal in smuggled antiquities, and I'm afraid I can't release both dolls to you just yet."

Paul groaned, immediately visualizing how Lau would react if he didn't show up with the dolls. "I have to return them. You don't know the character I'm dealing with."

"Hang on, Paul. We have a plan of sorts. It'll just mean a delay of about twenty-four hours. You can go ahead and give back Kimi, but hold back on returning Yoko. The agent has assured me Yoko will be ready for you, with the authentic jade bi-disc removed and replaced with a very good copy, plus a little something extra."

"Let me guess, a tracking device of some sort?"

Murph deflated at the accuracy of Paul's guess. "Hmm, yes that's right. If we can have them believe we haven't seen what's inside and, if they don't think we're on to them, we should have a better chance of finding out what's up."

With a lot to think about now, Paul knew he'd have to be creative to keep Lau hanging for yet another day. While he knew that reporting the possible stolen or smuggled item had to be done, he regretted the involvement of more authorities.

Paul was anxious to be on his way. "Murph, thanks so much for all your help, I'll be in touch, but I really need to be going, so if I could take Kimi now?"

"Oh, right. Yes, she's just about ready for you." The coroner turned his back, made his way through a connecting door.

Paul could hear him humming as he rummaged with plastic wrapping and returned with one large bag.

"I'll let you know as soon as Yoko is ready to travel," Murph said, handing Kimi over.

Gingerly carrying Kimi to his car, Paul made good time traveling home. Turning into his driveway, he remembered the slip of paper with the new alarm code. True to Dorothy's word, he could see a folder of information just inside the door, which he quickly scanned to find the reset directions. Satisfied all was in working order, he made a quick supper and then readied himself for the return of Kimi, and to find an excuse for not returning Yoko.

The setting sun threw long shadows down the driveway of Alanna's home. As before, the gates silently opened to allow Paul entrance. Coming to a stop at the front steps, he wasn't surprised to see the door opening, and the determined Ms. Scolfield there to greet him. With a very theatrical gesture her arm was stretched out to Paul.

"Darling, you're right on time. How lovely to see you."

Joan Crawford is alive and well, mused Paul as he pecked at the proffered cheek. At the same time he was looking around for signs of Victor Lau as he entered the home.

"Now, before we see Victor, he mentioned you had a package for him. Shall I have Johnson bring it from your car?"

"Mr. Lau doesn't waste any time does he? That won't be necessary, Alanna. There's been a change in plans."

Alanna's grip on Paul's arm tightened and she turned to him with trepidation in her eyes. "Don't you have the package he was expecting? He explicitly said to bring it to him when you arrived."

Gone was the relaxed hostess. Alanna had tensed up

and was waiting on further words from Paul as she kept looking over her shoulder.

"What's wrong?" Paul responded, not unkindly. "You seem apprehensive. Don't worry about explaining to Victor, I'll take care of that."

Alanna stood frozen, as if waiting for permission to move ahead. Paul gently took her arm. Alarmed to discover she was trembling, he was about to ask her what was going on when the door was thrown open by Lau.

Before Paul had a chance to say good evening, Lau bellowed, "Alanna! What took you so long? I need a refill," demanded an irate and obviously inebriated Victor, brandishing his glass. He then shifted his focus from Alanna. "Ah it's you, Webster. I won't offer you a drink—this should be a quick visit. Deliver my property and then leave."

Alanna moved quickly to fill his glass. She took Victor's arm, led him back into the room, and tentatively made an effort to put her arm around him, which he coldly brushed off. He managed to down the drink before sitting down, hard.

"Victor dear, we can't rush off our guest," she said in a placating tone. Not missing a beat, she handed Lau another drink. And then she entreated Paul to sit down. "You'll have a drink. Scotch, isn't it?"

"Just a glass of ice water please, Alanna, I won't be staying long."

Her face fell slightly. "As you wish."

"Mr. Lau, I'll come straight to the point. I've brought only one of the dolls this evening, the one which has been damaged."

Victor made a move to rise from his chair but couldn't quite make it to a standing position before he fell back. The drink he held slopped over the edge of the glass.

"This better be good Webster," he said in a slurred but still threatening voice. "You're putting my business in jeopardy with this delay. Where's the other doll? You've no right to hold on to my rightful property."

"I've taken quite an interest in these dolls since they were so unceremoniously put into my care." Paul chose his words carefully and sipped at the ice water he received from Alanna. Putting down his glass, he continued. "I've had research done on different art collectors. Seems that these dolls' worth may be different than I've been told."

Victor didn't respond, but narrowed his eyes as Paul continued.

"Now Yoko is certainly exquisite and undamaged, but I'm not convinced of her worth just yet. I'll return her tomorrow after I've one more evaluation made. In the meantime, maybe you can arrange for me to meet with *your* collector?"

Paul stalled for time and watched Lau once more attempt to rise from his chair. This was no time for false heroics. Alanna looked ready to flee.

He really is a nasty piece of work, thought Paul.

"Victor, I just had a wonderful idea," she offered in a conciliatory tone. "The party we're having in honor of Lily and Dominic will be just the time to introduce Paul. And—and he could return the other doll then," she finished with a hopeful note.

Paul looked at one then the other, wondering if that had been a wise thing for her to suggest.

Victor finally managed to struggle to his feet and held on to the back of his chair for support. He appeared to draw on some inner strength as he pulled himself upright. "Be careful, Alanna," he said in an icily calm and quiet voice. "Your usefulness to me is wearing thin." Still holding on to the chair, he then turned his focus to Paul.

His face was an icy mask as he spoke through tightened lips. "Mr. Webster, you have once more failed to return my merchandise. I find that more than disappointing. I believed you to be a man of your word." He leaned more heavily on the chair and Alanna was poised to offer assistance. "As Alanna pointed out, our guests of honor will be Lily and Dominic Qu. So, this is not a request. I expect you to be in attendance with the rest of my merchandise, and it better be intact. Understood?" He swayed on his feet and barked at Alanna. "Have Johnson bring in the package from Webster's car on his way out."

Dismissed, Paul was happy to make an exit but, before he reached the door, he turned back. "Oh, by the way, as I already had a date planned for that evening, I hope you don't mind if I bring her. That way, after I've met with your collector friends, I can enjoy the rest of my evening. Goodnight."

Glad to be leaving that nest of vipers, Paul drove away from the grounds and pulled into a nearby parking lot.

As he reached for his cell phone, dialing Dorothy's number, he realized he was more than anxious to hear her voice. After several rings, he feared the call would go into her voice mail, but she answered at last.

"Hey there, my partner in crime, how are you?" he said in greeting.

"I'm good. How did things go? I assume you got out of there in one piece."

He wanted to fill her in on all that had taken place at the lab and at Alanna's but spoke in general terms about the meeting and finished up by asking if there was a chance they could meet for coffee, to which she readily agreed.

A few minutes later, she pulled into the parking lot of a local Starbucks and went inside to join Paul, who'd been watching for her arrival. He provided details of the meeting and finished up by asking, "Care to be my date for cocktails at Alanna's? It's a good opportunity for you to see close up the charming and loveable Mr. Lau. Though you best make sure you have some anti-venom on hand."

"Well, how can I resist such an appealing invitation?" she said. "Sounds like it could be worthwhile and perhaps even entertaining."

"I just hope Murph will be able to release Yoko to me tomorrow, I don't think I can stall Lau any longer. In reality, the sooner I can sever connections with that group, the better."

"I've been busy doing background checks and the opportunity to actually meet Mr. and Mrs. Qu is exciting. I also talked to Murph. You can relax, plans are in place for Yoko's release. It's a golden opportunity for the feds to eavesdrop on the inner sanctum of these collectors. Seems they've been on their watch list for a while. Some of these so called import/export businesses are not much more than an elaborate front for money laundering and smuggling activities."

He sipped on his coffee and realized how glad he was to be having this time with her, even if it was for business. "So you'll be my date? I'd used the excuse that I already had the evening planned, so I'd be bringing along my date and that we'd leave at some point to continue with our planned evening."

"I look forward to it. Should I be making Ms. Scolfield jealous, hmmm?"

"However you want to play the part is entirely up to you, Dorothy. Just keep in mind that Victor Lau would appear to be a man not to be crossed." Changing topics, he added, "Tomorrow I'll be finalizing business details of my company's merger with Yashito."

"Exciting time for your company, I take it? Will there be a name change?"

"Indeed, it is. And yes, our new name will be Webster Yashito. We're forecasting an increase in revenue within eighteen months, which will enable us to expand our staff."

"It doesn't bother you that you'll no longer have full ownership of a company you've worked so hard to establish?"

"Times change, and I'll still have majority control, but I'm the kind who thrives on challenges, and it's time for the company to take a new direction. Either that or risk going stagnant and having the business wither. That, I'm definitely not in favor of."

"Well then," she said with a twinkle in her eye, "looks like you'll have a reason to be celebrating after all. The perfect excuse to be leaving Lau and company early, don't you think?"

"I like the way you think, Ms. Dennehy."

The interruption of her cell phone wasn't welcome, but business was business.

"Yes?" She listened to her caller, and, as her brow furrowed, she motioned for Paul to finish his coffee.

They needed to leave, now.

Chapter 9

He quickly down the rest of his coffee. "What's up?"

"That was HB," she explained as they headed to the parking lot. "There's been some excitement at your office, and we need to be there. I'll follow you, but now's not the time for a speeding ticket."

Paul raised an eyebrow. "Really?"

She smiled. "Don't go into your underground parking. We'll meet HB outside first. He'll likely be parked just across the street. Let's go."

And with that, Dorothy got into her Jeep, waiting for Paul to take the lead, and leaving him with unanswered questions about this latest development.

They pulled up behind two police cruisers—lights still flashing. A small crowd of curious onlookers had gathered. Sliding in beside Dorothy, Paul tried to downplay his concern. His gut said whatever was going on in the building was connected to the dolls.

"What now? Shouldn't I let them know I'm here?"

"Hold tight, there's HB now. Let's talk to him first."

Paul followed her line of sight and was taken aback. The man approaching looked nothing like Paul had envisioned a seasoned investigator would.

Short in stature, with a wiry build, he easily sprinted over to one of the squad cars and flashed a badge at the cop on duty. After a few words, he came over to Dorothy's jeep and jumped in the back. Although not a big man, his keyed-up presence managed to fill the space in the small vehicle. Paul noticed his black cap covered a bald head and the face beneath it showed signs of a life lived hard.

"Hey, boss lady, just had a word with an old pal and you're cleared to park here for a while." Without missing a beat, he turned to Paul. "Hi, you must be Mr. Webster. Pleased to meet you, finally."

Paul experienced a vise-like handshake. "Good to meet you too, HB. What's going on here that the police were called?"

HB craned his head back toward the office building and pushed at his sleeves. "When I'm not watching your house I switch with Raymond to keep an eye on this location. Need to cover the bases because the boss tells me you're dealing with some *bad dudes*. I've been keeping an eye on your office since mid-afternoon. About half an hour ago, I needed to stretch my legs, have a coffee. Then all hell broke loose when alarms tripped on your floor. Nice office, Mr. Webster but your security stinks. Nothing personal. Checked it out yesterday. A few areas need tightening up." The staccato delivery completed, HB's manner relaxed.

Paul wondered at the story behind the man.

"Have you been up to the office yet?" asked Dorothy.

"Went straight up there after checking the lobby camera" HB made a face. "The security guard had already called the cops. Someone's certainly been in the office but they may have tripped the alarm on the way out. Like I said, you do need an upgrade, Mr. Webster."

"It's Paul, please, and thanks for the timely advice. Changes will be made. So what now? I suppose we have to talk to the authorities and—"

"No worries, I've had a word with the uniforms, told 'em it might be something regarding a case I'm working. They're fine with that but they're sending a guy from burglary anyway to check things out. So, you'd better head up there before he arrives. Check for anything missing. I'll try and grab the surveillance tape before the cops do."

"Great work, HB. You're the best," Dorothy said as her lead investigator concluded his report.

He sprang out of the car, as if he'd been ejected, and dashed to the front of the building where he disappeared inside.

Paul was ready to follow just as Dorothy's cell phone rang. Touching his arm, she mouthed, "One sec." She listened. "Right, Dad, stay where you are and call me back in half an hour, unless things escalate."

Paul's questioning glance received a response.

"Yes, Dad's working for me tonight, I needed an extra body. Surveillance duty at Alanna's house. Seems all's not peaceful in Paradise."

"Why, what's happened?"

"Let's walk, I'll talk. We need to be there before burglary shows up. Even though they can be notoriously late because most of these calls are false alarms, let's not waste any time."

"What's the scoop on HB? He looks like he could be working for the wrong side of the law."

"Don't let appearances fool you. My dad recommended him to me, on condition I don't ask too many questions—in turn he'd give me nothing but hard work and unfailing loyalty. I've never regretted hiring him and the advice paid off. I do know he's an ex-cop, like me, has a black belt in Karate, and knows his way around a fight arena. That gives him a good edge for this line of work, and he's gifted at blending in with a crowd."

"Someone good to have in your corner, so to speak."

She nodded, and they quickly made their way to lobby reception. Being after hours, Paul wasn't recognised by the guard, and they both had to show ID and sign in before being allowed access to the elevators.

Once behind closed elevator doors and out of earshot, Paul voiced his concern. "So what's going on at Alanna's? I had a bad feeling when I left there tonight. She may be able to take care of herself, but she's mixed up with a cold and calculating man who'd stop at nothing to have what he wants."

"And you want me to *schmooze* with him at their party?" Dorothy laughed. Turning serious, she continued. "It seems about twenty minutes after you left, there was shouting, yelling, and the sound of breaking glass. Then silence. Just as Dad was going to call it in as a domestic, Alanna came out the front door and lit a cigarette. He said she appeared quite agitated, and she was pacing. She really jumped when more yelling came from inside the house. He'll let us know if there are any further developments."

"So, she really is frightened of him. That makes me want to clip his wings. His type shouldn't be at large."

Exiting the elevator, Dorothy returned to the matter at hand. "How do you want to handle this? You'll have to give the police something to work with. I've a feeling someone might be after documents or proof of your merger with the Japanese. Do you have specs on the fabric, or the manufacturing, that's important to this whole deal?"

"Let's see what damage has been done before I make a guess at what they're after." Paul had lowered his voice as they arrived at the glassed in entrance to his executive suite of offices.

One door stood open but was defended by an elderly security guard. He glared at them and demanded identification.

"Evening, Pete, how are you? You've had a bit of excitement around here tonight."

"Oh, hullo, Mr. Webster. Sorry, I'm not used to seeing you this time of night." Momentarily thrown off stride, Pete continued in a defensive tone. "I was patrolling as usual and didn't see anyone try to enter your office. The last one to leave was Miss Innis around seven. Oh, I do like that girl. She always chats with me before she leaves but she was in a big hurry tonight. Now that other—"

"Pete, sorry to interrupt. Thanks for the info, but we have to go inside and see if anything's missing. You know what the cops are like, and they'll be snooping around soon enough."

"Of course I do. Anything else I can do for you tonight?"

Before Paul could reply, Dorothy stepped up and extended her hand. "Pete, I'm Dorothy, a friend of Mr. Webster's. I'm here to help him out. You started to say something about another person being with Ms. Innis?"

Paul suppressed a smile. He could see she'd pegged Pete's character and extended just the right amount of male flattery with her warm smile.

The elderly guard visibly straightened, hitched his pants in what could only be a long-standing habit, and focused on her. Clearing his phlegm-filled throat, he grinned. "Yes, doll, you're right. Miss Innis did have company with her. Fellow made my skin crawl. Might have been dressed in a suit, but didn't look like he was comfortable in it, if you know what I mean? Asian, but I don't know if he was Chinese, Japanese, or Korean. For-tyish, maybe, good build, but stocky. Face looked like it didn't even know how to smile. Miss Innis didn't look too happy being near him either."

"That's very helpful, Pete, thanks for being so observant. Anything else you might have seen on your rounds tonight that looked suspicious?"

"No, can't say as I do, but if something comes to mind, I'll let you know." The old lecher looked at Dorothy with undisguised interest in his rheumy eyes.

"Thanks, Pete." With a quick tug at Dorothy's arm, Paul maneuvred her into the reception area and went straight to his office. "Why, that old devil. Making a play for you like that. I think you even enjoyed the attention. I've known him for years and there's not a woman here he hasn't propositioned."

"Jealous?" she teased.

"Sorry, but I've seen that old reprobate in action too many times. That's why he's on the night shift now, less chance of offending anyone. Okay, let's have a look."

Dorothy confidently went ahead of Paul into his inner office, motioning him to stay behind her. She glanced around the room, relaxed. "All clear, just wanted to be safe."

"You know, based on Pete's description the guy sounds a lot like the heavy who accompanied Victor here yesterday. He never said a word but I got the impression he was more of a bodyguard. If there's anything captured on the surveillance camera, I'll know for sure. But still, what the heck was he doing here, with Laura? That reminds me, did I tell you that Laura admitted to being a close friend of Alanna's?"

"No, you hadn't mentioned that—might have a bearing on things, so you'll definitely need a word with her tomorrow, ideally before the police do."

Dorothy grew silent as they surveyed the surroundings. While nothing visibly seemed to be out of place, Paul knew items on his desk and cabinets had been moved, if only slightly. A folder lay on his desk, which he was sure hadn't been there when he left. He reached for it, but Dorothy stopped him. At the same time, she pulled a pen from her pocket, carefully lifted one corner of the file, and flipped it open. "Have a look but try not to touch it."

"Oops, I should have known better, sorry."

He glanced at the first page of the open file and recognized a report he'd been waiting for, from Laura.

"I think this is all right, and probably the reason Laura was up here. She often works late."

Dorothy nodded and closed the file. Putting her fingers to her lips, she took out a piece of paper and wrote, *Bugs?*

Paul nodded, not really surprised.

Speaking out loud, Dorothy said, "Okay, Paul, so everything looks fine? It may have been a false alarm, but we'll wait downstairs for the police to arrive. Let's go."

They left the office, and said their goodbyes to Pete, still on guard. For a moment, Paul thought the old fellow was going to salute him.

In the elevator, Dorothy took a deep breath. "I think it best to tell the police it appears to have been a false alarm. You've checked and nothing seems to be missing or disturbed. Agreed?"

"Great minds think alike, I was about to suggest that myself. I mean we already have the feds involved with the smuggling angle, so it would only complicate matters to bring in another level of law officials."

"They may question my presence here, so I'll try to avoid them if possible."

"Sounds like a plan."

Reaching the lobby, they exited the elevator, relieved to see no police in sight.

He touched her shoulder. "Why don't you go on? I'll stay here until they arrive and then give you a call."

"Might be best. Plus, I want to find out what happened at Alanna's tonight. We'll talk shortly and I'll advise HB."

Paul watched as she left the building, swallowed up in the darkness outside.

"Your girlfriend ditching you then, Mr. Webster?" enquired the guard at the reception desk.

"Something like that. I'm just going to hang around for a bit. Hope the cops show up soon so I can tell them it was a false alarm."

"Yeah, you'll probably have to wait. Once they've been called, you can't cancel the alarm. Oh, here they come now."

An unmarked car pulled up at the curb and one of the uniformed officers went over to talk with the newly arrived detective. After a few moments, the detective made his way into the lobby.

Paul decided to strike first and extended his hand. "Paul Webster. It was my office security system that was tripped, but I think it's been a false alarm."

The handshake was returned and a badge extended to identify Detective Franklin Hyatt, a tall man whose face fittingly resembled a bloodhound, with slack fleshy jaws and droopy brown eyes. "Good to meet you. Hope you understand I still have to come and have a look see."

"Of course, not a problem. I can take you up if you like."

"How'd you hear about the alarm going off, does the company notify you at home?" Detective Hyatt asked.

Paul hadn't thought about that. And how would he explain without involving Dennehy Investigations? He quickly considered his options, but realized he'd probably have to involve them, after all. Besides, it wouldn't take much questioning of the security guards to discover that Dorothy had been with Paul.

"No, not quite. Dennehy Security & Investigations have been assessing my security needs, and we're in the process of upgrading the system. They were the ones who alerted me." He thought that should be enough without having to go into much detail. "In fact, I believe one of the firm's agents already let the officer outside know about it."

The elevator opened.

"So, why do you need your security system upgraded?" With notebook at the ready, the detective was busier scribbling than looking at Paul.

"My company's recently merged with another large firm, and there's always the potential for trouble when a third party is interested and sees their own business hopes disappear."

"I see. And you say that you've looked over your office and nothing appears to have been taken or disturbed?"

"Yes, that's right. I'm sure it's just a false alarm. When Dennehy has finished upgrading things, that should eliminate any further occurrences of this nature."

Pete was at the ready and had the office doors open as the men arrived, uttering a brief, "Good evening."

They entered Paul's office and Hyatt glanced around. "Well, sure doesn't look like the place has been disturbed. My desk always looks like a bomb went off. Still, we may want to take a look at any security tapes you have."

"If you want them, I can drop them off to you first thing tomorrow."

"That'd be fine," Hyatt agreed. Taking a last look

around Paul's tidy office he said that he was done, for now, and would be on his way. He handed Paul a business card. "Should you discover anything missing, give me a call. And I'll look forward to seeing that tape."

The tension Paul had been feeling diminished as the detective and uniformed officer finally left. Saying goodnight to the lobby guard, Paul returned to his car.

He called Dorothy to update her. She advised she hadn't much more to report on the Alanna situation, but that she'd really like a look at the security tape which HB had grabbed, before it was handed over to the police.

"I'll come by your office tomorrow morning, after I've picked up the tape from HB," she said. "We'll look at it and finalize details about our 'date.'"

Paul had almost forgotten about the get-together, but readily agreed to meet with her in the morning. "I think you've earned the rest of the evening off. See you in the morning."

"You too, Paul. Please be careful. Even though we're watching your house, with its new alarm system in place, don't let your guard down."

The call ended and Paul made his way home, where he found a message waiting on his phone.

"Paul, it's Laura. Please call me as soon as you get this message."

Chapter 10

He called her right back. "Hi, Laura, it's Paul. I got your message. What's up?"

"Paul! Thank you. I've been anxious to talk to you all evening about something that happened back at the office."

He knew where this was heading, but let her continue.

"I was working late and, just before seven, a very strange man came by my office looking for you, or at least looking for your office. This guy was quite intimidating. He made me nervous, especially as most everyone had gone home. And I wondered how he got past lobby security. Anyway, I explained you'd left for the day but asked if there was something I could help him with."

"Chinese fellow?"

"Yes, how'd you know? Oh, then this does have something to do with the merger? That's what I thought when he mentioned Victor Lau."

"Perhaps. Go on, what happened next?"

"He said that his boss, Victor Lau, had been to see you earlier and was sure he'd left some papers behind in your office. I know I probably shouldn't have, but I offered to unlock your office so he could have a quick look.

I was on my way there, anyway, to drop off a file."

"Which you did?"

"Yes, I'm sorry, Paul—he made me so uncomfortable, I just wanted him gone and thought the sooner I could hustle him out of there the better."

"Laura, don't worry about it. After you let him in, did he touch anything?"

"No, he just walked over to the sitting area and checked the chairs and under the sofa. He didn't find anything, so he apologised for taking my time and left."

"You watched him the whole time?"

"Yes. No, wait, about that time, old Pete, the night security guard arrived, and he wanted to talk a bit, so I chatted with him for a moment. But it couldn't have been more than two or three minutes."

"Interesting. Listen, Laura, you may as well know there was a false alarm at the office this evening. The police were there, but I don't think anything was taken. The two may be connected, not sure yet, but I'm sure they'll be in contact with you. Just tell them exactly what you've told me."

"I'll feel dreadful if this is connected. I've let you down."

She sounded dejected, and he was quick to reassure her that it wasn't her fault. He understood how the situation developed as it did and tried to lighten her mood. "See, I told you, working late every night isn't good for you."

"So I'm not fired?" she joked back.

"Not likely, you're far too valuable to this company for that. Now forget about it, and I'll see you in the morning."

ℰↄℯↄ

Tuesday dawned gray and damp. A light rain was

falling and the forecast promised more of the same for the rest of the day. Paul was anxious to view the security tape from the night before, knowing he wouldn't have much time before handing it over to the police.

Arriving at his office, he began to prepare for the day ahead. Within minutes, the phone rang.

Dorothy had picked up the tape from HB and would be there as soon as she could. She reminded Paul to use the boardroom. The call was short and sweet. He was savvy to the fact she didn't want their conversation in a bugged office.

For a moment, he contemplated what it would be like to work with her. She was always just one step ahead of him, and he admired her more and more. A knock on his door startled him out of a pleasant daydream.

A weary-looking Laura poked her head around the door. "Paul, can I have a word?"

"Of course you can. Is there a problem? You look beat. The report you left me was perfect, if that's what's worrying you."

Laura acknowledged the comment with a small smile. She moved into the office, but Paul rose quickly. "Do you mind if we talk in the boardroom. I'm heading there. I'll grab us a coffee, and you can tell me what's troubling you."

"Thanks, I sure didn't sleep well last night, and I could use a coffee to help me wake up."

Sipping their java, she told Paul of another call she'd received since she last spoke with him.

"Alanna called me, quite upset and probably a little drunk. I suspect it's because of Victor Lau. If you know Alanna at all, not very many men get the better of her, so that's out of character for her. But what disturbed me most was the fact that she knew about the guy who came to your office and wanted to find out if he got what he came for. Those were her words, and I was so surprised I didn't give her a concrete answer. While she's a very good friend, that friendship won't interfere with my loyalty to you and this company. I hope you know that?" She sipped distractedly at her coffee while waiting for a response.

"I appreciate your loyalty. It means a lot. Maybe she was with Victor when he dispatched his associate to my office. Let's not jump to conclusions." Laura seemed relieved and he continued. "I'd like you to meet Dorothy Dennehy who's a private investigator. I've hired her to scrutinize certain business matters. I think it'd be beneficial for you to repeat all this to her and let her ask you about what happened last night."

"Why on earth do you need a private investigator?" she questioned, coffee forgotten.

"I'll tell you later. For now, you'll just have to trust me on this. Don't go anywhere yet." Paul smiled at her in encouragement as he left the boardroom and pulled out his cell phone. "Dorothy, I need to speak with you outside the office before we look at the tape."

She agreed to meet him in the lobby.

Paul hurried back to the boardroom. "Laura, can we meet back here in…let's see…thirty minutes? I've a few things to do before we meet with Ms. Dennehy."

If she had any questions, she kept them to herself.

Paul hastened to the lobby in time to see Dorothy enter. His breath caught in his throat, and he realized how much he enjoyed working with this amazing woman, but he was also coming to see that he wanted more than a business relationship.

Her enthusiastic "Good morning" brought him back to the present. "And how are you today? Slept well, I hope."

"Good morning, Dorothy," he responded, gazing into

her beautiful eyes. "I'm fine, thanks, and yes not too badly, all things considered."

She smiled. "So, what did you need to say before we head up?"

He told her of the development which Laura had revealed. His suggestion that Dorothy could question her more regarding last night's events was readily agreed upon.

"I've had a quick look at the security tape. You should be able to easily identify your visitor."

"Great work. Now, I don't know if I should be concerned that Laura's a close friend of Alanna's, whether she might compromise any information. I don't think she would intentionally reveal any business dealings, but..."

"You'd like to be sure? Of course. From what I've determined, Ms. Scolfield is an accomplished people user. So definitely it'd be in order to talk with your colleague."

"Alanna Scolfield may have found her match in Victor Lau, judging by how I've seen him treat her," he said. Arriving back at his office, Paul introduced Dorothy to Catherine. "Please see if Laura can join us now in the boardroom."

While waiting, Dorothy set up the security tape.

"I'll have to take this over to Detective Hyatt as soon as we're finished here," Paul reminded her.

"Not a problem, there's really only a few minutes or so on here that's of any interest, and probably really only to us. Unless—"

"Yes?"

"Unless your visitor is recognized by the good detective, in which case, we might have a bigger problem on our hands."

She seemed about to say more, but was interrupted by Laura's arrival. Introductions were made then Laura came straight to the point. "Nothing personal, Ms. Dennehy, but I've worked with Paul a long time, and we've never had to use the services of a private investigator."

"You're quite right, Laura," Paul agreed. "This merger with Yashito has led to some unexpected and unorthodox situations, which, in turn, led me to Dorothy and her firm. At this point, it all centers around Victor Lau, and by association, Alanna. Dorothy is still investigating, but once I have the full picture, you and the rest of the team will be brought up to date. I'm not intentionally trying to keep anyone in the dark, but I do want to be sure of my facts before releasing any information." Laura seemed to need more reassurance, so Paul continued. "In light of last night's events, don't you think we should upgrade security around here? Dorothy can help us with that. In fact, she has already improved my own home's security."

"Well," Laura said, "some extra precautions around here probably does make sense."

Dorothy smiled at Laura. "Please feel free to ask me any questions and, as long as the information doesn't compromise my investigations, I'll be glad to answer."

Laura seemed appeased and agreed. "I've never had reason to mistrust Paul's business dealings, so I'm not about to start now."

With that, Paul explained about the tape, and they settled to watch. Thankfully Dorothy had sped up the process by targeting the specific time they were interested in.

Within seconds, Laura appeared on screen. There was no audio, but it was apparent she was talking to someone just behind her, and then the unnamed visitor came into view.

Paul grunted. "Yep, just what I thought. It is the fellow who was here with Victor Lau the other day. They didn't bring any papers to my office, so it's obviously a ruse to gain entrance."

"I should have known better, Paul. I'm so sorry."

"Laura, remember, I said not to worry. We may have bigger fish to fry, anyway. Let's see if we can tell what happens next."

The scene revealed her opening Paul's door after greeting Pete. With some amusement, they noted the old guard's interest in Laura once her back was turned. Even Laura had to smile at that, it was so obvious.

Laura had stood aside while the nameless man entered Paul's office, apparently to look for misplaced papers. She then entered. Reappearing a moment later clearly she was anxious to lock up Paul's office, as she stood tapping her fingers against her arm. Waiting for the unwelcome visitor to exit, Laura's attention was diverted as the video showed her turning and talking in Pete's direction. Unfortunately, the camera angle did not give privy to what was going on in Paul's office, but, only moments later, Lau's man appeared in the doorway. His mannerisms and the scowl on his face suggested he was disappointed to not find what he was looking for.

"At this point," Laura explained, "he told me he must've left the papers someplace else. You know, I remember now, thinking he was quite rude, because he never thanked me for letting him into the office, and it was almost as if he was disappointed in *me* that whatever he wanted couldn't be found."

"And you were glad to see him leave the place, I'm sure," Dorothy consoled.

"That's an understatement."

Dorothy glanced at Paul and intuitively he knew what she wanted. Addressing Laura, he said, "The tape gives me what I need to know, and I'd best drop this off to Detective Hyatt as promised. I'd like you to stay here with Dorothy and tell her all that you remember from last night. Take your time."

Leaving the two women, Paul exited with the tape.

"So, Laura, how long have you been friends with Alanna Scolfield?"

"Oh, a long time. About ten years. Funny, I don't really know why we're friends, we're so different from each other. Maybe I see behind the facade, because I think there's a somewhat insecure person behind all that. But, as I said earlier to Paul, even if she and I are good friends, I'd never compromise my position here, because of my respect for him."

Dorothy nodded in understanding and had Laura recount the previous night's events and her phone conversation with Alanna. By the time she was done, Dorothy felt confident that Laura would not reveal any sensitive business information to her friend. She left Laura a business card and the invitation to call at any time if she felt she had anything else to add.

Paul had not yet returned, so Dorothy informed his assistant that she would be in touch. "But before I go, I'd like to check something in Paul's office if you don't mind."

Crouching down on her knees once inside his office, she swept her hand beneath both the sofa and chairs, and there it was—a small listening device underneath one of the chairs. She wasn't surprised and left the bug in place.

Leaving the building, she went on her way to attend to other matters and then began to focus on how she was going to prepare for her date night with Paul. She used her cell to leave a brief message for him. "Can you meet me about six-thirty this evening, at Max's. That'll give us a little time to talk, but otherwise I'll be out of touch till then. And I did find what we suspected in your office so be cautious. Bye for now."

❦❦❦

Paul met with Detective Hyatt and passed over the tape. Just as he thought, Hyatt advised him not much would probably come of the apparent false alarm. Unfortunately these things happened all the time with no end result. Especially since nothing was taken. So he wasn't about to tell the detective his office had been bugged. Dorothy would handle that end.

Heeding her advice to be cautious, Paul decided on a change of venue for a scheduled meeting with Archie James. Returning to his office, he asked Catherine to have Archie join him at Benson's Palm Court at noon instead.

"I have to go out again but I'll be back after my lunch with Archie."

"Are you expecting any calls I should let you know about?"

"No, unless the building's on fire, you shouldn't have to contact me. You can tell Archie that if I arrive first, I'll order his usual. Oh, and give some thought as to how we can have a proper celebration with our new partners. You know, do it up big and invite the media for some press coverage."

Paul left the building. It was a fine May day. The sun was nearing its peak, the sky a pristine blue, and even in the city after the rains, he could tell the onset of summer wasn't far away. Strolling among the busy people of Portland, he aimlessly let his mind wander.

As the distance covered grew, he decided to hail a taxi to take him to the Art Museum. An earlier search on the Internet detailed their current impressive Asian collection. Curious by nature, he felt inspired to immerse himself in all things Asian since learning about the jade artefacts. He'd need as much ammunition as possible for the evening's gathering when he and Dorothy would be meeting the art collectors.

That started him thinking about how they'd play it at the party, wondering what Dorothy might have planned. Arriving at the Museum, he had no more time for reflection as he tagged on to a boisterous, but organized, line of school children waiting to begin their tour.

He headed toward the Asian exhibit where, for the moment, all was quiet. He spent the next hour wandering and absorbing the feel of an ancient and beautiful collection. Wall murals, intricate lacquered boxes, and all manner of jade trinkets filled walls and display cases. Satisfied, he left the museum and started walking.

He made the few blocks to Chinatown and wandered by an amazing variety of fruit and vegetables piled on sidewalk stands in front of the small grocery and convenience stores, many of which were also restaurants. When he came to Third Street he entered a store called the Great Era. Not sure what he was after, he looked amongst the miniature jade ornaments and found a small brown quail. It was not overly expensive but the shopkeeper assured him it was indeed genuine jade. He tucked it into the inside pocket of his jacket. His intention was to give it to Dorothy when the Yashito merger, and dealings with Victor Lau, were resolved.

Leaving the shop, he hailed another taxi and headed toward his lunch destination. Settling into the back seat, he patted the tiny bird in his pocket. The cab pulled up in front of the Benson Hotel. As Paul paid the driver, he spied Archie ambling along the sidewalk in his direction. The men greeted each other, and Paul apologised for the change in venue.

"Ach, not to worry, laddie, a change is as good as a rest, they say. Any occasion I can order one of their grand single malts is fine with me, long as you're picking up the tab?" The eyes beneath the bushy brows twinkled, but Paul knew the older man would be quite happy if he indeed did pay for lunch.

"And now the skies have cleared, it's a good day for a walk. So why did you bring yourself along in a cab?"

Paul chuckled. "You don't miss a thing, do you? Well, I'll have you know I didn't come here straight from the office, or yes, I'd have been walking too."

The Palm Court offered an elegant but casual lunch in the lobby. Saturated with old world charm, it had been a fixture for many years.

Drinks were ordered—the large single malt for Archie, knowing his boss would pick up the tab, and Paul's choice was the dry vodka martini the bar was famous for.

"So Paul, you've got your merger. All the details ironed out?"

"Pretty much. We'll have a celebration event in recognition of the change. Involve all the staff and those from Yashito, maybe some media. I think they bring a solid component to the table and now, with the exhibit later this year, it's like a bonus I hadn't counted on. With the right development and marketing, I think we've got a winner on our hands. Exciting times." He paused and gently swirled the cocktail glass in his hand. "Hope you can postpone your retirement long enough to help us get things off the ground. I really count on your expertise which will be critical in the early days."

"I'll not leave you in the lurch yet, but, on the other hand, I'm certainly looking forward to some time away from the daily grind. Although I'm thinking I may pursue something in the private consulting area. Nice to be able to pick and choose what kind of projects I'd like to be involved with. I'll always give you a discount, though." Archie chuckled at his own comment.

Paul smiled. "I'll keep it in mind, but if I know you well enough, I won't be saving much on any discount you might offer."

"Ach, laddie, I am mortally wounded at the comment, true as it might be."

Their meals arrived and lunch was spent reminiscing about their early days together and mapping out some general goals for the coming months.

"And what's been happening with those two dolls you told us about? Do you still have them or were they returned to their rightful owner?"

Paul hesitated about how much to reveal to Archie, and decided on just the bare details. "One was returned and the other I decided to keep for a day or two longer. They stirred my interest in Asian collectibles and I wanted to do some research. Tonight, I'll be returning the other one. I'm to attend a cocktail party at the home of Alanna Scolfield and will meet the couple who collect these dolls."

"Will that Victor Lau character be there?"

"I imagine so, and I'm not exactly his favourite person—seeing as his offer lost out to Yashito—so it might be a bit uncomfortable. But I don't plan staying late, anyway."

Paul sought to change the subject before he revealed more than intended, so he steered the topic back to Archie and his adored grandchildren. Soon, it was time to return to the office.

After he finished for the day, Paul wished Catherine goodnight on his way out.

Shortly before six-thirty, he found himself at Maxwell's Bar and Grill. Dorothy had not yet arrived and so he settled against a far table to wait. He loved to people watch, and this was a good place to do just that. The atmosphere was visibly charged. Those out for a night on the town were dressed up more, and Paul enjoyed watching the interplay between couples.

He was musing about the evening ahead when his attention was caught by a drop-dead gorgeous woman who'd just entered, alone. Her choice of clothing bordered on cheap, but provocative. The short white skirt and hot pink tank top certainly drew one's eye. Well-tanned legs were supported on impossibly spiked open toed shoes.

But it was her hair! Paul hadn't seen anyone other than Cher manage to wear jet black long hair that well.

He laughed to himself. *Someone's in for a hot time tonight.* And then, to his chagrin, he realized this apparition was heading in his direction. As she drew nearer and removed her designer sunglasses, he realized with a start that it was Dorothy.

"Hi, sailor, mind if I join you?"

A quick side glance told him other men in the room were disappointed she hadn't come their way.

Playing along, he grabbed at his necktie and nervously pulled at it, while half rising from his chair. "Um…yes, please, have a seat."

After a few moments the room settled back to its routine, and Paul was glad to resume a normal conversation. But he leaned forward and let out a heartfelt "Wow, lady, you're good."

She smiled. "You don't think it's too much?"

"Heck, no. When Alanna catches sight of you, she'll either laugh or strangle you."

"All part of the plan, and you'll just have to play along because I think there'll be some adlibbing, especially with Mr. Lau. You ready for it?"

"I'll do my best." He shook his head. "I can't believe how different you look. Don't let anyone see me handing you any cash, or I'll be spending the night in a jail cell."

Dorothy tilted her head and raised one eyebrow. "That would never do, sailor." She grew serious. "A couple of things to tell you before we go. First, I've picked up Yoko and she's in the car ready to go. With her added bonus of course. Which reminds me, our suspicion about your office is confirmed, but for now we'll let things stay in place, might be useful to plant some misleading information."

"I thought that would be the best route to go myself, use it to our advantage if need be. Anything else?"

"Oh yes. Pay dirt! My team discovered the person responsible for the surgery on your Kimi, and we have him secluded in a safe house."

"What?" Paul wasn't expecting this news.

"Yes, seems he has ties to Henry Yamada. Listen to this. He was working for Yashito, but went undercover for Jinan Import and Export. Industrial espionage is a common business practice, as I'm sure you know, and that's what our investigations found out. It would appear he was planted there to learn all he could about their manufacturing process, but inadvertently learned of the smuggling side business. That's why the doll was gutted. The greedy boy wanted what was inside. But now he's learned that Victor Lau also knows about his involvement, and as you can imagine, he's worried about Lau's reaction."

"Does Henry Yamada know the extent of his involvement with the smuggling?"

"That, as they say, is the sixty-four thousand dollar question. If he knowingly condoned his employee's actions, it doesn't cast him in a very good light with Yashito. On the other hand, perhaps he's still not aware of what this fellow was up to. David Matsumoto is his name, by the way. And as you can imagine, both Yashito and Jinan would like to have a chat with him."

Paul winced. "I don't think I'd want to be in his shoes. And you have him safe somewhere?"

"That we do, but for your sake, I'm not going to reveal…" Dorothy's words trailed off as her attention was diverted by a commotion growing at the front entrance.

A man's slurred voice was raised in threatening anger. "Dorothy Dennehy!" he yelled, clenching his fists. "I know you're here!"

Chapter 11

Paul tensed, his leg muscles ready to propel him to his feet, but Dorothy's hand quickly covered his, and, catching his eye, she breathed, "Don't move, just watch."

Sure enough, coming up silently behind the intruder was Max Dennehy.

"Dad still has the touch."

They watched Max grab the trouble maker's arm and twist it behind his back. Without a word, he was propelled toward the exit.

The small stir caused by the commotion soon subsided as the pub's patrons went back to their business.

Dorothy watched the retreating figures. "There goes trouble," she said. "Bo Hanson. I thought I was done with that clan. If I know Dad, he's already got the guy calmed down and will tell him I'm no longer to be found in these parts. One of Dad's strengths on the force was as a negotiator, and there aren't too many situations he hasn't been able to defuse. I'm still learning from him."

"Is this guy a former client or something?"

Dorothy was amused to watch him purposefully relax back into the chair. *I think he'd have come to my rescue.* "Not exactly. His wife was. She had me investigate him for what she thought was just a simple case of cheating. Turned out he was quite the special hubby and master pimp, with a predilection for Texas Hold'em. Doesn't take losing well, as you might imagine. He's got a younger brother following in his footsteps, and it seems about every six months or so, one of them shows up around here, looking to settle a score with me. As if I was the reason Bo's wife divorced him, sheesh! So Dad usually has a friendly little chat with them, reminds them about restraining orders, and the like, and they usually tuck their tails between their legs and slink away. Now, where were we?"

She saw the smirk, thinly disguised, cross Paul's face as he spoke. "A good thing you're in disguise—or are you heading to your second job later?"

"Guess you'll just have to wait and see."

"Is that a promise or a threat?"

"Yes."

He laughed and the sound was music to her ears. The room had returned to normal. She smoothed the skin tight skirt and grinned at him.

"You make it difficult to concentrate on business," Paul said with an approving smile. "So, you have David Matsumoto in a safe location?"

"We do." Glancing at her watch, she changed the subject. "You know, we'd best be getting a move on and can talk more in the jeep."

On their way out, they passed Max tending bar, who nodded at Dorothy, as if to let her know the threat had passed.

"Should I introduce you as Dorothy, or do you prefer Cher to go along with the hair?" Paul joked as they settled into her vehicle.

"Hmmm, let's see, how about Cherie. Cherie Markle?"

"Cherie, it is. Hope I can keep a straight face when Alanna lays eyes on you. I'm not bragging, but she's been making a play for me, so you'll be competition in her eyes." Snapping his fingers, he grinned. "And you're my blind date."

"Good idea. You can truthfully say I'm the cousin of a friend if anyone wants to know."

Paul asked if she wasn't going to be a bit chilly with her attire, now that the evening had turned cool.

"I've a sweater in the back seat."

As the drive continued, they discussed their strategy for the evening. Arriving at their destination, they followed a gleaming burgundy Cadillac into the driveway of Alanna's home. A middle aged, non-descript couple emerged as Dorothy parked beside them.

Paul and Dorothy looked at each other.

"Dominic and Lily Qu perhaps?" he said.

"Only one way to find out. Ready?"

"Let's do it, Cherie." He came around to open the door for her.

Anyone watching would have seen first one, then another, gorgeous long leg appear. As she stood, she leaned into the side view mirror for a final make up adjustment, not that it was needed. Tossing her head to settle her glossy black mane, she emphasized her perceived importance to Paul by clasping both arms possessively around one of his. As if joined at the hip, they approached the front door and were greeted by Johnson, who led them in.

Laughter and strains of music grew louder as they approached a large, informal entertainment area. Several people were hovering about Alanna and Victor, partially blocking Dorothy's view of them.

The moment Alanna spotted them, she swiftly made her way over. She barely hid a look of disdain toward

Paul's date. Ignoring her, Alanna greeted him. "Paul, how wonderful you're here. I've been so looking forward to seeing you this evening. How are you?"

"Alanna, let me introduce you to Cherie Markle. We already had a date planned and will be leaving shortly. I did tell you earlier."

"Pleased to meet you," was the dismissive response.

But Dorothy was ready.

"Oooh, Ms. Scolfield, I am so honored to meet you! I saw you on the news just last week, you know, and I love the clothes you were wearing. One day, I'm going to be able to afford the very same style, and dress like you," she gushed. "I can't tell you how excited I was when Paul here told me our first date would start out at your home." Cherie turned adoring eyes upon him.

"How nice for you, dear," was the ice queen's saccharin response. Her attention flew back to Paul. "Let me get you a drink. Then I want to introduce you to some of Portland's more-important people."

Dorothy wondered if Alanna even knew how successful Paul was and that he probably was already acquainted with many of the same people. She seemed to underestimate his standing in the business world.

Victor had turned at the sound of Paul's voice and observed the exchange. He came forward and introductions were made. Dorothy gave a little start and raised her voice. "Oh! You don't have a cat here do you? I mean, I'm really allergic, you know, I get hives and all wheezy. But it sure looks like you have a mean kitty if he put those scratches on your face."

Victor raised a hand to touch deep, parallel scratches that ran down one side of his face. "Please do not concern yourself, Miss Markle," he said, grimacing. "That cat will not make an appearance this evening."

Dorothy didn't miss the look he shot toward Alanna.

Then he pivoted his attention away. "Mr. Webster, you have my property?" As usual, there were no social pleasantries.

"Of course, it's in the car, and you'll have it before we leave. Are Mr. and Mrs. Qu here yet? I'd like to meet them. Seems I've developed an interest in Asian art. They should be able to answer some questions I have."

Alanna, smooth as silk, had managed to insert herself between Dorothy and Paul. She assured Paul a meeting could be arranged.

Dorothy excused herself from the group and began to explore the room, making casual conversation as she went. She'd picked up on the tension between Alanna and Victor and was sure Paul was aware of it too.

Not my idea of lovebirds, she thought.

A male guest practically leapt toward Dorothy in his haste to make her acquaintance. She positioned herself to make small talk and still observe Paul with their hosts.

Victor, apparently tiring of Paul, had moved away to greet another new arrival.

Dorothy watched as Alanna steered Paul toward a handsome man and introduced him as Portland's finest cosmetic surgeon, if not the entire state. Dorothy felt certain the good doctor counted Alanna among his clientele.

She continued to guide Paul about the room, and eventually they came upon the couple who had arrived in the Cadillac.

"Dominic, Lily, please meet my very good friend, Paul Webster."

Dorothy coaxed her chatty admirer a little closer to where Paul and the Qus stood, in order to listen in. Cheri's cover was blissfully unaware that he didn't have her full attention.

សេ

Dominic Qu was in his late fifties, showing the softness of an easy lifestyle. Intelligent brown eyes peered at Paul from behind stylish glasses. His suit, while of good quality, was at least a decade out of date. His wife and partner matched his age, and she looked uncomfortable in this social scene. Her graying, short cropped hair emphasized pinched features and cold eyes.

"Ah, Mr. Webster, Victor has spoken of you. We are pleased to meet you."

"Likewise." Paul dipped his head as a show of respect to the couple. "I understand you're the owners of Bamboo Fine Imports? If you're open to the public, I'd love to see your merchandise." Smiles were replaced by uneasy looks as Paul continued. "And you have a private collection as well. Any chance for a viewing? At your convenience, of course."

While Paul was speaking, he noticed Alanna had moved away and was now engaged in a discussion with Dorothy, sending her would be suitor on his way. Dorothy appeared to be somewhat agitated, despite Alanna's attention.

What's up between those two? he wondered. His thoughts were cut short as Dominic Qu spoke.

"Do you have a particular area of interest, Mr. Webster? We have many items that have come our way, some for sale."

"Jade's a favorite, especially carved. And lacquered objects interest me, too." He decided to go for broke and hoped for a reaction. "Recently, I saw a collection of beautiful dolls, dressed as Geishas. You must be familiar with these as well."

"We would be very pleased to assist, or educate you, on any of these objects, especially if you are interested in a purchase," Dominic replied in a guarded tone, showing no visible reaction to Paul's bait. As if by magic, a business card appeared in Dominic's hand for Paul. "Please come by during business hours any time."

Paul was disappointed at no forthcoming private invitation, but perhaps that would come in time. He thanked them and excused himself.

Not seeing Dorothy or Alanna in the room, he approached Lau, who stood off to one side. Paul resolved to bring this evening to a close. "Cherie and I will be leaving. I'll go bring back the item now."

"About time. I will accompany you."

With no further conversation, the men left the room.

೧೨೦೧

Dorothy stood facing Alanna in a small room. On the pretense of needing a bathroom and not feeling well, she'd managed to draw the hostess into a conversation.

When they'd first arrived, Dorothy had immediately noticed what Alanna's expert make-up failed to cover—the remnants of a nasty bruise along her jaw line. Now that she had the woman away from her guests, Dorothy offered to commiserate with her.

"Now, hon, I noticed right away that you've got yourself quite the bump on your face there. I know from experience how that got there, no shame in it either, you know? Some men, they're just...well, they're just men, you know what I mean? And no man, I mean *no* man, is worth putting up with that!" Somewhat amazed, Dorothy realized Alanna's eyes were glistening. She waited while the ice queen took a deep breath and blinked several times. Dorothy softened the tone of her voice. "If there's anything I can do, hon, I'm more than glad to help. And it's not because you're some big name celebrity, this is just a woman to woman thing, okay? It doesn't take a genius to know that you gave as good as you got, right? I knew right off those weren't any old cat scratches on that man's face!"

Although Alanna seemed to teeter on the edge of confession, she shook her head. "Thank you for your concern, dear," she responded brusquely, "and I do appreciate your offer of help, but I can take care of this myself. Now, if you'll excuse me, I must see to my guests."

Dorothy didn't push, and the women rejoined the party, just as Paul came back with Victor.

Dorothy made a bee line for Paul. "Oh, there you are. I thought you'd gone off and left little old me."

A pout was followed by her arm wrapping through his.

Alanna barely disguised a raised eyebrow as Paul began saying goodnight.

"Alanna, thank you for the invitation, and I'm glad to have met Mr. and Mrs. Qu, but we need to leave."

Their host merely nodded, as if not trusting herself to speak. She offered a bright smile and walked them to the door. A brief wave goodbye, and she closed the door as the couple returned to their car.

Once the car doors were closed, they both exhaled a big breath and started laughing.

"You've returned Yoko, I take it?"

"I have."

"How did that go? I've news for you, too."

Paul recounted the doll's return and the unveiled displeasure of Victor Lau. The man had insisted on seeing the doll in all her glory. "So I unwrapped her and handed her over. Lau could only grunt. He went over her with a fine tooth comb. He's satisfied, I hope. No 'thank you,' not really a surprise, and then he marched back to the house with her. What a charmer."

"Maybe I'll get him a book on etiquette for Christmas."

Paul laughed. "Couldn't hurt. Anyway, I followed him back, even though he ignored me. Here's hoping the transmitter works. I suppose they'd have picked up any conversation between Lau and me, had there been some," he said wryly. "He's one of the most unpleasant characters I've ever met. Let's hope I don't have to see him anytime soon."

"Sorry, Paul, it might not be the last time you see him if you're needed as a go-between. But I'm confident that, if there's any conversation taking place around the doll, we should be able to record it from here on in." Traffic was light, and Dorothy kept a close eye on her rearview mirror. "The more information we can gather, the better. You friend Alanna might be of help. With a little commiserating and a manly shoulder to cry on, she may open up to us—or at least you."

"I wouldn't classify her as a friend, and who is *we* exactly?"

Stopping for a red light, Dorothy turned to Paul. "The FBI's JAG section, who oversee gem thefts, has given me permission to follow through on any leads I have. They've put me on the payroll as a consultant until the investigation wraps up. Which means—" She laughed. "—that your bill will be subsidized by the tax-payers."

"How did you manage that?"

"Lucas and Murph put in a good word for me, and Dad may have lent his weight as well. I prefer to work on my own, but it's always nice to have friends in high plac-es."

Paul nodded. "A move we should celebrate, with a side order of details about your time with Alanna."

"How about the *Aye* for drinks and a quiet supper, unless you have other plans? I don't particularly want to be seen anywhere decent in this outfit. And I do have an ulterior motive for going to my place." He smiled. "You can take that naughty smile off your face, mister," she said. "Now the transmitter's been placed. The feds will get the same feed. I also need to connect with HB and the rest of the team. You don't mind, too much, do you?"

"Fine with me. I enjoy watching you work."

"Not so fast. I also have an assignment for you. Details to follow with your meal."

Confirming with one of her operatives that the coast was clear, she continued on to the *Private Aye*.

Kicking off her killer stilettos, Dorothy ran along the ramp and disappeared inside the boat with Paul not far behind. "Make yourself at home. Pour us some wine. It'll take me a few minutes to clean this make up off and feel like myself again, so I think a shower's in order."

Paul settled himself with a glass of wine while he waited for her to reappear. He turned on a light and closed the blinds.

She soon emerged from the back room. With her hair wrapped in a white fluffy towel, she was dressed in blue jeans and a black tee. Under Paul's admiring eyes, she busied herself in the kitchen, making sandwiches and sipping from the glass of wine Paul poured for her. "Hope you don't mind it's not anything fancy," she said, bringing plates to the table. "Ready to settle down and go over a couple of things?" Dorothy enjoyed teasing Paul. "I think the best plan," she said, "is for you to woo your new friend. You can complain to her that your blind date Cheri was not quite what you expected and you'd prefer a real woman."

"Woo?" Eyebrows raised, he gave a dramatic shudder, that was only half fake. "You aren't serious, are you? I don't entirely dislike Alanna, but to deliberately flirt with her—"

Dorothy was on a roll and cut him off. "And when

you are busy *wooing* Alanna, Cherie will be mincing along, clinging to Victor Lau. Or didn't you catch the hungry looks he was sending my way this evening?"

"Yeah, like a shark after a seal. I noticed."

"Did you also notice that Alanna's recently received a punch on the jaw? I suspect from Victor. She had it cleverly camouflaged with makeup, but I noticed it right off. That would likely be from the altercation Dad overheard, and I'd bet Victor received his scratches that night too."

Paul smiled as he put his empty wine glass down. "Very observant."

"Perhaps," she answered and then rose to her feet. "Time to check in with the boys and see if there's been any action." She moved into her operations room with Paul right behind her. A click of a switch and multiple screens came to life. She reached HB first, putting him on speaker. "Anything to report?"

"Hey, boss. Yes. I just sent you a report with an update on our new guest. In a nutshell, he's been a busy boy, playing on both sides of the street, if you get my drift."

"Got it. We'll probably have to hand him over shortly. JAG's involved now, and we don't want to be seen as obstructing their investigation either. I appreciate they're letting us work with them, so I don't want to jeopardize the relationship." She scrolled to her email. "I have the report. Are you still keeping an eye on the party house?"

"Yes, ma'am, doing that as I speak. Looks like most of the guests have left, and it's quiet. You want me to hang around all night?"

She considered. "No, stay for about an hour after everyone has left and, if nothing seems out of the ordinary, you can call it a night."

"Sounds good. I'll check in before I split."

Dorothy focused on another screen showing GPS tracking. "Yoko's not moved yet," she said, pointing a finger to the center of the screen.

"Once she's on the move, an audio signal will alert me, and the feds. In the meantime, let's see what HB's report says." She quickly scanned and printed the contents, not making any comments until she was finished. As they moved back to the sitting area, she spoke. "Well, it seems that David Matsumoto has been busy indeed, but maybe his value lies in the fact that he probably has a very good idea of how the smuggling works. He hasn't divulged much information, probably doesn't want to trust *anyone* right now." Continuing to read from the documents, she recounted more details. "Henry Yamada had hired him independently of Yashito's official payroll and got him employed as skilled technical labor with Jinan, in an effort to find out trade secrets regarding their knock-off new fabric. Better to have as much inside info as possible. Apparently, David stumbled upon the smuggling operation while doing his job."

"Any chance we can pry more from him before he's handed over to the FBI?"

"The feds may pull rank on us, but we'll stay involved for as long as we can. Now back to Mr. Matsumoto. Let's see...ah, yes. Evidently, it was his plan to steal Kimi and Yoko. His story being he thought they'd be valuable to Henry and Yashito, but in reality, he really wanted what was inside the dolls. Figured he could do some smuggling of his own. He must have whatever was inside Kimi, but didn't have time to steal Yoko's secret cargo.

Paul stroked his chin. "And now he has the pleasure of Victor Lau being extremely angry with him, not just for discovering the smuggling route, but for having the nerve to steal what he was trying to smuggle. Ironic."

"He's also been caught in a dishonorable state of lying to his own boss," Dorothy added. "I don't envy him. The best that might happen is some kind of immunity from the government if he's instrumental in bringing down this operation."

"I wonder if Mr. Yashito knows what Henry was up to," Paul reflected. "If not, then I'm thinking Henry may be out of work before long. I got the impression that Mr. Yashito's an honorable man, in the traditional sense, and perhaps Henry is too Americanized for his own good with that company. Which brings us to Alanna. How involved is she? Or is Victor just using her, as part of a respectability cover on his part?"

Dorothy handed him a phone. "Here's your chance to find out. Give her a call and see if she's willing to meet you. Don't worry, this phone number's blocked."

He took a deep breath and made the call. "Alanna? Paul Webster here. I wanted to thank you for the invite earlier and—" He hesitated.

"Go on!" Dorothy whispered.

"—to see if you'd like to have lunch?"

Dorothy's lips twitched in amusement as she watched the emotions playing across Paul's face. From the eye rolling to the grimaces, it was quite the show.

"Wonderful, I'll see you then...Yes, I will. Goodnight." He sighed. "Noon, on Monday," he said in a defeated tone, handing back the phone.

She reached out and gave his shoulder a jab. "Oh, relax, Paul, I'm not asking you to marry her. Unless, of course, that's an option you want to consider."

"As if!" he retorted.

She smiled, rose, and walked to the other room while unwrapping the towel. As she brushed out her hair, they discussed a plan to best use their connection with Alanna to find out what she knew. Returning to where Paul sat, her hair back to normal, Dorothy stopped in front of him. "Well, do you prefer the black hair or the real thing?"

Paul's breath caught in his throat. Her hair was loose and flowing over her shoulders, laughter danced in her eyes, and the wine had produced a slight blush on her cheeks. Not speaking, he reached for her hand and pulled her down beside him on the couch. For a long moment, he gazed into her eyes. Slowly, she closed them as Paul pulled her to him and softly met her lips with his.

"What have you done to me?" he whispered when the kiss came to an end.

"I might ask the same of you," she murmured.

Not resisting, she allowed herself to cherish the moment as he gently kissed the side of her neck, feeling the tremor inside as his lips awakened feelings long held at bay. As he caressed the side of her cheek, she could feel the tenderness in his touch and knew he would never hurt her.

Growing bolder, she returned his kiss and traced the outline of his face with her fingers, their eyes never losing sight of the other. Until she spoke.

"Paul, it's been a long time. I don't know if I can." Regretfully, she pulled back. The wounded look on his face stabbed at her heart.

"What's wrong, Dee?"

The concern in his voice gave her courage and she drew a deep breath. "I need to tell you about my marriage—and if you think less of me after, I'll understand."

He held her hands. "You have my undivided attention. I'm not about to judge you."

She gave him a small smile and squeezed his hands. Feeling more confident, she began...

"Angelo Moretti and I met at the Academy. I fell for him and fell hard. Once we were assigned to different precincts, we began dating, and I couldn't believe he'd consider me worthy, out of all the females he had to choose from. I'm not kidding," she said when she noted Paul's raised eyebrows. "Within a year, we got married. Can you imagine the size of a combined Irish-Italian wedding? Not only was my dad a cop, my husband's family had more than the average share among its clan. Did I mention his nickname was Angel? He had a reputation for being the sympathetic officer at domestic calls and accident scenes, but I need to tell you that, once he walked through the door of our apartment, he was less than an angel toward me."

She felt his hand tighten over hers as she spoke.

Emotions came flooding back as she rehashed those times again.

"Like every domestic abuse case, it started out small. And if I'd been smart, I'd have paid attention to the warning bells that went off the first time he pushed me. 'A friendly shove' he called it. Right."

"Dee, you don't have to tell me if it's too painful."

"I know, but you've shown me we deserve to be upfront with each other, and it's time you know all the facts."

He nodded. "Go on."

"So, first it was a shove, then a couple of slaps. Those he put down to frustrations at work. Funny, I had the same frustrations, but slapping the man I loved never crossed *my* mind. Anyway, it soon escalated, and I had to create excuses to explain the bruises and occasional breaks. I'm sure my dad knew what was going on, but he followed my lead and, if I wasn't saying anything, he acquiesced. And of course who could I report it to? His fellow officers would never believe it, and his own family? Well, I'd be lying if I told you I wasn't just a little scared of what they might do. The story would definitely all be one-sided."

"Catch-22."

She nodded and took a deep breath. "And then he got into gambling, and there were money problems, which of course were somehow my fault and just more fuel for the 'deserved' abuse. I'm ashamed to say this carried on for almost five long years. More than once I tried to leave, but there was no way he was going to allow that. The only thing I'm grateful for is that there were no children. One of the more severe beatings put an end to that possibility once and for all."

"I'm so sorry, Dee."

"Things came to a head one night. He came off shift and had stopped at a bookie's on the way home. No good news there. The supper I'd left for him had grown cold and how dare I be watching television and not fixing him a hot meal. He was in a vile mood, and I was once again afraid for my life. Maybe I'd had a flash of instinct earlier, but my service revolver was on the table beside me. While he ranted and worked himself into frenzy I grabbed it. By the time he was ready to take that first swing at me, I had the gun pointed at him. Can you believe it? He laughed! Said I'd never have the guts to pull the trigger, that I'd never find a man like him ever again, and I should be thanking my lucky stars that he still came home to me every day." She saw him clench his jaw, but he didn't interrupt. "He kept advancing on me, despite my warnings to stop. Paul, he wouldn't listen!" A sob escaped her throat, but she fought to regain her composure. "He got close enough to reach for the gun. We struggled and it went off. I—I—killed him."

"No one would blame you Dee. It was self-defence."

"You'd think so, but if killing my husband was a nightmare—the investigation and accusations that followed was pure hell. The brothers, both blood and uniform, stood together, and while I wasn't mandated to leave the force, it sure got mighty uncomfortable. So when the opportunity arose to come out here with my dad, I jumped at it." She paused and swallowed hard. "And now you know."

"Which explains your empathy toward Alanna."

"Yes."

Paul held her close and she looked into his eyes.

"Listen, Dee, your past, like mine, is just that. It's the past. Nothing can change it, and it will always be a part of who we are. It changes nothing of how I feel about you, except to help me understand you better."

Relief flooded through her and she folded herself into his waiting arms. "Thank you for listening—and not judging. There aren't many I've told about this. I guess, on some level, I feel ashamed."

"Hush now. I'll never hurt you, and I won't rush anything until you're ready."

In answer, she reached up, and turned out the light.

Their soft murmurs synchronized with the gentle movements of the boat as the evening tide rose.

Chapter 12

Look at the *time!*"

Dorothy had rolled over to look at her watch, but when she realized Paul was beside her, she lay back on the pillows, a contented smile on her face. Sometime during the night they'd made themselves more comfortable by extending the sofa into a double bed.

"Morning, beautiful," came the sleepy response from the other side of the bed.

"Good morning yourself, sailor. You sleep on this old tub? Not seasick are you?" she teased.

In answer, he pulled her close and nuzzled her neck. She started to respond then reluctantly changed her mind. Swinging her feet onto the floor, she turned to him. "Mr. Webster, as I am in your employ, I feel the client/employee relationship has been severely jeopardized by all these shenanigans, and I don't know how impartial I can now be in your best interests."

He chuckled, grabbed her hand, and pulled her back to him. "I promise to resume our proper client/employee relations if you promise we can have more shenanigans later," he murmured as he finally released her.

Dorothy just smiled and moved away. She didn't have to go far to put the coffee on and then jump in the shower. Soon, she was down to business in the small kitchen area.

"I'll start on breakfast if you want to use the shower. Dad will be here shortly to deliver supplies. Then I'll tell you both what I've been thinking."

Paul stood behind her, his arms about her waist. "Coffee will be fine for me. But I didn't know we'd be having company so early." He tapped her playfully on the behind as he made his way to the shower.

In next to no time, they were sharing a coffee, each finding an excuse to touch the other's hand, communicating with no words. Approaching footsteps on the deck outside brought their intimate respite to a temporary halt.

"Good morning, my darlin'," Max sang in his Irish brogue. "Oh, and who do we have here? Well, if it isn't Mr. Webster visiting first thing. No, don't get up. I hope you like a big Irish fry up for breakfast. You do know it's the most important meal of the day?"

The man's enthusiasm was contagious, and it was hard to begrudge him the interruption he'd caused.

"Good morning to you too, Max. Coffee's all I need." Paul raised his mug in salute to the older Dennehy.

"No good arguing about breakfast, Paul, you don't stand a chance," Dorothy advised as she helped her dad with the stores he'd brought.

Max unloaded bags, filled the fridge, and rattled cooking pans. His large frame filled the little galley kitchen, and it wasn't long before the tantalizing aroma of bacon and sausage brought Paul's appetite to life. Max explained he'd done a stint in the navy and was used to small quarters. He maneuvred around like a ballet dancer, talking all the while. Before long, they were sitting at the small table.

They brought Max up to date with the doll situation, Victor Lau, and finally David Matsumoto, who, Dorothy confessed to Paul, was being kept in a house, just a few doors away from his own home. She crumpled up her serviette and dropped it on her empty plate. "I've a plan, so hear me out and let me know what you think. Keep in mind we don't have a lot of time to play with."

She had their full attention.

"Matsumoto is acting very nervous, according to Raymond and HB, who are watching him. The fact that he's not tried to run makes me think he's afraid of Victor Lau but doesn't appear to realize the predicament he's in with JAG. The feds will only wait a short time until they pull him in and do their own interrogating, and I feel we could use this to our advantage."

"What do you have in mind, love?" Max prompted, pouring more coffee.

"Glad you asked, Dad. I know this is a little irregular, but I'd like you to act as a JAG agent to see what you can pry from Mr. Matsumoto. You won't need to say you're from JAG or that you're a federal agent. HB will set the scene. Your tough guy presence is what we need. If Matsumoto falls for it, maybe he'll give us the information we need. Of course, anything we learn will be given to the feds so they can deal with him. It just might give us a good lead on Lau."

"I like the idea. Think you can pull it off?" Paul asked.

"JAG has given me carte blanche. Dad and I have our routine down pat. Just like *Starsky & Hutch*. Right, Dad?"

"Could be fun, darlin'. What do you want me to find out?"

"What we really need to know is where and how the Chinese are marketing their textiles. Maybe he can give us more on Henry Yamada too. His involvement's not really clear. So, what do you think? You'd have to be in a suit, Dad, and I'll be your partner. I think he'd be more willing to talk to you than answer to a mere woman."

Max rubbed his hands together. "When do we get this show on the road?"

"No time like the present. I'll set things up with HB and Raymond. Then I think a visit this afternoon is in order. What do you think, Paul?"

"You seem to have thought this through, I'm definitely on board with it."

Dorothy jumped up and headed to work in her office. "I'll need to keep my black wig on standby. Cherie is anxious to meet up with her friend Victor," she said over her shoulder.

"Well, boyo, if I have to put a shirt and tie on, I'll be on my way. Give me a call, Dorothy, when you're ready to move," Max shouted, leaving the houseboat.

A soft spring breeze had cleared the sky of any clouds, and the fresh air seemed to bring a sense of purpose to the afternoon's activities. Paul opened the kitchen window.

Dorothy was absorbed with work, her fingers flying over her keyboard. A small cough made her look up.

Paul stood in the doorway.

"How long have you been standing there?"

"Only a minute, or three." He smiled and gestured toward the kitchen. "Dishes are done, and I'm on my way. Catherine will be wondering what the heck happened to me. I've called a cab and will be anxious to hear how your chat with Matsumoto goes."

"I'm sorry. I didn't mean for you to clean up. Guess I got sidetracked in here." She looked apologetically at her desk. "But thank you." She stood and came to him, arms ready for a hug. "I think I'll miss you," she whispered into his ear.

He smiled. "I *know* I'll miss you. But, for now, we both have work to do."

A gentle kiss on her forehead was his goodbye, knowing they'd be together again soon.

ຂຈຂ

Dressed in a conservative gray suit, Max Dennehy presented the demeanor of a seasoned official, and his daughter was suitably attired in a modest skirt and jacket, with hair pulled back and no makeup. With her sensible shoes, no nonsense was written all over her. The moment they entered through the front door of the safe house, they were all business and introduced themselves to HB, who gave no hint of recognition. "We've come to see David Matsumoto," Max announced with little preamble.

"He's in the next room." HB led the pair down a short hallway. Without knocking, he opened the door to reveal a sparsely furnished room, whose window had been boarded over. Sitting dejectedly on a narrow cot was a slight man, pale and barely able to control a visible tremor, which threatened to overtake him completely. On a chair next to him sat the remains of an earlier meal, picked over.

"Mr. Matsumoto, I warned you the feds would be involved," HB said to the man, "especially the Jewelry and Gem boys. Looks like your time's up."

Turning back to Max and Dorothy, HB barely nodded. "Call if you need anything. I'm right outside the door."

The door closed behind him, and Max introduced himself as "Mac Connors and my partner, Jill McPhee."

The detainee looked up at them uneasily. "Please, if I may see some identification," he said, just above a whisper.

Obligingly Max and Dorothy produced official-looking credentials. Glancing without really seeing, Matsumoto just nodded and once more allowed his head to droop.

Grabbing a nearby stool, Max situated himself directly in front of the subject, while Dorothy leaned casually up against a cabinet in the corner.

"Now then, Mr. Matsumoto, it would seem you've found yourself smack dab in the middle of a situation which doesn't have a lot of healthy options for you."

There was no response, other than an increase in the nervous tremor.

"I'm sure that Victor Lau would be most interested to know your whereabouts," Max taunted, receiving the response he was looking for—David Matsumoto grew paler. "If you fail to co-operate with us," Max informed him, "you'll be deported, and that fact will be made public very quickly."

The man's mouth opened. "I have brought great dishonor to Yashito Design and Textile. I am disgraced."

"Why are you disgraced?" Max asked.

"You would not understand."

"Try me."

Matsumoto sighed. "For many years I have been honored to work for the Yashito company. Many opportunities were given to me, and my responsibilities grew. Sometime ago, Henry Yamada handpicked me to be part of a team developing a new product. I was so pleased to be felt trustworthy of such a position. And now I have let down that trust, all because of greed..." His voice trailed off.

Dorothy stepped into his line of sight. "Mr. Matsumoto, I understand a little about Japanese honor, and, while my partner and I need to know what's going on, we also want to help you. It'd probably be better to deal with us than Victor Lau. If your information leads to his downfall, then I'm sure something can be worked out that would lesson your punishment."

Without looking at her, Matsumoto shrugged. "There is only one punishment fitting what I have done. I am not afraid of your American justice."

"Jill, how about you go find us a coffee, and I'll continue the chat with our little friend here," Max said, dismissing his daughter.

Giving him a practiced look of extreme frustration, she turned and left the room, slamming the door hard on the way out.

Immediately, she joined HB and they both listened in on the conversation being taped. With Dorothy out of the room, Max launched his next tactic.

"I'm thinking you'll feel more like talking without a woman in the room, am I right?" There was no response. "Let's see how much of the story I can provide and you just fill in any of the missing pieces," Max continued. "So Henry Yamada handpicked you. His intention was to uncover the inside scoop on Jinan Import and Export and their process. You were to gather information that would enable them to better compete with, or expose, the counterfeit merchandise Lau has made in America. He managed to find you a good position within Jinan. And, for a while, you did just fine, funneling information back to them. How am I doing so far?"

Matsumoto gave a brief nod of affirmation.

"But then something else happened that really got your attention, didn't it?" Max asked. "Thought one little item wouldn't be missed from the cache of gems and historical artefacts being smuggled out of China. Actually stolen objects, if we're going for accuracy here. You know, that's a serious crime in this country—smuggling of antiquities, especially stolen ones. Where, or who, was Lau's source? Who's his connection here in America? And what's he going to do with you when he finds you? No doubt, he's aware that you have in your possession a very valuable object, and he wants it back. Then Henry Yamada has to go to his boss and explain what a failure you've been. Do you think he'll shoulder any of the blame, or expect you to take the fall?"

Max bombarded the man with question after question, not waiting for a reply, just relentlessly hounding him until there was nothing left to ask, except one last question. He allowed a moment's silence before the final jab.

"Well, friend, if you're not going to provide any information, then it will be up to us to decide who to inform of your whereabouts and give notice that you'll be deported. Will it be Victor Lau or Henry Yamada?"

Pride, disgrace, and tradition seemed to be at war within the man, and he appeared to visibly grow smaller as the realization of what his future held finally settled in.

Glancing at his watch, Max started to rise. "Can't say we didn't try to help, and I wish you luck."

As his hand reached for the doorknob, Matsumoto finally spoke. "Wait, please. If I tell you what I know, what guarantee do I have that I will be safe from Victor Lau?"

Dorothy and HB shared a hopeful smile and waited to see what beans would be spilled.

An hour later, Max emerged from the room, a triumphant smile on his face. "Well, Jill, happy with the results? I'm glad he's agreed to be moved under the jurisdiction of the feds. They can pick him up anytime. From what we've learned of Victor Lau, he'll fare better with them and may be granted some immunity. Looks like the guy got in over his head, but one bad lapse in judgement is all it takes, and down you go."

"Glad to see you haven't lost your touch, Mac. We'll call in the JAG contact now and turn Matsumoto over." She glanced at her watch. "Paul's probably home now—if you want to drop me off there, I can make my own way home later. I know he'll be anxious to hear how things went."

"I can do that, darlin." Turning to HB, Max commended the agent on his set up with their house guest and said he was sure Dorothy'd give him the night off, once the Feds picked up Matsumoto.

Her playful punch connected with Max's arm. "I was just going to say that—I know how to keep my employees happy. We've got copies of the tape, so I don't think we need to horn in on the feds angle any more. They're welcome to Mr. Matsumoto. If you need me, though HB, you know how to reach me."

"Got it, boss, and thanks."

A few minutes later, Dorothy stood at Paul's door, finger poised to ring the doorbell, but the door was thrown open as if its owner had been watching and waiting.

"Well, how'd it go? Learn anything useful?"

"JAG are on their way now to pick him up. It worked like a charm, and Dad was his usual persuasive self. I have to hand it to him. He knows how to play the part. And by the way, it would appear your premises are clean, no bugs about."

Dorothy was on a high. She paced back and forth, as she related how Henry Yamada's hireling, David Matsumoto, in addition to his industrial espionage, was doing a bit of thieving on the side. He very much regretted the lapse in judgement and was in way over his head.

"The feds may overlook the industrial espionage. It seems to be accepted practice in business today, but not so the smuggling of stolen artefacts. If he cooperates and helps them bring down Victor Lau...well, they may be lenient. He gave Dad quite a few names and contacts. We think he was going to use them himself but has decided his life is worth more if he coughs up what he knows."

"Great job, Dee. All that hard work deserves some kind of reward."

"No time yet for that. There's still work to be done."

He cocked an eyebrow. "By the look on your face, I'd bet you have something up your sleeve. However, before anything else, I want to show you something upstairs in my bedroom."

"I told you, rewards will have to come later." Her smile softened the admonition.

"You have it all wrong, young lady. I really do need to show you something from my bedroom window."

He took her hand, led her upstairs, and walked over to the window.

"Just move the curtain a little and tell me what you see."

Parked opposite the safe house just a few doors up, was the same car that had been seen many times over the past few days.

"They pulled up about five minutes after you and your dad showed up, so I'm guessing they'd have seen you leave."

Dorothy assessed the vehicle and could see that its two occupants appeared to have a camera aimed at the house. She whipped out her cell phone and spoke to HB, informing him of the situation, and then called her dad. "Dad, see if you can bring some uniforms over here to clear off Victor Lau's goons before the feds arrive. I'll see if JAG can postpone the pickup for half an hour. I don't think they'd appreciate being photographed. Thanks."

In silence, they stood at the window observing the car while waiting for reinforcements.

Breaking the silence, Paul said, "I'm concerned for your safety when you finally rendezvous with Lau. Cherie is good, but he's devious and a serious threat. Will you be armed?"

She made him look her in the eyes. "Don't underestimate me. This is my life and I'm good at what I do." She could see the worry on his face and wanted to put his mind at ease, but she also needed him to understand she could take care of herself. "I'll be covered by the guys from JAG, and I've my own surveillance people around all the time. Why do you think I'm so expensive? I'm never without backup, and Dad's always looking out for me. No worries—got it?"

"Understood and I apologize but you know—"

Dorothy's eyes were now riveted on the window and commotion on the street below. A patrol car had arrived, and an officer was asking the two occupants to get out.

She compromised with a quick kiss on his cheek. "Sorry, we'll continue this later."

She was back on the phone, her eyes never leaving the scene below. Voices were now raised, and there appeared to be a heated argument about the need for identification. The officers were obviously not satisfied with their answers to their questions of why they'd be taking pictures of an empty house.

"Looks like they're taking them in, HB, so let's have a look at the car before the feds arrive, or it's towed away. Won't be long now. How's our guest?"

"The man is more than a little nervous and downright jumpy," HB advised her. "But he obligingly wrote down a few more names. It seems that most of the people concerned in the smuggling originated in Beijing."

"Good work, HB. Listen, I hate to do this to you but can you cancel your night off?" She made eye contact with Paul. "I'd like everyone to meet here at Paul's place after Matsumoto's been removed. If Lau's guys are in custody, at least for a few hours, then I'd like to have a conference with all concerned. Raymond, too."

"No problem, boss. But when this job is over there's a small island in the sun with my name on it, just waiting for me."

Chuckling, Dorothy ended the conversation and went straight into another call, this time to her JAG contact. She spoke briefly to him and brought him up to date.

He agreed to join them at her impromptu gathering— once Matsumoto was in custody and a quick debriefing held. Finally taking a breather as she ended the call, she turned her attention to Paul. "I better bring Dad on board too. I hope you don't mind me using your home as a meeting place. It just seems a convenient and 'clean' location for us to gather and map out what's next."

"No complaints here. I said it before, I'm in your capable hands. However, the vacuum and duster are in the hall closet."

He held up his hands in mock surrender, and Dorothy moved toward the door, but then she turned with a grin. "If you're a good boy and behave, I may stay over tonight, unless the thought of me cozying up to Lau is a deterrent? Let's see what we can map out when everyone's here."

Paul managed a very theatrical sigh. "Well, I'm not sure if I want to play second fiddle, but if that's the best you can do."

"Stop pouting and tell me about your day while I was next door impersonating the FBI."

"Aside from the minor affairs of running a business,

Catherine and I worked on more of the merger celebration. It would be great if all this trouble with Lau and company was wrapped up before then—it'll put a real damper on things if not."

"Let's be optimistic. We've had a good breakthrough with David Matsumoto today." Her phone rang. "Hi, Dad, listen, we may have been observed, even photographed, leaving after our interview with Matsumoto, by those two in the car. Any chance you can find out what photographs might be on the camera they had?...Thanks, Dad. I'll do that." She hung up laughing.

"What's so funny?"

"He's concerned we're not eating enough, and I've a feeling he'll be remedying that when he arrives in a little while. He wants the 'lazy good for nothing' next door to go and pick up some beer as well." Then she turned a mischievous smile on her client. "Well we have about an hour, did you have any plans, Mr. Webster?"

Chapter 13

Paul smiled. "The plans I have in mind would need more than an hour. How about I put on a pot of coffee, instead, and we enjoy a few minutes peace and quiet before your party arrives."

"Sounds good to me, but I'm intrigued about what kind of plans you might have. Any chance of a discussion in the near future?"

"That's for me to know and you to find out," he countered with a laugh. "Come on, lady, I could do with a coffee."

He had just poured them a second cup, when the doorbell chimed. As instructed, there stood HB and Raymond, each with a six-pack of Max's favorite brew. Behind them, Max was pulling into the driveway.

Dorothy helped her father in with food he'd brought. They came back into the kitchen and set about putting together a meal for those who'd attend. Paul's mouth watered as the aroma of yet another home-cooked meal reached him. A large pot of chili was put onto the stovetop to keep warm.

"Another of my favorites, Paul. Irish chili," Max explained.

"*Irish* chili? Do tell."

"Well, son, let's just say that you'll be more likely to find potatoes in my chili, than beans. But still perfectly acceptable, so I'm told."

A large loaf of still-warm soda bread, wrapped in a tea towel, was set out with a dish of fresh butter.

Paul grabbed dishes and glasses for the table.

"Should be plenty for your JAG friends, if they're hungry when they arrive," Max advised. "Go on, help yourselves. And, I'd like to propose a toast. Here's to health, peace, and prosperity. May the flower of love never be nipped by the frost of disappointment, nor shadow of grief fall among your family and friends."

Beer glasses were raised in agreement.

For a few minutes, it was almost as if they'd forgotten the reason for gathering at Paul's home, until the doorbell let them know the rest of the guests had arrived. Dorothy excused herself to greet them.

She returned with two agents and made introductions.

Jim Addison was thirty-something, fair haired, tall and slender. He looked very confident in his tailored suit. His partner, Ashley Flores, matched him in height, but as fair as Jim was, Ashley was darker. Her serious expression quickly disappeared with her first smile. They both fit in easily with the group assembled and were more than glad to help themselves to Max's Irish chili.

Casual conversation soon gave way to more serious matters.

Jim Addison asserted himself as the authority in charge.

"Max, Dorothy, first let me thank you both, on behalf of the FBI's JAG Division, for your help in apprehending David Matsumoto. We're sure this will help in finally putting together the pieces behind the increase in one particular area of Asian smuggling. And,

Paul, you may be interested to know that your doll has now made its way to Bamboo Fine Imports. It's transmitting some interesting conversations."

"So the Qus are involved?" Dorothy asked.

"Indeed, very much so."

"We need more information on Victor Lau and hope you might be able to help us," Ashley said to Dorothy. "Your good friend, 'Cherie,' may be an asset. Also, Paul, you're having lunch with Alanna Scolfield on Monday, is that right?"

With a mouth full of chili, Paul merely nodded.

"Great. A golden opportunity for you to glean more information that she wouldn't perhaps share with the authorities." When he didn't comment, she offered reassurances. "If you have reservations about doing this, there's no obligation. It's different for Dorothy. She's on the payroll, so to speak. Although I'd heard that Alanna really has the hots for you," she said, grinning.

"Don't believe everything you hear," Paul countered. "I can handle a lunch date with Alanna. I'm not unsympathetic to her, and I have a vested interest about her involvement, if any, with the smuggling. For her sake, I hope she's not aware of Victor Lau's criminal pursuits."

The group's focus moved from conversation to opening more beer and refilling bowls with chili. Max humbly received accolades for his culinary creation.

When they'd settled down again, Jim Addison took over the conversation. "Paul, you've concerns regarding Alanna. Here's what we know so far. We've had our eye on Victor Lau for a very long time, including anyone connected with him. We knew something was afoot with Dominic Qu and Bamboo Fine Imports, but, as you found out, he and his wife portray a very unassuming couple, and we could never pin anything on them. Until the transmitter was hidden in the doll. And while we're successfully gathering evidence from that source, it would strengthen our case if we had concrete confirmation of direct involvement."

"How can I help?" Paul asked, jumping in with no hesitation.

"We thought maybe a visit with Alanna to the Qus' would give us the ammunition we need."

Paul sought Dorothy's eyes for affirmation but she seemed deep in thought, stirring the remnants of her chili.

"We have no proof that Alanna's involved with the smuggling or even knows about it," Ashley said, picking up the conversation. "Victor's likely using her, both as a cover for respectability and as a hostess for his entertaining. He needed someone in the fashion world to promote his version of the textile, and she was flattered by his initial attention. Maybe he made financial, or other, promises. Personally, I feel she may now regret her involvement. We've gathered from our sources, she's not a happy person at the moment. Max informed us of their latest fight. She may be willing to confide in a sympathetic ear, Paul. You know the saying 'Hell hath no fury like a woman scorned'?"

"So if you don't think she's involved, what do you think she can tell Paul that will be important to your case?" Dorothy asked.

"Perhaps she's overheard conversations, even if she's not aware of the significance of them. With the right prompting from Paul, she may unwittingly reveal inside information. Especially if Victor's wounded her ego, or vanity, she may be more than willing to confide in Paul. A visit to Bamboo Fine Imports could provide a catalyst."

"What do you think?" Dorothy enquired, turning to Paul.

A grin tugged at his lips. "I've been told my charms are persuasive. Let me give it a bit of thought on how I might handle things."

"Don't hesitate to call on me, if I can help," Max offered. "I'm not just another pretty face you know."

"And a talented chef to boot," Paul complimented. "But seriously, Max, I won't hesitate. Otherwise, I'd have to contend with your daughter giving me what for."

The conversation grew more casual as the meal came to an end and all made ready to go their separate ways.

"Will you need a ride back home, darlin'?" Max asked as the last of the meal containers were gathered up. HB, Raymond, and the JAG agents had left, and the house had settled back into a peaceful mood.

"I'll see she makes it home safe and sound, Max. We need to go over plans on how to deal with Victor and Alanna. All right with you, Dorothy?"

"You read my mind. Here, Dad, I'll help you back out to the car with all this. I think your chili was a big hit, thanks for making it."

"Well! Here's your coat, what's your hurry? Right, darlin'. I can take a hint. I'm off, and I'll leave you to enjoy your evening." He smiled as he spoke, showing he wasn't really annoyed.

With Paul's help, all that Max had brought was neatly stowed away in his car. They waved as he drove away.

Returning to the house, Paul locked the door behind them. He grasped Dorothy's hand and pulled her to him. "Now then, Ms. Dennehy, I believe it's time to talk about that ancient Irish tradition."

"My father's Irish chili?"

"Shenanigans…"

CROSO

Wrapped in Paul's bathrobe, Dorothy curled up contentedly beside him on the sofa. "Now this is the way to end a day. I could get used to this," she murmured as he stroked her hair.

"Couldn't agree more." He hesitated before continuing. "I hate to kill the mood, but we need to discuss our next move with Victor and Alanna. I think I'll take her shopping with me after our lunch on Monday. A good excuse to get into Bamboo Fine Imports, and then I'd just have to ad lib it from there."

"It would be a start," she agreed, giving in to a lazy stretch. "I, on the other hand, have to gear up to ingratiate myself in Victor's good graces."

He fixed her with an injured look. "As long as you don't wear one of *his* bathrobes—"

"Not a chance. Besides, the wig will be long enough to keep me warm," she teased. And, with that, she moved off the couch and retrieved her handbag. Taking out her cell and a small note book, she punched in some numbers. Paul sat transfixed as he saw her change from Dorothy to Cherie before his eyes.

"Oh hi, um…can I speak to Mr. Victor Lau please. Tell him it's Cherie Markle calling. Thanks so much!" She winked at Paul as she waited for Victor to pick up the call. "Mr. Lau? Gosh, I'm glad you're there. I didn't know if I'd be able to reach you this quickly, you being so important and all. But I just wanted to let you know how much I enjoyed meeting you. And, well, this might be a bit forward on my part, but if you're ever looking for a friend, I wouldn't mind going for a coffee, or something. Pardon me for saying, but I got the impression you weren't all that happy with Ms. Scolfield, and maybe you just need someone who'd listen and offer a sympathetic ear."

Paul almost felt a twinge of sympathy for Victor

Lau, as he imagined the man enduring the rapid fire of Cherie's speech.

She paused and appeared to be listening intently, and then a knowing smile spread across her face. "You would? Oh, wow, I mean, yes, that would be great! Sure, I can dress a little warmer. Yes, I know where that is. Meet you there at four tomorrow afternoon. Paul? Well, gosh, you know, it was only a blind date. Didn't really turn out the way I'd hoped...Why, thank you. I don't think anyone's ever said that before." And she actually managed a giggle that was so unlike Dorothy, Paul had to refrain from laughing out loud. "Bye, bye for now."

He shook his head in admiration. "Meryl Streep had better watch out. You are definitely competition." He reached for her. "Come back over here, you. I think we've discussed enough of our plans and we can spend some more time on us."

∽∾∾

The next morning dawned dull and rainy. After a breakfast of toast and coffee, they lingered in Paul's kitchen going over ideas on how they'd deal with their respective dates.

Paul laid out his plan to let Alanna know he'd sensed an immediate attraction between them and couldn't help but notice how unhappy she was at their last meeting. If she was receptive, he'd ask her just how much she was involved with Victor and offer a shoulder to cry on. He'd build up her ego with all the wonderful things he'd heard about her business.

"How am I doing so far, any of this sound plausible?"

Dorothy smiled as she watched him pace across the kitchen. "You're doing great. Maybe when you take her to the Qus, you could coach her to ask questions about the doll collection. I wonder if they've discovered the dummy artefact yet. Hopefully they may not have noticed it's not the genuine article."

"Well, I'll do my best to woo her but I don't want to scare her off. Maybe we can look at some jewelry, and I'll gradually talk to her about Asian artefacts and see if anything twigs. There are lots of scenarios but I'll have to play it by ear—using all my charm of course," he finished with wry smile.

"Hmph. First you're going to woo her and then use all your charm. Perhaps I should be on hand in case you need rescuing—from yourself, Mr. Webster. Be careful you don't give away the game."

"I can play the game, Dorothy." The easy bantering crashed to a stop. He moved to refill his coffee cup. After a moment's silence, he continued. "What're your plans and where are you meeting with Lau?"

Before responding, Dorothy moved from the kitchen and called over her shoulder as she ran upstairs, "Let me have a shower first, then I'll tell you. I have to bring Cherie back and do some prep work before meeting with her new boyfriend."

She leaned over the banister and teased with a smile. Paul couldn't resist returning it. "I'll be waiting."

When she reappeared, she was all business. Calls had been made to meet with her operatives to go over the meeting with Victor. She'd meet him at the airport, where he was scheduled to join some executives who were flying in on a business layover.

Paul looked at her pointedly. "I trust you'll have coverage at the airport? You know I won't rest easy till I hear from you."

"Yes, I'll have cover and I'll be wired. If you can slip away from the office, you're more than welcome to join the guys at the *Aye* and listen in as Cherie Markle has her date."

Her tone may have been business like, but inwardly she was warmed by the genuine concern he showed.

They lingered in a tight embrace, but then it was time for her to leave.

Chapter 14

Cherie's cab arrived at Portland International Airport just after three-thirty. Handing over the fare, Cherie instructed HB, who sat behind the wheel, to be on standby for a later pick up.

Merely nodding, he accepted the cash and, without a backward look, drove away, leaving Cherie at the curb. She caught sight of admiring glances as she made her way through the airport doors. Her flowing black wig did not detract from the emerald green two-piece pantsuit she wore. Its form-fitting cut accentuated her shapely figure. She strode with confidence through the airport concourse, making her way to the Oregon Market. She soon found the Rose City Wine Bar, her destination to meet Victor Lau.

Stopping several yards from the entrance, she pulled a mirror and lipstick from her handbag and, under pretence of touching up her lipstick, spoke quietly to an unseen companion. "I'm just about to enter the Wine Bar and hope you're receiving this okay."

"Affirmative."

Jim and Ashley were sitting in a nearby customs office, out of sight but in touch.

Right, Cherie girl, this is it. Let's see how we handle Mr. Victor Lau.

With a toss of her jet-black mane, she confidently headed toward the bar's entrance. Once inside, she scanned the interior and quickly found her man, sitting at a corner table. He rose to greet her.

"Miss Markle. I am glad you suggested we get together. Please, sit, and I will order you a drink. What would you like?"

"Why, thanks. I'll have a Mai-tai please. And it's Cherie to my friends." She slid onto a chair directly across from Victor. "Gosh I'm glad to be here too, with such a gentleman and all. You said you have friends coming too? Almost like another party."

"Correct. They should be here any moment. I hope you don't mind that I have had to combine business with pleasure, but they are only passing through and this is merely a courtesy visit. So there will be no dry business discussion to bore such a beautiful lady."

Cherie demurely lowered her eyes and managed to look flattered. "Oh, I don't mind at all. I always like to meet new people."

As her drink was placed in front of her, a cell phoned chirped. Victor looked startled and reached into his jacket, "Excuse me, I must take this call."

Once he said hello, he lapsed into an Asian dialect, and Cherie was disappointed and unable to understand the nature of the call. Victor kept his tone quite even. She hoped that the agents monitoring her would be able to interpret the conversation at some point.

Victor looked apologetic as he put his phone away. "Please forgive the interruption, but it appears we will be on our own. My associates have been delayed and are unable to meet."

"Oh, say, that it is too bad, I guess. Or maybe not."

She gave a little giggle and raised her glass. "Cheers."

Victor merely sipped at his own beverage and remained silent.

"Um, I hope I wasn't too forward on the phone yesterday when I mentioned what I'd seen between you and Ms. Scolfield? Glad to see the scratches are healing nicely, though."

"Alanna is a very…determined…woman. Usually an attribute I admire, but there are limits. However, for now, our relationship is back on track, but I thank you for your concern. Now then what about you? I find it hard to believe an attractive woman such as you is not married."

Cherie managed a grimace. "Not for lack of opportunity, I'll say. But, nope, I have to say I prefer the single life. I enjoy my fun, if you know what I mean." And she swiftly downed the remainder of her cocktail.

"Would a short trip on a private jet qualify as fun in your books, Cherie? Only a short walk from here."

She had to think fast, this was an unexpected turn of events.

The voice in her ear confirmed. "Too risky. Stay on the ground."

"Wow, normally I'd say, sure. But for the last couple of weeks, I've been having some ear infection problems, and I think that would really aggravate it, you know?"

"A shame. Well then, perhaps you'd care to just come and have a tour of my jet? I'm quite proud of it, and it would perhaps give us a little more privacy." The implication was clear as he caught her eye and held it for longer than necessary. Dorothy felt her skin crawl and hoped her expression didn't betray her.

As she hesitated with an answer, he sought to reassure her, "You're not nervous, are you, Cherie? You can trust me. Besides, I have some beautiful art from my own home on board, which might interest you. I noticed you paid a lot of attention to some pieces at Alanna's the other night."

"Oh, I just loved the vases she has, and those shiny black boxes."

"You mean the lacquered chests? They are quite beautiful, aren't they? And very valuable, too."

"Oooh, I'd love to see more of them. I guess a visit to your little plane would be all right, but I can't stay long. It's a work day tomorrow, you know."

Her ear piece came to life. "Change of plans, Dorothy. Coming up."

"Wonderful, let's go now, shall we?" Leaving money on the table to cover the drinks, he rose to his feet and took Cherie's arm.

She made a determined effort not to flinch, for she found him as appealing as her late husband when he'd had too much to drink.

They made their way back to the concourse of the busy terminal. Victor led the way, keeping in close contact with his date. Crowds of people, overloaded with luggage, were milling all about them. Out of the corner of her eye, Cherie realized a woman with a large duffel bag and a super-sized container of soda was headed straight for them. Something about her was familiar, but before Cherie could place her, the woman careened into her and cold sticky pop spilled all down the front of Cherie's outfit.

"Oh no! I'm so very sorry," the woman exclaimed in a distraught voice, "I didn't see you. Oh, your beautiful suit will be ruined. There's a washroom right here. Let's go and see if we can minimize the damage." Then Cherie knew, it was Ashley Flores. Quickly catching on, she agreed to accompany the woman into the washroom.

Feigning supreme disappointment, Cherie turned to Victor. "Nuts, Victor, I really am going to have to take care of this, or my clothes will be ruined. Looks like the rest of our date will have to be postponed—for another time, I hope?"

Frantically dabbing at the spreading wetness with sodden tissue, she couldn't help but notice that he had stepped back quite quickly when the liquid was en route and not a drop had touched his expensive suit.

A small crowd of onlookers had gathered, and he appeared uncomfortable. "A disappointment, but I understand. I feel somewhat responsible and will gladly pay for any cleaning costs."

"Oh, shucks, that won't be necessary, the washing machine will do the job. Just have to pop it in there as quick as I can. But thanks. Can I call you again?"

"Of course." Victor turned and quickly disappeared into the crowd.

Ashley and Dorothy headed into the washroom, where Ashley exhaled a large breath. "That was close!"

"I don't understand, Ashley. What happened?"

"Thankfully, nothing." Before offering an explanation, Ashley reached into the large duffel bag and retrieved a nondescript pair of sweat pants and tee shirt for Dorothy. A pair of blue crocs finished off the outfit.

As Dorothy went into a stall to change, Ashley explained. "The call your date received a few minutes ago? Good thing we had an agent who understood what was being said. You were being set up. There was never any intention of other business associates meeting you. The call was confirmation that Victor's suspicions about you were well founded. He suspected you're working with Paul and looking for information. According to the phone call, he ordered his jet be made ready for a brief flight about an hour offshore and then back again—and you wouldn't be on board when he landed."

Dorothy shuddered, glad to know the wettest she'd

be that afternoon was from the deliberately spilled soda.

"Your taxi's waiting, but unfortunately your cover is blown on this case," Ashley continued. "Sorry."

Dorothy was matter of fact. "It happens. I just hope it doesn't jeopardize Paul's meeting tomorrow. What do you think?"

"We'll need to regroup and go over strategy. I think the stakes have been raised and personal safety may be compromised. We need to be sure Paul can handle the situation. If anything happens to him, we're ultimately responsible. Now that Victor has been rousted, he may be even more of a threat."

Ashley made a move to the door as Dorothy stuffed her wet clothes into the duffle bag. "Do you mind if we meet back at the *Aye*? It's private enough, and Paul's already there. I'm sure he'll be glad to see you after this little episode."

She took the bag and told Dorothy she'd leave separately then meet her back at the houseboat.

Dorothy waited a few moments more before navigating through the terminal for the taxi and HB.

ℰↄℰↄ

The *Aye* was packed. All aboard were keyed up over Dorothy's airport escapade. Max's fatherly concern equalled Paul's relief at seeing her unharmed. After she reassured both men that she was fine, Paul and her father began to relax. The fact Dorothy had narrowly missed being dumped into the ocean was not lost on any of them, least of all Max.

As usual, he made sure all were looked after but that didn't stop him asking questions. "Now, darlin', what the heck happened out there?"

Max hadn't been there to hear the conversation being

taped. Before Dorothy could answer, Philip Yee, who had been brought in at the last minute to interpret, gave an account of the incident. Yee was American of Chinese ancestry and had been with the FBI for several years. Although only thirty, he'd proved himself invaluable. His linguistic skills were unparalleled. As well as Mandarin, Cantonese, and a few other Chinese dialects, he was fluent in eight other languages. After introducing himself formally, he gave his account of Victor's call from unknown quarters.

"After I was briefed by Jim about this case," he stated, getting everyone's attention, "it should be no surprise to you that we're dealing with a very dangerous man. The informant spoke Mandarin, but with a dialect I'm not familiar with. I'll take the tape back to the lab to try and pinpoint where he comes from. It might reveal more about him."

Phillip continued to relate what had been learned from overhearing Lau's call.

When he'd finished, Dorothy straightened. "Thanks for your quick interception, and great teamwork. I'm a pretty good swimmer but that would have been one long trip. Now, what's next? I can be a watchful eye over Paul when he lunches with Alanna tomorrow."

"Hold tight, Dorothy," Jim cautioned as he moved over to her side. "We need to discuss a few things first. For now, how about giving us a tour of this very impressive set up of yours?"

Not needed at the moment, HB and Raymond left, agreeing to check in with their boss later. Phillip, interested in the scope of Dorothy's agency, elected to stay as the houseboat became a little less crowded. Dorothy took the three agents into her operations room. As she explained some of the equipment's functions, there were favorable comments, and all were impressed.

Phillip also took his leave, promising a report as soon as possible. The others moved back to the main cabin, where Ashley took charge, and they began to work out a plan for safeguarding Paul when he met Alanna for lunch.

"Before we agree to let you go on this fishing expedition, we need you to promise some things. One, no heroics. Two, if at any time you feel in danger, you will leave. And three, we need you to wear a wire."

"Agreed." Paul nodded. "Anything else?"

Ashley glanced at Jim. "Jim and I talked at length with our superiors, and it was agreed you need to sign a waiver absolving us from responsibility should anything happen to you. You have to keep in mind that it is very not customary to allow civilians to carry out our work. However, because we are aware of your background and appreciate your involvement in this case, concessions have been made. You've made progress where we might not have been able to."

All eyes turned to Paul, who looked to be weighing everything very carefully. When he spoke his tone was cool. "I've worn a wire before, and I am fully aware of the unexpected which can occur. I may be a civilian right now, but having some experience with the military in covert operations, I'm confident that I won't let you down. This is very much a team operation and, as such, I assure you I won't take unnecessary risks."

"Thanks for the reassurance, Paul. I didn't mean to offend you, or underestimate your abilities, but we just need to let you know our side of things. From what we've observed so far, you are more than qualified to undertake the appointment with Alanna Scolfield tomorrow." Ashley had wanted to soothe any ruffled feathers and, judging by Paul's expression, she was successful. She then turned to Dorothy. "I know you want to be included but, for now, it will have to be at arm's length. I propose you be with us in our surveillance vehicle tomorrow. You at least have had some dealing with Alanna. We've had none, and you may be able to read her a bit better."

"Anything I can do is fine with me," Dorothy quickly agreed.

"Hey, don't forget about me," Max reminded them.

"As if we could, Dad. I'm sure your presence will come in very handy."

"No worries, Max, you'll be involved. But, like Paul, you'd have to sign a waiver. So if you're agreeable, you're in."

Max reached into his shirt pocket and brought out a pen with a flourish, eliciting a laugh from the group.

"Duly noted," Jim said. He then turned to Paul. "I'll come by your office about eleven tomorrow morning, to suit you up and do a sound check."

"Perfect. I should call ahead to Bamboo Fine Imports to ensure the time is right for taking Alanna shopping. We'll have lunch first—think I'll take her to Madame Butterfly's on Stark Street. So, ideally, we should be at the Qus' about one thirty."

"We'll have our surveillance vehicle set up well in advance of your lunch. Actually, your choice of restaurant works well because it's not that far from Bamboo Fine Imports, and we'll try to station ourselves midpoint between them both," Jim said.

Further instructions were given to Dorothy, and they wrapped up their debriefing session.

Soon the houseboat was quiet, and Paul anticipated some alone time with Dorothy. As she saw her father off the boat with a promise to be around later that evening, Paul stood behind her.

When she turned, he wrapped his arms around her. "Dorothy, if anything had happened to you today, I don't know what I would have done. You gave me such a scare. I can't tell you how relieved I was to see you walk through that door." Before she had a chance to reply, he cupped her face in his hands, "Do you know just how special you've become to me?"

The answer came in a deep and hungry kiss.

Gazing into her eyes, he sighed. "I can't say I'm sorry you won't be having any more planned contact with Victor Lau."

"It was a close call, but everything worked out. Besides, the shoe will be on the other foot now. *Tomorrow*, I'll be worrying about *you*!"

"Yes, you're right. I promise to be careful and not agree to any plane trips."

She swatted him on the arm and, laughing, pulled away. "Right then, I'll clean up from the soda spill. Give me about twenty minutes. Then we can go grab something to eat and try and forget about today's events for a little while."

"Best offer I've had all day, Cherie," he replied, grinning from ear to ear.

∽∾∽

Friday morning found Paul in discussion with Catherine, going over details of the upcoming merger celebration. As usual, his assistant ensured everything was on schedule.

True to his word, Jim Addison arrived to see Paul promptly at eleven. Leading Jim to the board room, Paul asked Catherine to bring Alanna to the reception area later when she arrived. They were not to be disturbed in the meantime.

Once the wire was in place, Jim took out his cell phone, dialled a number, and simply said, "Testing."

Paul repeated a brief sentence. Jim listened and confirmed all worked.

"Looks like we're all set, Paul. I'm going to hang back here and watch as you leave, and then I'll meet up with the team. We'll be listening closely and, just remember, at the first sign of any trouble, move Alanna and yourself out of harm's way, right?"

Paul gave a mock salute, assuring Jim he'd not jeopardize Alanna, or the investigation.

When Catherine knocked to let him know Alanna had arrived, Paul slipped out, leaving Jim behind closed doors.

Heading toward his office, he spied Alanna waiting in the reception area. He didn't know a lot about fashion, but guessed the cream-colored suit she wore was silk and probably worth more than he wanted to think about.

Even though she looked like she'd just stepped off the pages of a magazine, he preferred Dorothy's more carefree style.

"Hello, Paul," she gushed and leaned forward to accept the kiss he carefully placed on her cheek. Close up, he saw not a hair was out of place. "I can't tell you how much I'm looking forward to lunch today, and, of course, some shopping afterward."

Behind her back, Paul caught a slight, but unmistakeable rolling of Catherine's eyes and had to bite the inside of his cheek to keep from smiling in acknowledgement.

"I'm looking forward to lunch as well, Alanna, and hope you'll enjoy the restaurant. It's a blend of Japanese and French cuisines, but somehow it really works."

"If you like it, I'm sure it will be wonderful. Shall we?"

They arrived at the eatery and were soon seated. Paul recommended the Yakisoba.

"And what's in that, dear?" Alanna asked, glancing over the menu.

"It's quite good. Hot noodles, stir fried with bite-sized pieces of chicken."

She quickly agreed. The menus were removed, drinks placed before them, and they settled into casual conversation.

"How long have you been interested in the fashion business?" Paul asked.

"Oh forever, it seems." She allowed the smallest tinkle of a laugh to escape her full lips. "But my real interest is in public relations, of course, and I've represented many high-end clients, both here in Oregon and across the Mid-West. The fashion angle is but one of the areas I chose to specialize in."

"Is that why Victor approached you?" Paul took a chance in mentioning him and was not surprised to see her face momentarily cloud over.

Her hand trembled slightly as she laid her fork aside. "Please, Paul, if you don't mind, I'd rather not spoil my appetite by talking about that man."

Point taken, he moved on to other topics, keeping the focus on her and not allowing her the opportunity to ask much about him. It wasn't a difficult task, as the indomitable Ms. Scolfield certainly enjoyed talking about herself. Glancing at his watch, he changed gears. "Dominic and Lily will be expecting us shortly, so if you're finished, we should be moving on."

"I can't wait to see inside their business." She began to chatter. "I've known them for a little while but have never found the time to pay them a visit. I'm hopeful they'd want some PR representation to strengthen their marketability, so this may be a very beneficial visit. At the very least, I'd like to add to my own Far East collection."

After listening to the woman prattle for most of the lunch hour, Paul was even more of the belief that she truly didn't have a clue what Victor was involved in. He wondered if the surveillance team was having difficulty staying awake. But then he thought of Dorothy as part of the team and an unbidden smile came to his face.

"I'm glad you enjoyed lunch. Perhaps we can have dinner soon?" She must have mistaken the smile as being directed at her.

"Anything's possible." He guided her out of the restaurant before she got any more of those ideas in her head.

A few blocks away found them outside a lovely older Victorian style home, in an area which had become commercialized over the years, but still retained the air of a well-established and comfortable neighborhood. Bamboo Fine Imports not only took up the original structure, Paul could see the building had been extended significantly at the rear. Parking for several cars was available and, as they exited his car, he noted a cable repair van parked down the street. *Probably the backup,* he thought.

Entering the main door of the establishment, he felt immediately transported back to the Far East. A subtle hint of incense hung in the air. He watched Alanna's eyes grow wide in amazement at jeweler's display cases of jade jewelry and intricate carvings. Bi-discs similar to the one found in Yoko rested on velvet.

Exquisite artwork adorned the walls. Beautiful geisha-type portraits, delicate fans, and peaceful landscape scenes were arranged in groupings.

"Welcome to our business," said Dominic Qu as he and his wife moved to greet their visitors.

As Paul turned toward the sound of their voices, he was disquieted. Sitting on a child sized chair in the corner, was Yoko.

Chapter 15

"Oh my, what a beautiful doll," Alanna said as she moved toward the small bamboo chair where Yoko sat. "May I?" she asked Dominic Qu.

"Ah, I see you have an eye for beauty, Ms. Scolfield. Please, allow me."

Paul smiled to himself as he watched the art collector effortlessly place himself between Alanna and the expensive creation. The message was clear. This was his territory and he was in control. But Alanna was not without her own charm.

"Dominic, please, I've told you before, call me Alanna. We're not just acquaintances," she said in a flattering tone as she carefully took the doll extended by Dominic.

Her manicured hands stroked the jet-black hair. "Exquisite. Do you have more? This is definitely something I could collect myself."

Dominic appeared disconcerted at her presumed familiarity. He focused his attention on Paul. "Would you care to see the other dolls we have."

"We'd like that," Paul said.

Dominic asked Lily to take their clients into the "Doll Room." Obliging, she ushered them through a pearl-beaded curtain. A muted tinkling sound accompanied them as they walked through the delicate drape, underscoring the ambience of the establishment.

Paul was awestruck as they moved into the room. Everywhere he looked there were dolls in all manner of styles and sizes, peering at him with their lifeless eyes. They were perched on shelves, tables, and encased behind glass display cases. Shimmering silk kimonos in every color adorned the replicated courtesans. An extensive collection of parasols, sandals, and hair decorations filled other display cases.

Moving right behind Alanna, he enthused about the room for the benefit of his listeners. "What do you think Alanna? Floor to ceiling dolls. This could be some little girl's fantasy room, couldn't it?" His question ended with a hearty laugh.

Alanna was oblivious to his over enthusiastic comments. When they were fully into the room, she was so transfixed by the beauty and abundance of dolls that she failed to notice a door slowly closing on the outside of the translucent pearl curtain.

Paul, however, was aware. "What the hell is going on here?"

He thrust his hand through the flimsy curtain and connected with a solid and unyielding door, locked. He aimed a well-placed kick but there was no give.

Alanna, preoccupied with the treasures in the room, was unmindful of the danger they were in. She hadn't noticed that neither of the Qus had come into the room with them. "Paul? What on earth are you doing? And where is Dominic. I want to ask his opinion on the investment value of these dolls."

"Damnit it, Alanna. We're trapped."

"You must be mistaken." She attacked the door handle, to no avail.

"Dominic. Lily!" she shouted through the closed entrance. "Where are you? We appear to have locked ourselves in here."

"Save your voice. This was deliberate. We're stuck in here."

"I don't believe it. There must be another way out. And I have a meeting later this afternoon so I can't be here."

Only half listening, Paul sized up the room. It wasn't so much large as it was high. Shelves rose to its ten-foot ceiling and covered all four walls except for the curtained doorway and another closed door on the opposite side. No windows either. He realized the chances of any transmission from the wire he wore were now slim to none.

"Let's see if this other door leads anywhere." Paul moved toward it. Before his hand reached it, the handle turned.

"Victor!" Alanna exclaimed, her attention finally diverted from the dolls. "What are you doing here?" Her expression rapidly went from one of surprise to that of guilt. "Paul and I—"

Victor raised a hand to silence her and focused a cool eye on Paul. "I am not interested in your explanations. However, I am most curious to have your friend explain his presence here."

"Hope we didn't interrupt you and Dominic in the midst of any business dealings," Paul responded, recovering quickly. Lau didn't answer. Paul kept his composure at Lau's unexpected appearance and attempted a diversion. "I'm glad to see Yoko on display. She seems none the worse for wear."

"Yoko? Oh, you refer to the latest acquisition of my friends. I want to talk to you about this doll."

"I really don't think we have anything further to discuss concerning the doll," Paul asserted, taking a defensive stance. "I returned her to you as agreed. And now, Alanna and I are leaving."

"Not quite so fast, Mr. Webster. Again, I need to remind you that I will not be played for a fool, therefore, we will have a discussion—now." Turning to Alanna, he spoke curtly, "You stay in this room and admire these priceless collectors' items. He and I have things to discuss."

Alanna merely nodded at his icy tone, her lips pursed firmly together.

"This way," Victor said, allowing Paul a glance at the revolver discreetly holstered under his jacket. He led Paul through the doorway. The next room was small, containing a desk and file cabinets. Two sturdy wooden chairs faced the desk, and Paul wondered if they would be sitting, as Victor made no move to go toward the desk. Again, there was no window or other sign of exit, and Paul's anxiety ramped up. This might be his only chance to get the thief to admit to his part in the smuggling of antiquities.

Hope the wire works from here. "What do you want to discuss, Victor?"

Lau tightened his lips before replying. "Do you know how much I dislike your familiarity with my name? It shows a lack of good manners on your part, but I'm not surprised."

Paul bristled inwardly, but didn't rise to the bait. He made no comment, preferring to wait and see where this conversation was leading.

"I will admit to being surprised to see you here with Alanna today." Lau paused. "And not with your Cherie Markel—or whatever her name is."

The statement was left hanging in the air with no response from Paul.

"Please, don't insult me with an explanation that will only be lies," Lau continued. "Shall I make a guess?"

"Go ahead, *Mr.* Lau."

"You are both too interested in my business affairs. Do you feel that, by spying on me, you can gain information that will assist you in your new partnership with Yashito? Do you hope to learn how to improve on our processes?" Before Paul could come back with a reply, Victor hit him again. "Or are you more interested in the doll—Yoko?"

"Perhaps," Paul admitted, realizing Lau had given him the opening by referring to his business other than the knock-off manufacturing. "There's more to her than meets the eye. There certainly was with her twin. Someone definitely wanted something hidden inside, any idea what that might've been?"

"So that's what brings you here. You have used Alanna as an excuse to gain access to the premises, I presume. This should not have happened."

"Oh? Why's that? Something to hide?" Paul's frustration grew. He couldn't steer the conversation around to any kind of confession or details of the smuggling.

"We all have something to hide."

"Some more than others," Paul countered.

Lau was silent for a moment. "Your accomplice with the black wig, what's her real name? I was briefly attracted, but once I suspected her motives, she became disposable."

Paul wanted to smash his fist into Lau's obnoxious face. "Her name's not important. I'm only involved because these dolls crossed my path, and I needed to find out why. Like I said, there's obviously more than meets the eye with them, more than just being collectors' items. What's the connection with them and the counterfeit fabric you have created?"

Lau's eyes narrowed. "I'm the one asking questions here,' he said in clipped tones. "You, on the other hand, know more than you are saying. Your merger with my rivals caused me a large monetary loss. Then I find my merchandise has been damaged in your possession. Do you know what I discovered?"

"That smuggling antiquities from one country to America is illegal? That you might be caught?" Paul's ire was rising. Lau was insufferable and Paul had just about had enough. He couldn't resist the barbs and waited for a reaction.

Ignoring Paul's questions, Victor sighed. "I discovered that yet another piece has gone missing, and not only missing but replaced with a counterfeit."

"Counterfeit? That's ironic."

Eyes flashing, Victor reacted with a solid slap across Paul's face.

Paul took the blow and stood his ground.

"Enough! This is not a game. For the second time in my dealings with you, I demand you return what is rightfully mine!"

Paul rubbed the side of his face where the imprint of a hand was forming. "Then enlighten me. What is it you're looking for?"

Victor clenched his fists but kept them at his side. "A jade bi-disc. A rare treasure of immeasurable value—you think you can fool me with a cheap copy."

"This disc, did it stay in Yoko all the way from China, ending up here?" Paul responded calmly. "How did you know it was there?"

"Because I put it there, you fool!" Victor spat.

Inwardly, Paul gave himself thumbs up. Finally, some progress.

Without warning, Lau reached for Paul's shirt and gave a yank. Buttons flew and revealed the wire. "It seems we both play this game of electronic eavesdropping. I assume your comrades are nearby and listening. Well, let them listen to this. You may have David Matsumoto locked up, but I have you, and Alanna. She knows nothing of my other business dealings and so her protests of being innocent should be believed. However, I don't care if she's killed in the process of us leaving here. You and Alanna will now be my *guests* and will be coming with me."

Paul assessed his chances of escape. He didn't know if there was anyone else on the premises besides Dominic and Lily Qu, but he had to assume Victor wouldn't go far without accomplices. If only Paul could be certain the conversation had been overheard and the feds out there would back off.

"The Qus will not be coming with us," Victor said, as if reading his thoughts, "but there are others who are, and our transportation is waiting. Fix your shirt and come with me."

They re-entered the doll room, Alanna was apparently unaware of Paul's dishevelment. That she wanted to get away from Victor was patently obvious.

"You must need to get back to work, Paul, so I'm ready to leave if you are."

He caught the tremor in her voice and didn't want to add to her anxiety. "Um, it seems we'll be having a slight detour first. We're going with Victor."

At those words, the locked door opened. Two heavily built men were revealed, who gestured them to follow. One of the men reached through Paul's torn shirt, severing the wires, as Paul began to speak "I thought we were going in—"

As Alanna began to protest, Paul firmly held her arm and told her to trust him and not make a fuss. The Qus were nowhere in sight and the brawny guards led the pair back through another part of the house, down several stairs to a heavy, locked door.

✲✲✲

Across the street, Dorothy and the agents listened in dismay to what had transpired. Nothing further had been heard since Paul told Alanna they'd be going with Victor. They debated on what action should be taken, the final consensus being that an unmarked car, already in place, would discreetly follow any vehicle seen leaving Bamboo Fine Imports.

Dorothy tried to quell her uneasiness. She knew Paul was capable of handling himself, but worried because she knew he'd put Alanna's safety ahead of his own.

"There they go," Jim announced, as a long, sleek, black limousine emerged from a garage at the back of the property. After instructions were given to the driver of the surveillance vehicle, Jim added, "We need more voice contact from Paul, but I guess Victor's put an end to that. We'll wait here a little while longer and then head back to your place Dorothy."

"Sounds good," she agreed, but longed to be in the surveillance vehicle instead.

✲✲✲

Meanwhile, Paul wondered what was on the other side of the door. Victor moved ahead of them and produced a key. Darkness yawned before them until a switch was found. A single bare bulb dangling from the ceiling revealed a dusty concrete floor and cinder block walls. Boxes, barrels, and other forms of storage stood scattered about, some draped in cobwebs and months of dust.

Paul and Alanna were pressed forward, and immediately felt the chill of this below-ground storeroom.

"A time out, Webster. Think of it as a chance to consider your options, which are limited."

Before Paul could respond, Lau backed out of the
room which was quickly sealed with a heavy thud.

Alanna looked petrified and clung to Paul. Her
stricken face was about to crumble. They didn't speak as
Paul ushered her over to some of the cleaner boxes.

"Alanna, sit down. You're cold, here take this." He
removed his jacket. Draping it around her shoulders, he
bent closer to her. In a hushed voice he whispered, "We
may be overheard. I'm sure Victor has this place bugged.
So don't say anything unless I ask you a question. Understand?"

She nodded, a dazed expression on her face. Paul felt
sorry for her, as she was indeed an innocent party. He and
the team had put her in this danger, without her
knowledge. If she was guilty of anything, it was vanity
and a need to be accepted. Paul took her hand and
squeezed, hoping the gesture would reassure her that
things would be fine. He struggled for a way to handle
this situation. The experience he'd gained during his
years with the military should have put him in good
stead, but at that moment, he was out of ideas.

Where's the cavalry when you need them? he wondered.

ের

Outside Dorothy and Jim waited on word from the
surveillance car. Jim had called for backup, and all were
on alert.

He told Dorothy he hoped the additional agents
wouldn't be needed, but the degree of danger had escalated when communication from Paul was lost.

Jim ran his hand across his chin, thinking aloud. "I wonder…"

"What is it?"

"Just a hunch, but Paul said 'they were going in' and then he was cut off." Contacting the surveillance car, he barked, "Stop the suspect car and hold the passengers until you hear from me. You've been following a decoy. Use caution. We've no way of knowing whether they're armed or not."

Dorothy called Max, asking him to meet at the Qus along with her other agents. "Keep well back, Dad. Jim has things under control, so we'll let them do their job."

"You keep back yourself, darlin'. I can't have anything happening to you."

Dorothy broke the connection as she listened to Jim fielding calls. Several cars had already driven into place intending to have Bamboo Fine Imports, and its property, surrounded. Jim was handed a megaphone as more cars, some with sirens blaring, screeched to a halt in front of the Qus' establishment.

Adrenalin coursed through Dorothy, and she said a silent prayer that Paul and Alanna were all right. Just then, the surveillance driver called to say that the Qus were the decoy passengers and had been apprehended. Victor had used them as a distraction. They'd both tried to resist being held but had now calmed down.

"Great job," Jim acknowledged. "Hang tight till I get there."

Jim picked up the megaphone. His voice carried across the street. "This is the FBI. The house is surrounded. Victor Lau, come out with your hands up!" Silence, while they waited for a response. None came, so he tried again. Phone calls to the house were unanswered.

Dorothy was starting to feel antsy, shifting from foot to foot. "What's going on in there?"

"One more try, Dorothy, and then we go in." Standing behind a car, Jim hailed Victor once more. When the man didn't surface, he ordered, "Let's go."

In addition to the garage, a couple of outbuildings stood on the property. All were completely surrounded when Jim and a handful of his special agents broke through the front door, weapons drawn.

Alarms rang but were soon cut, leaving an ominous silence hanging in the air. No running footsteps, no yelling, or sounds of anyone trying to get away.

"Where the hell are they?" Jim's frustration was growing. "I want this place searched with a fine toothcomb—*Now*! They're still here."

The house crawled with agents, searching for any kind of hiding place. It was a warren of small rooms laden with treasures of all description and, to the uninitiated, quite overwhelming.

Jim returned to the car where Dorothy continued to pace.

"No sign of them yet, but we'll find them."

She looked at him. "I'm glad it's you in charge."

"Bring the Qus back to the house," Jim barked into his phone. "They'll be able to tell us of Victor's plans. If they're not still holed up in this funhouse, they left another way we haven't discovered."

Ashley joined Jim and Dorothy while the other agents continued their search "I don't believe Lau would be alone," she commented. "He'd have a couple of henchmen with him. He must know Paul would put up a fight in the right circumstances."

Just then, the Qus arrived and were bombarded with questions.

They made quite a racket, fluctuating between Mandarin and English, and demanding a lawyer—or at least Lily was. She was the most vocal, and the more she was questioned, the more she denied ever knowing what Victor's business was. Dominic seemed to have shrunk and looked like a man with much on his mind. Dorothy thought he'd aged considerably since she'd last seen him.

"Mr. Qu, Victor Lau and your two 'guests,' Paul Webster and Alanna Scolfield, where are they?" Ashley said. "You're aware there's a penalty for kidnapping and forcible confinement? Along with the charges of buying and selling smuggled artefacts, you'll be going away for a long time."

Both Qus paled and Lily began sputtering. "I—I know n—nothing, nothing. I want a lawyer, I want a lawyer."

"All in good time, Mrs. Qu, when we formally arrest you will be soon enough," Jim said briskly. "Now then, once more. Where are they? We can't wait here all day."

Dominic started to speak in a soft voice. All ears tuned in to listen. "I—I—my wife knows nothing," stammered the cowed man. He continued in a defeated tone of voice, and they had to strain to hear what he had to say. It was a tale of fear and intimidation. The threat of having authorities discover Lily Qu was in the country illegally was all Victor needed to blackmail Dominic. They claimed to have been running a legitimate business for many years until they met Victor Lau. According to Dominic, Lily knew nothing of the extortion. The more he helped Victor, the deeper his obligation to him grew.

"We'll keep your stories for later Mr. Qu. Right now tell us where Victor's hiding them," demanded Jim.

"Tell them, tell them!" exclaimed his agitated spouse.

"It will be easier if you follow me," Dominic said.

"Right. Ashley you stay here with Mrs. Qu. Everyone else, let's go. Dorothy you can follow, but stay back until I give the all clear, understood?"

She nodded, but her whole being was coiled like a wound spring—she had to find Paul.

Back through the house, over territory already covered in the initial search, went the group.

"We've been down here, sir," said one of the agents as they started down a small flight of stairs into what appeared to be a storage area. "It's only shelves and storage."

"All is not what it seems," Dominic contradicted. He walked over to one of the laden shelving units, moved a package, and began searching for something. He quickly stepped back as the shelf began to move outward, revealing a locked door.

Unperturbed by this revelation, Jim merely asked Dominic for the key.

"Mr. Lau keeps the only key. I do not have another copy."

As if expecting that answer, Jim went up to the door and banged on it, "Paul? Are you in there?"

"Jim! Is that you? Man, I'm glad to hear your voice. Alanna's with me, and not to hurry you, but it's chilly in here. So the sooner you get us out of here, the better, and there'll be an extra bonus when you do."

Paul's voice was muffled, but Dorothy was very relieved to hear it.

"We're working on it. Just give us a few minutes." As he spoke, Jim assessed the strength of the door. He turned to one of the agents. "Call a locksmith and as a backup, an explosives expert."

"I'm on it, sir." An agent ran back up the stairs to carry out his task.

Dorothy put her hand on Jim's shoulder. "I'm going to see Dad for a few minutes, don't go anywhere till I get back."

"Oh, I think we'll be here for a while yet, at least until we get a good locksmith. This is one secure door."

Dorothy found her father waiting across the street and updated him. Then she added, "I think there's going to be a need for hot coffee, and maybe some blankets when they're finally free. Would you mind? I know I could do with a large java myself."

"No problem, love, I'll go get a couple of thermos filled and be back in two shakes of a lamb's tail." He gave her a peck on the cheek and drove away.

Dorothy leaned up against a nearby vehicle and exhaled a long pent up sigh of exhaustion. Relief at finding Paul, and Alanna, mingled with disappointment at not being able to get their hands on Victor Lau. Agents were fanned out at the airport and docks in hopes of apprehending him.

Flexing her shoulders and straightening up once again, she returned to the house and it's scene of activity.

She knocked on the door. "Paul? It's Dorothy. I've got some hot coffee coming for you two. Hang in there. We'll soon have you out."

"Oh, coffee sounds great! We won't go anywhere."

Footsteps were soon heard approaching, and a middle aged man in work clothes and baseball cap which read *Speedy Lock Service*, appeared on the scene. Without a word, he set to his task, arranging the tools of his trade near the door. Jim and the others moved back to give him room and didn't interrupt as he made his attempts at unlocking it.

The growing tension was finally released when the locksmith uttered an "Aha!" and stepped back. "Yup, she's all yers now, gents."

He quickly gathered his tools and left as silently as he arrived.

Jim took the honors of opening the door and Dorothy was gratified to see two relieved faces. The chill of the room hit her like walking into a freezer, and she could see the occupants were starting to shiver.

Paul came forward. "Man, am I glad to see you guys!" But his eyes searched out Dorothy as he spoke.

She was relieved to see that they were unharmed, other than slightly chilled, and hoped Max was waiting outside with hot coffee and blankets. Then she looked past them into the contents of the room. Her eyes grew wide.

Paul offered an explanation. "While we were waiting, we decided to poke around in here, and look what we've found."

Chapter 16

Jim and Ashley hastened into the room where Paul and Alanna had been held. Dorothy, needing reassurance that Paul was not hurt, fell close behind. Their eyes met, and his face brightened.

"I'm fine, I'm fine, but I think Alanna needs warming up," he said quickly, answering Dorothy's questions before she could voice them.

Jim asked Dorothy to take Alanna outside.

"Yes, of course," she agreed, although she felt reluctant to leave Paul so soon. Turning to Alanna she asked, "If you'd like to come with me, we'll find you a blanket and some coffee to warm you up."

"Good idea. Alanna, go ahead, I'll catch up with you in a few minutes," Paul reassured her as Alanna seemed to hesitate before leaving with Dorothy.

Once outside, Dorothy handed Alanna over to Max, who immediately draped a blanket over her shoulders. "Let me pour you a coffee, darlin, you look right chilled," he said. His Irish brogue was gentle and comforting.

Seeing her father hand Alanna a cup of hot coffee, Dorothy asked, "Dad, can Alanna stay here with you? I'd like to go back and take Paul a coffee."

Alanna, cupping the warm liquid close to her face, gazed intently at Dorothy. "Have we met?"

Dorothy hesitated. "Yes, as a matter of fact we have. But, if you don't mind, I'll have to explain later. You're in good hands now. Paul and I'll join you shortly."

Not waiting for a reply, she dashed back inside, carrying a thermos, and soon crossed the threshold of a small room that was cold and uninviting. A space, she knew, which easily could have been a tomb for Paul and Alanna. Shadows bounced off stark walls from the agents' flashlights. The solitary bare bulb was not enough to illuminate the myriad of boxes that held the agents attention. Although there was only Jim, Ashley, and Paul in the room, it felt crowded.

Dorothy moved over to Paul's side, the thermos forgotten as her eyes took in the contents of the room. "Geez-louise, look at all this!"

Box after box of lacquer and porcelain objects, a multitude of jade pieces, and traditionally dressed dolls were all now exposed. That they'd been carefully wrapped in a colorful silken fabric was obvious, as the material had spilled over the edges of the opened containers. A seemingly endless array of other containers stood, as yet, untouched.

Paul nodded. "Alanna and I opened just a few, so can you imagine how much is stored in here?"

Jim ran a hand through his hair. "A thorough inventory is definitely needed, with lots of photographs. Ashley, you're in charge of that if you don't mind."

"Yes, boss," Ashley agreed, giving her partner a mock salute.

Jim turned to Paul. "Time to fill us in. The last we heard from you was that Lau was going to take you and Alanna somewhere, and then we lost the connection."

"Let me have some of that coffee," Paul said with a

longing look toward the thermos still in Dorothy's hand. "I trust Lau is now in handcuffs?"

"Wish I could say yes," admitted the fed. "At this point, he's given us the slip. We've been watching the airport and docks, but I imagine a character of his ilk and resources would have other means of escape."

"Damn. That devil needs to be caught. He wouldn't have thought twice about leaving Alanna and I in that room, permanently."

"The day's not done yet, Paul. We'll find him."

"He has no regard for others, if they're a threat to him," Dorothy said, remembering her recent narrow escape at the airport. "It wouldn't surprise me to find a body or two in his wake."

Just then an agent came to Jim with a question. "What about the tunnels? You don't suppose he escaped that way?"

They turned to the young agent.

"What tunnels?" they all said in unison.

"Never heard of the Shanghai tunnels? In the mid-eighteen hundreds, they were used to move goods. People who frequented the docks were often 'shanghaied' and literally made into slaves. The tunnels run parallel to these buildings and I just thought...well, maybe he'd hatched an escape route or at least somewhere to hide."

"Personally, I haven't heard of them, but I'm not from around here. See what you can find out and if they could be connected," Jim said to his protégé. "Good thinking by the way. Everyone's on high alert to find him. It may take time, but he'll trip up, and then he'll be all ours. In the meantime, we build a good case against him."

"Do you suppose the stuff we found here has been smuggled?" Paul asked. "Because I have a hunch about the material it's been wrapped in."

"Oh?" Jim asked. "Go on."

"It will need confirmation, but it looks similar to a fabric design my company is involved with. Long story short—we'd recently learned that there has been a concerted effort by a Chinese business to produce a counterfeit fabric to undercut us. I'd say we've stumbled on the bulk of their supply. Using it as a material to pack these items in."

"And that's probably the main focus behind Victor getting established here with the fabric so close by with his business friends, the Qus," Dorothy added.

"Making a few extra bucks along the way with smuggled cargo wouldn't hurt either, I suppose," Jim noted.

Dorothy grew concerned. "Paul, do you think this will have any effect on your new business? There's bound to be inevitable bad press."

"I really haven't had the time to think through the implications. Then again, sometimes bad publicity turns into a good thing if it's handled right."

Just then a familiar voice hailed them, "Dorothy, darlin'? Are you down there? Your friend out here is anxious for some news."

Dorothy threw a guilty look toward the voice, "Oh, sorry, Dad! I'll be right there."

Jim told Dorothy and Paul they could go, and that they'd meet up again shortly.

Heading back toward the entrance, and seeing no one else around, Dorothy stopped dead in her tracks.

"What's wrong?" Paul asked as he nearly bumped into her.

"Just this." She put her arms around him and gave him a kiss, as if he were a long lost lover. "I couldn't do this when I first saw you down there. I was so thankful to know you were safe, that's all."

"Who knew there could be such great perks to being kidnapped?" Paul chuckled. "Do you treat all your clientele with such loving concern?"

"Oh, you! Come on, we'd better see to Alanna. I think she recognizes me, too. So I'll have to explain."

Out into the welcome sunshine, Dorothy nudged Paul as they observed Max and Alanna across the street. Max seemed totally absorbed in the woman's intense one-sided conversation.

"Do you think he needs rescuing?" Paul teased as they crossed the street.

"No, take a good look. I think he's actually enjoys listening to her."

It certainly appeared as if Max wasn't suffering, even though the closer they got Alanna's protests over the days' events became more vocal.

"…and the room was so cold! But Paul, he's such a dear. He offered me his jacket. It helped a little. For the life of me, I can't understand why Dominic and Lily would have any part in wanting to harm us. They're such a nice couple."

Her conversation was erratic, however, she had Max's undivided attention. He barely seemed to notice the arrival of Dorothy and Paul.

"Alanna, better now? Warmed up some, I hope. Feels great to be out here in the sunshine, doesn't it?"

"Oh, Paul, thank goodness you're free from that horrible place. Max here has been so kind, providing coffee and a very patient ear. I must be boring him with all my chatter." Even as she spoke to Paul, her eyes never left Max's face.

He, in turn, offered reassurance that she was not boring him in the least.

And then Alanna realized there was another person present. "And you are Max's daughter, I believe." Her eyes narrowed. "But I've met you before haven't I?"

Dorothy extended her hand, "You're right, Ms. Scol-field. The last time we met my hair was a little darker and much longer. And the name was Cherie."

She waited for the pin to drop and was amused to see the change in expression as Alanna put the pieces together.

"Oh. No. You and that blathering Barbie doll are the same person? I don't believe it. You certainly had me fooled—"

"Ladies, I have a suggestion," Paul said, clapping his hands. "Let's go somewhere quiet to talk about what's happened. Out in the middle of the street is probably not the best place."

"Grand idea, son," Max agreed. "Let's hop over to the marina. This time of day it won't be too busy. Is that agreeable?"

There were no objections so Dorothy made a request. "Paul has his car here so I'll hitch a ride with him. Would you mind bringing Alanna, Dad?"

"My pleasure."

Dorothy could hardly suppress a smile as she watched her father escort Alanna to his car.

"Well, well, stranger things have happened," Paul observed with a laugh.

Back at Maxwell's, they settled comfortably around a corner table.

Over the next little while, Alanna came to learn of Paul's involvement with Yashito Design, Jinan Import and Export, the dolls, and the reasons for bringing Dorothy on board as a private investigator. To the business-woman's credit, she managed to keep her interruptions to a minimum until all the facts were in. "I've been conned by Victor, haven't I?"

"Taken advantage of perhaps, but certainly I don't

believe you would be easily conned," Max said, trying to comfort her.

"What happens now? I've no firm to represent, if Jinan Import and Export is not legit. I should distance my company from them immediately, so I need to talk to my legal department."

Paul nodded. "Likewise, I'm not sure how this will affect my company's recent merger with Yashito. Victor Lau's done a great job of interfering with many plans." He sighed. "I hate to break this up, but I must call Catherine and the others. They'll be wondering what the hell happened to me. The last she saw of me I was heading to lunch." He reached for his cell phone.

Pushing her chair away from the table, Dorothy agreed that she also needed to leave. "Can we drop you back home, Alanna?"

The quick glance Alanna sent Max's way didn't go unnoticed.

"Now, darlin', don't you be worrying about Alanna, I'll make sure she arrives home just fine."

Dorothy's cell phone rang as they were leaving Maxwell's. Jim Addison had news. Dorothy put the phone on speaker so Paul could hear.

"He's given us the slip all right. We checked the tunnel angle, but that's not how he escaped. We found an abandoned vehicle, registered to Jinan Import and Export, at a small airport outside of Portland. They tell us a helicopter took off a couple of hours ago, flight plan specified Seattle, but they've never arrived."

"He's a slippery one and we can't underestimate him. Keep me posted, Jim. I'll be at the *Aye* with paperwork. Do you need an analysis of the fabric we were telling you about? I can have Paul send your forensic team a sample of the Japanese fabric. We're assuming they'll discover the difference, but can't be certain."

"Good idea, thanks."

"Oh, and Jim, can you keep my involvement out of the media? I prefer to work behind the scenes and don't want to compromise future opportunities."

"Don't worry, nothing is going to the press just yet, but I'll keep you out of it. Unless there's any more breaking news, I'll probably not call you tonight. My team will be busy with the inventory of that storage room and questioning the Qus. We may turn up some leads from them as to where Lau has gone but I have my doubts. Why don't you take a little down time and we can meet up again tomorrow?"

"Sounds good. Talk later." Dorothy closed her phone and threw a smile Paul's way. "How does dinner at my place and some shenanigans sound to you? You heard him, my boss on the ACT team has given me the evening off and I should let HB and Raymond off the hook too."

"An offer I can't refuse. Remind me to thank Jim. When I spoke with Catherine, I asked her to assemble the management team for an emergency meeting this evening." He glanced at his watch. "With luck, they'll all be arriving shortly, I need to hustle over there. Our legal rep's on standby, so I may be busy for a while. Could be after nine o'clock before all's done, is that too late for you?"

"I'll be up, just remember to bring a toothbrush."

After dropping Dorothy at her floating office, he sped off to his own.

What a day. Weariness was setting in, but he had to prepare for his new role as director of the merged company.

ജേഷ

Meanwhile Max and Alanna hadn't gone far. They'd

left the bar and moved upstairs to Max's flat where he was regaling her with stories of his years on the force and in the services. Anyone who was aware of her reputation as the reputed Ice Queen would be surprised to see her looking so relaxed and contented.

Max pottered in the kitchen, preparing a meal and humming a tune while he worked. At his insistence, Alanna had taken her shoes off and was lounging on the sofa petting Houdini. The cat was purring contentedly and, to all appearances, so was Alanna.

ↄↄↄↄↄ

Boarding the *Aye*, Dorothy kicked her shoes off as well. Coming home to her own space afforded her down time to think about the day. Immediately, her thoughts turned to Paul. In a tranquil frame of mind, she wrapped up loose ends at her desk and planned the evening ahead.

She gladly informed her team they had the night off. One last phone call resulted in a delivery from the local deli where she'd ordered food for a late night meal with Paul.

Satisfied that she'd covered everything, Dorothy had a long hot shower and prepared for an enjoyable evening with a man she cared for very much.

ↄↄↄↄↄ

Back at Bamboo Fine Imports, the activity continued. More agents had been called in to help with the inventory when it became apparent there was more to catalogue than expected.

"Jim, this is going to take a while. How about ordering in some dinner? Experts are going to be needed to help evaluate this hoard. It's like Aladdin's cave in here,"

Ashley said as she brushed dirt from the knees of her pants.

She wore gloves for both protection of the artefacts and for warmth. A few stray cobwebs were attached to her, and when she gave a shiver, Jim realized they could use some heat as well.

"Good suggestions, Ashley, you've got it. I'll call in JAG as well to go over the jewelry." He cocked an ear toward the sound of raised voices. "Listen to that noise out there—the press would love to hammer down the door, but I'd like to keep this under wraps for now. Do you think—"

She smiled knowingly. "I could speak to them using my womanly wiles?"

"I'll owe you one. You know how I dislike dealing with the press."

"What do you not want me to say to them? They've surely seen the FBI vehicles and police cars, the Qus taken into custody, all the activity here. What shall I tell them?"

"As little as possible and that, as soon as we have more information, they'd be the first to know, etc., etc. You know what to say. After all, you're still the best liaison officer we have."

"Flattery will get you everywhere."

Brushing the cobwebs from her hair and shoulders, and glad of the break from the frosty room, Ashley walked confidently out the front door and into the blinding glare of lights set up by a local television crew behind the yellow police tape. Their lead reporter could smell a good story a mile away.

As if scripted, Ashley said all the right things. Admitting nothing and keeping what she did say to generalities, she hoped to appease the reporters. Even with microphones pushed into her face, she smiled charmingly and assured them that, as soon as she had a story, she'd relay details back to them.

છ

Catherine had gathered everyone into the boardroom just before Paul arrived. His legal counsel, Rolin Montase was on his way. She'd filled him in and he'd shortened a previous appointment to be there.

"I also tried to locate Henry Yamada at your suggestion he be here as well. But all I get is voice mail."

"Perhaps he'll get the message and arrive shortly." Paul turned to address the assembled group. "Thank you all for coming in—on a Friday night, no less. There are some developments that may jeopardize our new company, so I appreciate any personal plans you've put on hold to be here this evening. Rolin will be joining us shortly. Please, help yourselves to some coffee, donuts are on the way."

Unanswered questions stayed on hold, while coffee cups were filled.

Laura searched out Paul. "Do you still want me on board with this? As far as I'm concerned, Alanna is still my friend, and I'm not about to change that."

Paul gave her a reassuring pat on the arm "Things are fine in that direction."

"Greetings everyone," came a forceful voice.

Pushing a mail cart laden with donut boxes was Webster and Associates' legal counsel, a playful grin nearly overshadowing deep brown eyes which had a sparkle to match the stud in his ear lobe. Built like a quarterback, Rolin owed his dark good looks to his Haitian mother and his education to his American father. His clean-shaven head, sense of style, and warm good humor met women's approval and fed into the insecurities of some men. Added to that was a sharp legal mind—an intimidating presence when needed in the courtroom. Paul walked over, shook his hand, and thanked him for being available at such short notice.

"As if I'd miss coming to see my favourite ladies," he said with a smile that impressed even the men, in spite of themselves.

Paul threw him a bemused look and steered the agenda back on track. "Thanks for the delivery, Rolin, but don't give up your day job just yet. With all that's gone on today, I need legal clarification as to the status of Webster Yashito. Catherine already provided notes for your review. You can advise us if you foresee problems down the road."

The room grew quiet in anticipation, although Archie appeared to be mumbling to himself and kept tapping the pipe in his top pocket.

Paul gave an account of the day's events and filled them in regarding Victor Lau as much as he was able to. The donuts were forgotten, even Archie had stopped eating. Paul had effectively captured their attention. Looks of concern and disbelief were visible on their faces.

Paul was confident that, due to his and Rolin's shared military background, his counsel would not be unduly concerned about the close call.

There was silence after Paul had spoken, and it was Patricia Barry who broke their concentration in her quiet and careful manner. "First of all, Paul, I'm sure I speak for everyone that we're very relieved to have you here none the worse for wear." She cocked her head. "Do you think the Japanese will have any problem proving they are the rightful, and original, creators of this material and design? We need to be cautious. What's your legal opinion on this, Rolin?"

The self-assured counsel rose to his feet and walked

around the table. He was a commanding presence and all eyes now diverted to him. "Yes, legally, the merger is a done deal. But if any evidence comes to light that legitimizes the Chinese fabric ahead of Yashito, we may have problems. My advice to you is go slow. Have the fabric investigated more thoroughly to determine origins."

At the mention of "origins" a resound slap was heard. Paul held a hand to his forehead. "Of course. These samples I gave you were from the dress of the dolls which belong to the Chinese. I'll have to ask Yashito for samples. Wish Henry had been able to make this meeting, he'd probably have answers. Obviously, time's important here. If you have thoughts or suggestions about the merger, call Catherine. For now, I say we call it a night."

Shaking hands with his staff as they dispersed, Paul asked Catherine to contact Yashito for samples to be couriered over as soon as possible.

Rolin waited to have a word privately with Paul. "Just want to reassure you, that I'll go over everything carefully so there are no surprises to trip us up. Keep me up to date on anything new, but for now go home and relax."

"It's good to have you in my corner. I'll be counting on you."

They parted ways and Paul drove home at breakneck speed, showered and made it to a florist before it closed. Tapping on the window of the *Private Aye*, he was all smiles, standing on the gangway with flowers in one hand and a toothbrush in the other.

Chapter 17

The door slid open, and Paul's heart tripped. Dorothy, obviously not long out of the shower, had her damp hair pulled back. Dressed casually, she looked as if she'd not a care in the world, and only had eyes for him.

She reached for the flowers and raised an eyebrow at him as she stood aside to let him in. "Lovely toothbrush, Paul. How did you know I needed a new one?"

He noticed the small dining table set for two, wine glasses at the ready. A salad and fresh rolls awaited their attention. He made as if to sniff the air. "Is that a steak on the grill I smell?"

"Well, there's just no fooling you, is there?" She leaned toward him and grazed his cheek with a soft kiss. "Beautiful flowers, thank you. Now, have a seat and tell me about the board meeting." She placed the flowers in a vase and then continued with the remainder of the late dinner preparations while Paul described the meeting.

"Will this cause harm to your firm?"

"Depends. Rolin thinks we may have a case if we find Yashito wasn't truthful. Honestly, I really hope they didn't mislead us, and that the merger stands. There's such potential for the marketing of this fabric, other than just fashion dollars. But…" His voice trailed off.

"Yes? But what?" she prompted as she placed a perfectly grilled steak before him, onions and mushrooms carefully added to one side.

"Wow, I'm so ready for this, thanks."

"Stop drooling, and don't change the subject. Go on, what else do you want to say?"

"My gut feeling is the merger will stand, and succeed. The financial reasons you can probably understand. My goal was always for the company to be successful. I've great employees and the potential for ongoing growth is wide open. It's just that—"

He turned his attention to the meal before him, and Dorothy waited.

Fork poised in one hand, he confessed, "—it's just that, all the events of the past few days have made me realize how much I missed my days in the services, dodging the bad guys, putting pieces of an investigation together. Do you know what I mean?"

"I think I just might," she said slowly. "Once that's in your blood, it's really hard to shake."

"Yeah, I thought you'd understand." Looking somewhat relieved, he put the fork to work. "Anyway, let's enjoy this dinner. It's wonderful. Your talents know no bounds."

"Glad you approve, now eat while it's still warm."

They ate companionably and swapped tales of past work-related adventures.

The evening lengthened and Paul couldn't believe his eyes when he realized the time.

"I don't know where the time goes when I'm with you."

"That's probably why it seemed like an eternity for me earlier today. Paul, I have to tell you, there were times after we lost the connection, that I was more than a little concerned about your safety. I couldn't decide what I wanted to do more, barge into the store and search every corner for you or race after the car we had under surveillance. Needless to say, I was relieved to hear your voice on the other side of that door."

"Not jealous I was locked up all that time with Alanna?" he teased.

"I don't think she's really your type. However, my dad seems to find her fascinating."

They shared a laugh, thinking back to how Max and Alanna had acted with each other earlier.

"I wonder how their evening's going," she mused.

Paul rose from the table and reached for Dorothy's hand. "Let's not talk about anyone else right now."

She responded to his touch and they moved over to the sofa.

The lights were dim and, with no further talk, they found themselves cuddling, enjoying each other's presence. All was peaceful until the persistent ringing of her phone could no longer be ignored.

"Can't you just leave it?" Paul asked.

"It's not my cell phone, so it must be business—or a wrong number," she added hopefully. "Sorry, I have to check, in case it's something to do with today."

Paul overheard one side of the conversation and deduced it was Jim, and then Dorothy called him to come and speak with him, too.

"He has news," she said in a very serious tone as she set the phone on speaker mode.

"Jim, Paul here. What's up?"

"Hey, Paul. Sorry to disturb you so late, but I thought you'd rather hear it from me, than on the news, or in the morning papers. We'd almost finished searching all the containers in the storage room of the Qus—"

"And?"

"We found something more than smuggled arte-facts—we found a body."

A chill raced up Paul's back. "Do you know who it is?"

"No. Not quite what Ashley was expecting. She was in charge of inventory and certainly wasn't prepared for that kind of discovery. All I can tell you so far, it's a male. Appears to be Asian. He had no ID on him. This is where your help might come in. You've met quite a few of the Yashito and Jinan players, so there's the possibility you may be able to identify him. I've a hunch our body has a connection."

"Anything I can do to help, count on it. So you think there's a good chance he's there because of Lau? Had he been there long? What about cause of death?"

"I'll answer what I can when I see you. Coroner's on his way, and I want to keep this low key for now. The last thing I need is the press finding out about a body."

"No kidding. I'm glad you called. Dorothy and I are on our way. Don't think I'll let Alanna know we spent the afternoon with a corpse," Paul finished with a grimace.

Ending the call, he turned toward Dorothy. She was already gathering her cell phone and car keys and grab-bing a light jacket against the cool evening air. She sighed. "Well, I guess our relaxing evening is going to be postponed. Sorry, sweetheart."

"Hey, not your fault. We're in this together, so at least we still spend the evening with each other, just not exactly as planned. But what to do about my toothbrush?"

She laughed. "Oh, I think it can stay put for now. C'mon, let's get this show on the road."

He was not surprised she'd caught her second wind. Her customary energy and enthusiasm were in full force, despite the lateness of the hour.

The traffic was light and, in almost no time, they were once again parking outside Bamboo Fine Imports. The building was well lit, inside and out, and two uniformed officers appeared to be on patrol. Not far away sat a CNN van and a local television station's media vehicle. Parked just ahead of them was a black van from the coroner's office.

"Looks like the doc's already here," Dorothy announced, putting her jeep in park.

An officer at the door checked their ID and then allowed them to enter. They quickly made their way back down to the storeroom. The earlier hub of activity had subsided to allow the senior coroner, Dr. Emery Davidson, to proceed.

Paul nudged Dorothy. "Look at all the stuff they've uncovered."

The sheer volume of Asian collectibles was amazing. And off to one side was a growing pile of neatly folded, multi-colored cloth.

"I wonder if they accomplished a double round of smuggling," he mused aloud. "If that's the counterfeit fabric, then Lau, or the Qus, managed to bring it into the country undetected."

Dorothy nodded. "Jim's team certainly has a lot of work ahead of them, cataloguing all of this and determining what's stolen and what's legit."

They grew quiet, looking into the room where the coroner attended his newest client. A long narrow crate stood open on the floor. Packing straw and more of the same colorful cloth spilled over the edges. The coroner crouched over the coffin-like crate.

Although Paul could see into it from his vantage point, Dr. Davidson's frame blocked the view of the victim's face, as he lay within the confines of the container.

Jim stood a few feet from the coroner, whose assistant was carefully taking photographs from various angles.

The doctor seemed oblivious to others in the room, so intent was he on gathering evidence and information that would aid in determining the cause of death. He began to speak, as if to himself, and Paul had to strain to hear what he was saying. "The deceased appears to be young Asian male, late thirties—early forties, no visible sign of trauma. Body temp indicates he's been dead quite a while, rigor has come and gone." He straightened up, and turned to address Jim. "Sorry, Jim, I really don't have much at this point, but I'll know more once I can complete a more thorough exam."

When Dr. Davidson stood up, the victim's face became visible, and Paul gave an audible groan.

"You recognize him?" Dorothy asked.

Giving a big sigh, Paul admitted, sadly, he did. "It's Henry Yamada, Mr. Yashito's right hand man. He seemed to hold so much promise and was excited about the marketing potential of the product. I'm really sorry to see him like this."

"Wasn't Henry Yamada responsible for planting David Matsumoto with Jinan?" she asked.

"I see where you're going, and that just reinforces my gut feeling that Victor Lau has no qualms about disposing of anyone who's ticked him off, or threatened his business." His voice was tinged with anger.

"When was the last time you saw Henry," Jim asked, with a notepad at the ready. The coroner was listening intently as well.

"Let's see…that would've been four or five days ago, the meeting just before I went to Alanna's and met the charming Mr. Lau."

He grew quiet as his attention diverted to the remains of Henry Yamada lying so still. He looked as if he was just sleeping, his body in perfect condition, except for the fact there was no life in him.

Dr. Davidson turned to Jim. "You say, when you found the body, it was wrapped in this cloth, like a shroud?"

"Ashley Flores was actually the one who discovered him. Everything up to that point they'd unearthed had been wrapped carefully in this stuff, so she didn't think twice. Had quite the shock when she pulled the cloth back and found a body. Why do you ask?"

"I'm just puzzled, and I really shouldn't comment until the full autopsy and toxicology reports are done, but my experience tells me this man has been dead for several days."

"Nothing unusual about that, is there?" asked Jim.

"Except that if he's been dead as long as I suspect, there should be marked decomposition of the flesh, even taking into account the chill in this room, yet look at him. It's as if he's sleeping without a care in the world, his body perfect."

Jim reminded the coroner that he'd need to see the report as soon as possible. Paul and Dorothy moved out from the cold room where Paul had nearly been interred. Jim had moved aside to let the coroner's assistants lift the body onto a stretcher for removal to the morgue.

"Doc, I'm sure you're aware that this is a high profile case. We won't be releasing the identity of our body until we're sure of the motives and nature of his demise."

"Naturally, I'll keep things quiet until you say otherwise, but a next of kin needs to be notified."

"Understood."

The older man picked up his medical case and left.

Paul felt forlorn, looking at the room which had become Henry Yamada's last resting place. The enormity of the task seemed overwhelming, there was so much booty.

"So, what's next Jim? Do you want me to inform Mr. Yashito of Henry's death?"

"Hold off a bit, Paul, until we have the coroner's report. We need to find next of kin and have them notified. If there is no one, then I'd say Mr. Yashito can be told. We still have to deal with Mr. and Mrs. Qu—more loose ends. They can wait until morning now, but I'm hoping they'll be able to shed some light on this. Ashley and I will handle the interrogation tomorrow. I'm sure she could use a break from this place."

"Let me know how I can help," Dorothy offered as they walked past jam-packed shelves of beautiful objects. Just as they reached the front door, Paul picked up Yoko and handed her to Jim.

"Here. I think you should take Yoko. You know, she and her sister became the catalyst for this entire investigation. She may yet have more to tell you."

"Thanks, Paul. Can I count on you both to attend a debriefing session with the rest of my team tomorrow? They may have questions you can answer, based on your involvement before we came on board. Experience has taught me it can be effective. Great minds think alike and many hands make things easier...or something like that." The agent stifled a yawn. "You'll be copied on the autopsy reports. And you both have my thanks, again, for your valuable assistance. So now, go home."

Dorothy reacted with a yawn of her own. "If you're sure there's nothing else, we'll go. It has been one long day, and I think it's catching up with all of us."

Walking out, they noticed CNN and the local camera crews had left the scene. Ashley, in her usual manner, had been able to put them off for a few more hours. She was a master storyteller and could bend the truth when she had to. Promises had been made to give them the whole story as it became available.

Agents would be working around the clock on the inventory, and now that the body had been removed, they were much relieved. The armed officers remained on duty, stationed at the front and back doors. An unmarked car was in the vicinity just in case Victor Lau made an unlikely appearance.

Fatigue washed over Dorothy and Paul as they drove back to the houseboat. Both agreed not to discuss the case anymore tonight. They crashed on the sofa where Paul, with a tired, but mischievous grin, said to Dorothy, "Now where were we?"

Chapter 18

Even though the next day was Saturday, Paul drove to his office to catch up on neglected work. He was grateful for Catherine's efficiency as he read through the file she'd left him, outlining details and progress for the merger event.

If it doesn't go off the rails, he thought wryly.

Sitting at his desk, he decided to call Alanna. He hoped she was recovering from yesterday's excitement.

"Scolfield residence," came the answer as the call went through.

"Good morning. It's Paul Webster. I'd like to speak to Ms. Scolfield please."

"I'm sorry, sir, Ms. Scolfield cannot come to the phone right now."

"Oh. Please have her return my call when she's able. She has my number. Thanks."

Dismissing further thought of her from his mind, he turned his attention to phone messages and email. But, unwillingly, his mind returned to the sad discovery from the night before, and he realized he was anxious to hear from Jim with an update. He soon gave up any pretence of work. Seizing the opportunity as an excuse to call Dorothy, he punched in her phone number.

"Hello?"

"Morning, again. Guess who?"

"Hey. I was wondering how long it would take to hear from you," she said, her tone softening. "What's happening?"

He smiled. "Well, that's part of the reason I called you. Have you heard anything from Jim, or other sources?"

"And the other reason?" He heard the smile in her voice.

"We can discuss that later, I'm sure."

"Can we now? Hmmm. Well, to answer your question. No, I've heard nothing yet, but I'm confident Jim will call as soon as he has anything to tell us. I believe he's likely involved with questioning the Qus right about now."

"Yes, you're probably right. Thought I'd come in to the office for a bit, but it's hard to concentrate on just regular business, you know?"

"I do know. Have you seen the morning papers? Headlines abound about the 'incident' at Bamboo Fine Imports yesterday. Rumors of stolen jewels, secret rooms, and a mummified body. I love it when you know the real story and see how the press choose to speculate." She paused. "Sorry, Paul, there's a call coming in from Jim on my other line, hold on if you like."

Paul waited silently, and then she was back. "The initial autopsy report is back, he's emailing a copy. He says there's some interesting reading. Would you like to go over it with me?"

"Definitely. I'm finished here now and on my way."

"Sounds good. See you shortly."

Locking up behind him, he was glad to be heading back to the *Aye*. When he arrived, the aroma of freshly brewed coffee welcomed him aboard, along with her greeting.

"Have a seat, I'll be right there," she called from her inner office.

Moments later, she entered the main cabin. Paul had poured coffee for them both, and they settled at the table to review the report.

"Nothing boring about this. Jim's highlighted a lot, so I'll refer to that first and then we can go over the details later. He'd like us to meet with his team in about an hour for a debriefing."

"Fine with me, read on."

"The coroner's initial report noted that Henry Yamada had been deceased for several days, stomach contents gave an estimation of at least six days. The body showed no obvious signs of trauma that would have resulted in death, but when the autopsy got underway, Dr. Davidson noted irregularities with his liver, spleen, and kidneys. Toxicology reports revealed traces of ricin—a toxin extracted from the castor bean. Dr. Davidson believed the victim had been exposed to the poison at least seventy-two hours before he died and would have developed breathing difficulties, fever, and nausea. When inhaled or injected, even a pinhead sized amount of the poison can kill an adult—"

"Isn't that the same stuff suspected of killing that Georgi Markov several years ago?" Paul interrupted. "Speculation was the KGB injected a pellet into him through an umbrella, if I recall."

"Could be—we can check on that."

"And another thing, now that I think about it. When I first met Henry, I thought he was coming down with the flu. Maybe he'd already been poisoned at that point. That would explain why he never showed up for the meeting."

"We'll let Jim know, for sure. Now let's see what else it says here. Oh, yes, this is pretty unusual. Remember the doc made a comment last night, that there should have been more decomposition visible on the body?"

Paul nodded. "And?"

"Says here, he wants to run further tests to determine why decomposition seemed to have been halted, or dramatically slowed. Even allowing for the coolness of the room, all the post-mortem changes were visible on the inside, but not on the outside of his body. So he's holding off on complete results until he can find some more answers."

"I'm no medical expert, Dorothy, so we'll have to wait and see what he finds out. But who would have poisoned Henry? At this point, the only logical person seems to be Victor Lau. Maybe he discovered that Henry had planted David Matsumoto in Jinan's production facility. Or, maybe Henry was playing both sides against the middle and his time ran out."

"Lots of unanswered questions."

"And I have one more. I wonder how Alanna is today. I tried calling earlier, but she couldn't come to the phone."

Dorothy nodded. She wore a mischievous smile. "I'm curious too. Dad's car was missing all night and he just drove by here about an hour ago."

Paul clued in. "Perhaps she'll come to the phone now if I call. I'll try again."

His call was successful and he was relieved to hear her sounding more relaxed and confident than the last time he'd spoken with her. She made a general inquiry as to his well-being. After exchanging pleasantries, he agreed to her offer to meet with Max and her for dinner later that evening at Max's residence.

"Oh, and can you bring Miss Cherie with you? I

hope to make her re-acquaintance," Alanna said with a chuckle.

Paul relayed the request to Dorothy. The look on her face when he informed her they would be having dinner at her own apartment was priceless.

She studied him with raised eyebrows. "Dad must have charmed her right out of herself."

"She's been through a lot. Let's give her a second chance. We can bring them up to date on Jim's reports if that's okay. I'd thought it would be nice to take Jim and Ashley for a drink tonight, but that can be postponed if we're going to your dad's."

"I have a better idea. I'll call Dad and invite Jim and Ashley for dinner. Although, I'll have to ask permission from Jim on just how much we can discuss regarding the case in front of Alanna. She was Victor Lau's partner, after all."

"Good idea If your dad's agreeable to having every-one over, we can ask Jim shortly. Can't wait to hear what's happened with the Qus."

"You and me both. I really want to know the depth of their involvement with Lau."

ຕ໌ເຕ໌ເ

Arriving at the FBI offices on First Avenue, they found parking in the underground lot and took the eleva-tor to the fourth floor after passing security. Jim stood ready to greet them as the elevator doors opened and showed them the way to a boardroom where he'd assem-bled his team.

Introductions were made all around and, taking a coffee handed to her, Dorothy spoke to Ashley while Paul moved over to speak to the young agent who'd explored the tunnel angle.

"I've an invite for you and Jim, don't let me forget."

"As if you'd forget anything, Dorothy." Ashley laughed. "Let's sit here."

They found seats at the large wooden conference table in the middle of the room. Off to one side stood a display board with photos of Victor Lau, Henry Yamada, and the Qus. Various close-up shots of items discovered in the store room took up a lot of space. Yoko sat silently on a chair nearby.

The agents were talkative and energized. It wasn't every day that such a big cache of smuggled goods were recovered, and now they also had a body to deal with. Coffee cups were strewn around the room and the atmosphere was charged with excitement.

"If I could have your attention please." Jim glanced round the room and coughed. He seemed to enjoy making them wait before starting. "First off, let me congratulate you all on the hard work that's been done in the seizure of the stolen artefacts, and the apprehension of Dominic and Lily Qu. No doubt there's work still ahead of us, and I'll provide more info on the Qus momentarily. We're far from finished with this investigation. The mastermind, Victor Lau, is still at large, and the trail's grown cold. We need to determine if there's a connection between him and the murder victim. I might add that the press are clamoring for details, but I remind you that no information is to be released until I give the say so."

Heads nodded and notes were taken as Jim spoke. Some side comments arose between agents.

Putting up his hand for silence, he continued. "Let's talk about the Qus for a moment. Since being taken into custody yesterday, we have, of course, been interrogating them. Not judging a book by its cover comes to mind. In the course of our interrogation, we've found that their quiet unassuming ways are a good cover, because it appears they're capable of anything."

All eyes were on Jim and voices were hushed.

He referred to his notebook then glanced at the crowd. "Background checks revealed that Dominic has no known criminal record, but his good wife Lily has a sheet as long as your arm, both here and in China. I have copies."

Handouts made their way around the room.

"Lily's been the one to spill the beans once confronted with her rap sheet, but Dominic is a hard nut to crack. When they met Victor Lau a few years ago, Victor recognized in Lily a kindred spirit, sharing the same characteristics of greed and cunning. What might have begun as a legitimate business for Dominic soon turned sour after they met Lau. We're still trying for more details from Dominic and will keep you updated. At this point, we've not been able to confirm any connection between the Qus and our victim."

Jim proceeded to read the autopsy report. He fielded many questions, especially regarding the cloth the body had been wrapped in, but admitted they didn't have all the answers yet. "In your handout, you'll see a copy of the autopsy report, and I'd like you all to study it and do some brainstorming. Put any questions up here on this board, and we'll see if we can come to a few conclusions. If anything comes to mind, I think Mr. Webster here could have a shot at answering questions. He's had personal dealings with both the Qus and Lau. So while you discuss and strategize, I'm heading back to the holding area to see Dominic. Let's hope he's been more talkative. We're going to let Lily stew for a while before we start again."

The meeting over, a few agents approached Paul with questions about the fabric, while others could be seen making lists on the board. Dorothy waited to speak to Jim and Ashley before they left. "Thanks for including us, Jim. I had my doubts about the Qus for a while so I'm glad to see you're making progress with them."

"No problem, you and your company have been instrumental in bringing this to fruition and Paul's help has been invaluable."

"All in a day's work." Dorothy shrugged. "Now, before we leave, are you two free for dinner tonight? My dad's making dinner at the apartment, and you're both invited. As a bonus, his hostess is one Alanna Scolfield, if you can believe it. However, if you feel it's not quite appropriate—she was Victor Lau's partner, after all— we'll understand. Seems Dad and Alanna have taken quite a shine to each other."

Ashley considered the invitation and its possible conflicts. "Should be fine. The background check we've done on Alanna pretty much puts her in the clear. In fact, I'm on my way over to Alanna's now to question her regarding Victor. She may have information that, in her mind, is not important, but could be of great interest to us. I really think she was just a dupe in this case."

"Well, I for one would like to be there. I remember your dad's Irish chili," Jim said with a smile.

Ashley didn't hesitate. "So, what time and where?"

"Seven at Maxwell's—the marina where I'm docked. Just ask the bartender to lead you to our apartment. I'll tell him to expect you."

They said their goodbyes. Dorothy returned to join an animated discussion the agents were having with Paul. She soon caught his eye and indicated they should leave. Reluctantly, Paul left the group of dedicated and enthusiastic young feds. They promised to let him know of any forensic results on the cloth, as they became available.

Paul felt invigorated after the debriefing and he

parted company with Dorothy, promising to see her later.

"I'd best give Dad a call and let him know to add two more places for dinner."

❧❧

Her father was happy with the news.

"Ah, now, that's great indeed. The more the merrier. It was Alanna's idea, you know? She wants to thank you both for freeing her from that situation with Lau, and I offered to cook," Max explained heartily.

"She'll be questioned by the authorities today, I hope you know that, Dad."

'Well, I suspected she would or they'd not be doing their job, now would they? I know she's willing to help. Such a lovely woman. I think you had her all wrong, Dorothy."

"If you say so, Dad, see you at seven."

Dorothy elected not to return to the houseboat right away and settled for a time of pampering at her favorite spa. On the way, she called HB to give him the night off and to let everyone else know to meet with her on board next day.

Her time at the spa was too short, and she returned to her houseboat straight from the drycleaners with an outfit she'd wear that evening.

Paul arrived not long after, carrying a bottle of wine. Smartly dressed in a light charcoal suit and blue shirt, he greeted Dorothy with a big smile and kiss.

She returned his greeting, but moved away from him with a sigh.

"What's up? You look very distracted. Can I help?"

She rubbed the back of her neck. "It's nothing or it's everything. I think someone's been on board. My fault. I've let my guard down and had no one watching. It's just a hunch, but I'm ticked off to think someone's been here uninvited."

Paul took her in his arms and this time she relaxed against him.

"Is anything missing or damaged? How long have you been back?"

"That's just it. I've only been here about an hour, so there's been no one here since early this morning—when we left. I don't see anything missing or out of place, but I've called HB back on duty to stay on board until I return. He'll check the files and equipment for me. He has a keen eye for that kind of thing and will notice anything even slightly off."

"Maybe it's just an overreaction to all that's been going on." Even as he spoke, his eyes swept the room looking for anything out of the ordinary.

"Sorry, just call it a feeling. Everything was locked up, but…" Her voice trailed away. Then she made a determined effort to shrug off what she was feeling. "I'm not going to worry about it. If there's anything to be found, HB will find it."

They didn't have long to wait for him to arrive. After apologizing to her faithful employee for reneging on his night off, Dorothy laid out instructions for him to investigate the possibility that she'd had an unwelcome intrusion to her space.

"Leave it with me, boss. If someone's been poking around in here, I'll find out. Now you two just go and have a good time. Raymond's out in the lot, keeping an eye on the place as well."

Rain had settled in for the evening, so they took Paul's car to travel the short distance to Maxwell's. Dorothy made a small gesture of acknowledgement to the occupant of a car who was now watching the houseboat, and his partner inside.

"They're very loyal where you're concerned."

"I lucked out in that department for sure, no complaints from me."

Arriving a few minutes late they were greeted by laughter and soothing Irish melodies playing in the background.

Dorothy nudged Paul. "You're in for a good time tonight. When Dad starts playing his music, the singing's not far behind."

Entering the living room, they came to a full stop. After observing the company already present, they turned, looked at each other, and began to laugh. Max and Alanna were wearing jeans and casual shirts. Jim and Ashley had also arrived in casual attire.

Max chortled. "Well, lookie here at these two in their fancy clothes. Didn't I tell you we're having a ceilidh?"

And, with that, he handed both a glass of his special twenty-five-year-old Irish whiskey.

The room looked festive and the table groaned under the weight of food. Flickering candles adorned shelves and side tables.

Alanna came forward to greet them both. Her transformation was amazing. Not only was she wearing jeans, she wore almost no makeup and her hair was loose and not shellacked with hairspray.

Dorothy wasn't the only one fascinated at the change. She saw Paul's face relax as he gave Alanna a hug. "Recovered from yesterday?"

"I'm fine, Paul, thank you. I'm grateful it was you with me in that awful room. And now that I know we shared it with a dead body. Well, what can I say?"

Alanna shivered slightly. She turned toward Dorothy and gave her a genuine smile, unlike any Dorothy had ever seen.

"I should have listened to you 'Cherie' when you

tried to warn me about Victor. This whole episode has made me take a second look at my judgements and priorities."

"All's well that ends well, Alanna. Cherie has now retired, at least for the evening. You've no idea how happy I am that you got away from that dreadful man in time," Dorothy said, giving her a hug.

They moved farther into the room and settled on the sofa opposite Jim and Ashley, who seemed anxious to talk to them.

Max cleared his throat. "If you'll excuse us ,we have some last minute preparations for this repast, and I think you have things to discuss, so without further ado…"

Jim appeared bursting at the seams, and, once Max and Alanna were out of earshot, he launched right into his afternoon spent with Dominic Qu. Paul and Dorothy listened with great interest, while Ashley nodded her head, as Dominic's story unfolded.

"Apparently, we've just scratched the tip of the iceberg with this case. Reports are now filtering into our offices concerning Dominic. As mentioned earlier today, we couldn't find any known records on him. However, a fingerprint match has now come back with a positive ID, and we're now going after a DNA test to back up what we've learned."

He took a drink from his glass. "We believe his real identity is Peng Xao Ping, formerly of the People's Republic of China and listed as a missing person, presumed dead, for the last thirty five years. His disappearance coincided with a major art collection theft in Hong Kong. The collection belonged to Sir Alfred Knowles, a retired British diplomat, living out his final years in Hong Kong. On staff in the Knowles household was a young Chinese girl, Lily, who also disappeared just after the theft. Apparently, she was the inside person, aiding Dominic in his scheme. None of the art surfaced for many years, nor was there any word on the thieves. It was as if they never existed.

"For almost fifteen years there was complete silence, and many began to believe that the thieves and their loot had met with an accident—perhaps the sinking of a boat as they tried to escape." Jim paused and Dorothy began to see the dots connecting. He caught her eye and nodded. "Then, about five years ago, Sir Knowles passed away. Within weeks, small pieces of his collection began appearing on the black market in Europe, sources unknown. Authorities began to hope that the thieves had been biding their time and would soon give themselves away by trying to unload larger pieces, but after only a couple of months, the trail once more grew cold. No more items became available and the mystery continued. Fast forward to this week."

"It's all coming together, isn't it?" Dorothy mused.

"Yes, it is. We've had an expert in Chinese art and antiquities start looking at what was found within the Qus'residence. And not just what was in the storeroom, but scattered throughout the building, and in the personal living quarters of the couple. It should come as no surprise when I tell you that this decades-old mystery is now on its way to being cleared up—"

"Jim, you mentioned something about a DNA sample?" Paul interrupted.

"Yes, I did, didn't I?" he teased. "We may have our connection between Henry Yamada and Dominic Qu. Dominic had an older sister and she married a Japanese fellow, whom we suspect was Henry Yamada's father. A possible theory is that there was a family betrayal with Dominic and his sister. So with family honor at stake, Henry was groomed to avenge the disloyalty Dominic had shown his family. We don't have all the details yet and may be filling in a lot of the blanks ourselves, but a story is starting to emerge that goes back a long time."

"So maybe it wasn't Victor who poisoned Henry?" Paul suggested.

"We did find evidence of castor beans in Dominic's kitchen," Ashley said. She let the implication settle.

"Still no word on Victor's whereabouts?" Paul asked. "It wouldn't surprise me if he was involved with Henry's death as well."

"Nothing yet, and the more time that elapses, the harder it is to find his trail. He most likely had at least one escape route planned and could be out of the country by now."

"Hmmm…" Dorothy murmured. "Smart man that he is, perhaps he only wants us to think he has left the country. Once he feels the threat has lessened, he may show up again." Before anyone could comment, her cell phone chimed. "It's HB," she said by way of explanation. "Hey, what's up?" She listened and her face grew serious as she heard what her number one operative had to say. "Good job, just leave things as they are, and I'll take it from here shortly."

Paul threw her a questioning glance, but before she could respond, there was a hearty "Dinner's ready!" from the kitchen. Max made his way to the dining table with a platter of roast chicken. Alanna followed behind him with more food.

The rest of the discussion would have to wait until after dinner, for now they were all more than glad to partake once again of Max's culinary skills.

Chapter 19

The dinner party was relaxed, a time for developing friendships and a much needed break from the intensity of the past days. The food, although simple fare, was delicious and more than satisfying. Over glasses of wine, they discussed their shared adventures. Alanna, surprisingly, was very open with details of her relationship with Victor. She was both lighthearted and mellow at the same time. She recounted time spent earlier that day with Ashley. How she'd vented her anger at Victor and railed against herself for being taken in by him.

"She helped provide a clearer perspective," Ashley added and then related what she had learned from Alanna. "According to Alanna, Lau came from peasant stock and any savvy business acumen he appeared to hold was all a sham. Acting was his strong point. He depended completely on advisors and others with whom he had business dealings."

"His façade dropped when he drank," Alanna said. "He provided a lot of opportunities for that. And then he'd give himself away."

Ashley patted her arm. "Some months ago, he'd approached her company. With lots of charm and suave maneuvers, he persuaded Alanna into a partnership."

Alanna shook her head in disgust. "I can't believe I actually fell for his idea. If I'd done more due diligence, I'd probably have discovered his counterfeit plans. I was so excited at first and eager to begin the promotional and marketing side of things. What an opportunity it presented. But things didn't seem to add up. He was secretive about other business dealings and wouldn't provide numbers or information that I needed for a successful campaign." She grew silent and the smile left her face. No one interrupted as she recounted the embarrassment of bearing the brunt of his displeasure when his plans didn't go as he intended. "He's a very angry man and any attraction I had for him in the beginning soon faded. As Cherie here—" She smiled at Dorothy. "—pointed out, he had started using me as a punching bag."

Dorothy admired Alanna's public admission and her ability to remain calm as the story unfolded. From her own experiences, Dorothy knew how difficult it could be.

"I have to admit to some guilt here, Alanna," Paul said. "It seems a lot of your troubles started when I held back the dolls. Money was at stake. Maybe he was under pressure from the Qus." He turned to address Jim. "I doubt we know the whole story yet. Just who is behind all this anyway? Lau, or Qu?"

Jim, by this time, had consumed an Irish whiskey and two large glasses of wine. Dorothy was bemused to see a silly, but endearing, expression light up his face. He rose from his chair and bowed theatrically to Max. "Friends, I have a confession to make. I fear I am a little unsteady right now and, therefore, will not be answering any further questions regarding Qau and Lu."

Max burst out laughing, and any further serious discussion was done for the evening. The group left the table for the more comfortable sofas and chairs by the fireplace.

Dorothy was unable to relax and soon headed to the kitchen to brew coffee. She knew Paul would want to know about the earlier call from HB. But for now, true to his nature, Max put on more music, and his deep baritone joined anonymous recorded voices singing beautiful Irish ballads.

In the kitchen, she was deep in thought as she began rinsing and stacking dishes while waiting for the coffee to brew. She didn't notice Paul enter the kitchen and jumped when he put his arms around her waist.

"What's up, Dee?" he asked with affectionate concern.

She dried her hands and looked into his eyes. "I'm sorry. I didn't want to mention it out there, mainly because I'm not sure if it's anything. HB says that someone has definitely been in the houseboat." His arms tensed around her waist and she sighed. "I don't need Dad involved, so I'm going to leave shortly and meet up with Raymond. He's still watching the place from the road."

"And I'm coming with you whenever you want to leave."

"No immediate rush, but I must say I'm anxious to go. Perhaps we should just have our coffee then take off—after a few renditions of 'Danny Boy,' of course. Dad's sure to sing that before much longer. Listen."

Voices from the other room were joined in song and, as the tune died down, the gentle opening notes of the beloved Irish ballad began.

Dorothy smiled and set about putting the coffee ready to serve. As she worked, she continued bringing Paul up to date. "I have to admit I'm a little unnerved to think my privacy on the *Aye* has been violated, and I'd planned to stay here because of that. However, it looks as if Dad may already have company planned for the night—" She tilted her head toward Alanna and finished wiping down the counter. "—and I don't really feel comfortable staying if that's the case."

"Any chance I could bunk in with you tonight?"

"You don't even have to ask."

"Somehow I thought you'd say that."

"Is that coffee ready yet?" Max bellowed from the other room.

"That's our cue." Dorothy swatted at Paul with a towel. "Let's bring their coffee and then we can go."

Joining the lively gathering and following along for a chorus or two, they then made their excuses to leave. Jim was half-asleep and Ashley assured them she'd call a cab for him.

The rain had stopped, leaving shrubs and trees a glistening green. The evening air was fresh and peaceful. The pair enjoyed the walk down to Paul's car. Dorothy reached for her cell to call HB, but it rang before she had the chance. Raymond's excited voice was audible to Paul.

The relaxed mood was swept away when she urged him to hurry. "We need to get over there."

Paul put the car in gear and pulled out of the restaurant's parking lot. "What's happening?"

Dorothy tapped her fingers on the dashboard. "Raymond saw a car near the docks not long ago. The driver parked close to a building across from the marina. Whoever was driving got out and snuck aboard the *Aye*."

"I thought HB was on board."

"Probably what the intruder was waiting for. HB had just left to pick up some equipment. Raymond's already called the police, who should be arriving at any moment. Whoever's there now can be charged with breaking and entering. This can't be a coincidence. Got to be connected with whoever was aboard earlier today."

Pulling up to the marina's car park, they jumped out of the vehicle. Approaching sirens could be heard wailing in the distance, growing louder by the second. Dorothy and her firm enjoyed a good rapport with the local police and, when they realized whose property was at risk, they wasted no time responding.

Squad cars squealed to a halt next to Paul and Dorothy. Doors slammed and officers rushed into position. HB's vehicle screeched to a halt behind them. He joined Raymond, who was keeping as close as he dared to the armed law-enforcement detail. Guns were drawn and orders barked. Two lead officers approached the gangway with caution and stopped abruptly when they heard a splash.

Catching up to the officers, Dorothy and Paul arrived in time to witness a bedraggled Victor Lau being fished out of the murky waters of the dockside.

As his soaked feet made contact with the solid surface of the dock, he began shouting in Mandarin. One dripping wet arm swung out in an attempt to block an officer's effort at restraining him. His partner's handgun was trained on Victor, who was soaked to the skin.

Tensions were running high, and Dorothy knew from experience that it wouldn't take much for a bullet to end this angle of the investigation. "Victor Lau!" she shouted.

In the split second that Victor's attention was diverted from fending off capture, another officer moved in and tackled the man to the ground. Handcuffs were quickly employed and Lau found himself being dragged to his feet, none too gently. Rights were read and he was hustled off to a waiting police car.

In unison, Paul and Dorothy exhaled a sigh of relief.

The officer in charge approached them. "Dorothy, another round of excitement I see?"

"Hey, Grant, good to see you as well," she joked. "I'm anxious to go aboard and see if anything's been taken or damaged."

"You'll have to wait for the all clear. Business first for my team." He tipped his head in the direction of the car where Victor was held. "Apparently, you know this guy, do you?"

"Once he dries off, you'll likely recognize him as someone you've been looking for—Victor Lau. He's wanted on charges of forcible confinement, and possible murder, among other things."

"Dorothy, once again you find yourself involved with the most unsavoury of characters," the officer said, sounding impressed. "It shouldn't be long till we can allow you back on board. And now that we've the prize catch of the day, so to speak, we'll get him off to the station pronto."

As the policeman finished speaking, he trained his eyes on Paul.

Dorothy winced. "Oh, I'm sorry, Grant. My manners have fled. Let me introduce you to Paul Webster, a good friend of mine. Actually, he's the reason I got involved with that fishy character you've arrested."

Handshakes were exchanged.

"Glad to meet you Paul. Any friend of Dorothy's…"

"Likewise, Grant. Knowing Victor Lau's safely in your custody will help some friends of ours rest much easier."

A few minutes later, Dorothy was given the all clear to board her houseboat. Stepping almost hesitantly into the main cabin, she was relieved to see that all seemed in place. "Looks as if he ran out of time to search for whatever he was here for."

"There's another possibility, Dee," Paul suggested, speaking softly. "What if he wasn't looking for something, but wanted to leave something behind, if you get my drift?"

She nodded. "All the more reason I'm glad to leave

that to HB. Does my suggestion for tonight's accommo-
dation still stand?"

"I certainly haven't changed my mind." A brief kiss
sealed the deal.

"I'll throw together an overnight bag."

Paul drove, and Dorothy left a message for Jim Addison, giving details of Lau's capture and which police
station held him.

"One more call and I'm done, promise," she said.
"Good news, Dad! Victor Lau's had his wandering spirits
thoroughly and literally dampened. Make sure you tell
Alanna she can relax now."

Paul groaned at her play on words. Once her phone
was tucked away, he reached for her hand. "I'm glad
you're coming back with me tonight. Let's see if we can
avoid talking about Lau, or dolls, or anyone but us."

"I like the sound of that," she agreed.

꿍ꀜꀜ

The phone's persistent ringing brought Paul awake.
He didn't need to glance at the bedside clock to know
he'd slept well. Sunlight peeked through the slats of the
window blinds.

Reaching for the receiver, he hoped he managed to
sound as if hadn't just woken up. "Hello?"

"Mr. Webster. Good morning. HB here. Sorry to
bother you so early, but I'm trying to reach the boss and
her cell keeps going to voice mail. I figured she'd be
there with you?"

"Sure, hang on." He put the phone on hold, gave a
mighty stretch and kicked his legs out from under tangled
sheets.

He only had to follow his nose to find Dorothy. Busy
in the kitchen, where a fresh pot of coffee awaited, she

was tending bacon, which was frying nicely in a pan.

"Busy girl, I see. HB's on the phone for you. I'll watch the bacon if you want to use the phone in the other room."

Wiping her hands on a nearby cloth, she turned from the stove and walked over to Paul. "Morning to you too, sleepyhead."

A quick kiss and she continued on her way to speak with HB.

A few minutes later she rejoined Paul. "You were right, Mr. Detective. Victor did leave something behind. HB found an explosive device underneath the control panel. Fortunately, he must have been interrupted in his task because it hadn't been activated and has now been safely removed. I'd bet anything he was the one in there earlier, although it's only a gut hunch."

She sat at the table where Paul had laid the breakfast of bacon, eggs, and fresh fruit. Steaming mugs of coffee completed the meal.

"Thanks for finishing up." She took her first sip of coffee. "HB's been thoroughly searching my computer files. He says he can tell that there've been attempts made to access them. Thank goodness for the password layers I'm religious about using. It's paid off this time."

"I'm glad you have HB on your side. Does that man never go home, or sleep?"

"Seems that way, doesn't it?" She paused. "Dennehy Investigations gained much more than an employee when he joined the team. He's invaluable, and I trust him completely."

Enjoying their breakfast they wondered aloud what the day would bring.

By day's end they found out, when Jim arrived at Paul's home. Before bringing them up to speed, he thanked them for a pleasant evening the night before.

"Although," he added sheepishly, "I could do without this headache."

"From the singing or the whiskey?" teased Paul.

"Yes." Jim grinned. "The FBI learned that the private plane Lau used for travel was in fact registered to Dominic Qu. More of the real relationship between these two men has come to light as the investigation progresses. It came as no real surprise to learn that Jinan Import and Export was a well set up front for the Qus. On the surface, Lau is the owner of the company, Dominic Qu is his silent, but deadly, partner. Qu was the one with the plan to develop a counterfeit fabric to compete against Yashito."

Dorothy nodded. "That fits. It would be too good of an opportunity to pass up."

"Exactly," Jim agreed. "Lau is one cold and calculating individual, showing no mercy to those who stand in his way. We'll build our case to include attempted murder, not just against you and Alanna, Paul. But also against Dorothy."

"For the explosive device?"

"That's one count, and then another regarding 'Cherie' and the foiled one-way air trip. It's great that we have *that* conversation taped."

"And where does Henry Yamada fit in with all these murder charges?" Paul asked.

"At this point, we don't have conclusive evidence of who's responsible. Castor beans have been found hidden in a false cupboard in the Qus' private apartment. Certainly, the evidence is leaning toward either Dominic or Lily. But I want to dig some more and see if we can't link Lau to that one as well." Jim paused for a breath. "All the usual legal bargains are being drawn up. An exchange of information against the Qus will offer Lau a lesser sentence. At this point, he seems more than willing to take advantage of this offer and is, even now, supplying us details on what the Qus have smuggled over the years."

Paul clapped him on the back. "Good work, Jim. Seems like all the pieces are falling nicely into place."

Jim nodded and turned to Dorothy. "Your help's been tremendous, Dorothy. It's been a real pleasure working with you and your team. There'd be no hesitation on my part to enlist your services in the future."

"So I guess that means I no longer have need of Dennehy Security and Investigations," Paul teased.

"Now, Mr. Webster, you still have a media event coming up, don't you? I think I should stick around and ensure there are no glitches with that, don't you agree?"

"I don't think I'd let her get away," Jim said as he made to leave.

∽∾∽

Enjoying a well-deserved day off, Dorothy stretched out on Paul's sofa. She caught up on some long-neglected reading with the latest Inspector Gamache mystery.

While she read, Paul was in a discussion with his office, Patricia Barry specifically. He brought her up to date. Even though she'd read about Victor Lau's capture in the paper, Paul gave her additional information she could relay to her colleagues. "Patricia, I'd like you to touch base with Catherine so you can be the number one go-to person for this merger event. I'd like you to personally talk with Mr. Yashito and keep him advised of all the details. Catherine has the invitations ready. We're just waiting on the time and date to be confirmed."

"Not a problem, Paul. Whatever needs doing, I'll handle it. Does this mean you've now settled on a date?"

"Right. I'm looking at a week Tuesday for the celebration. We may not have all the RSVPs but that should

be enough time for definite interest in our announcement."

"Got it." Patricia hesitated. "If you don't mind me
asking, I know how much you always stay on top of these
things, and I'm a little surprised that you seem to be
handing off details you'd normally cover. Is everything
okay?"

"I have no concerns about leaving this with you.
Next to me, I doubt there is anyone who understands this
company as well as you do. But, yes there is a reason I'm
delegating this time around. I'm going to be out of town
for a couple of days." Patricia waited, expecting more
details, but instead he touched on current events. "When I
know more details, I'll let you know. For now, the world
stays a better place with their activities curtailed."

"Well, I, for one, I'm glad I never had to meet Victor
Lau. I'm sure he's not someone you'll soon forget."

"Too true, Patricia. We still need confirmation on
how the fabric was instrumental in preserving Henry
Yamada's body. That information should also be con-
tained in the coroner's report."

"Thanks for all the info, then," she said. "You won't
have to worry about anything while you're gone. Going
anywhere special?"

Paul knew her too well. "Yes, as a matter of fact, I
am. For now, you'll have to keep your curiosity at bay
until I return." He laughed. "But when I do return, be
prepared for some heavy discussions with you about the
future of this company."

"Guess I'll have to wait then, but you've certainly
got my attention," she said. "In any event, we'll deal with
other matters when you return."

Phone call ended, Paul turned around to find Dorothy, book in hand, looking at him with a quizzical expression on her face.

"Going away? Not that I was eavesdropping, but—"

"It can't be helped, I'm afraid. Sorry, I meant to tell you before I spoke with Patricia. It's only for a couple of days."

"Oh."

Seeing her crestfallen face, Paul took the book from her hands and pulled her close. "While I'd love to have you come with me, there are things I need to take care of and have been procrastinating over. However, if all goes to plan, you and I will be taking a few days away very soon—if that's agreeable with you."

"Take care of what you need to and then get back to me." She kissed him. "I'm most agreeable to some time away with you."

Chapter 20

Paul's three-day trip came to an end, and he was anxious to see Dorothy. They'd agreed to meet at Maxwell's to catch up.

Paul grabbed a table on the deck outside, overlooking the water. The time away had given him a chance to step back a little. To see both his business world and the relationship he'd developed with Dorothy more objectively.

Staring out over the water, he didn't see her approach.

"Hey, sailor, haven't I seen you here before?"

He stood and hugged her, whispering in her ear, "I've missed you so much."

"Me you too. It's been a long three days. Was the trip a success?"

He nodded. "I believe so. And now it's back to reality for me. The merger celebration is on track, and you'll be working a new case before long."

"You must be psychic. I do have new clients lined up, but my first order of business today is to submit my invoice to Paul Webster and Associates for services rendered. I assume you'll no longer need my professional assistance once the merger is complete?"

He concentrated on his drink while he mulled over the reply. "Don't be too hasty on that, Dee."

Dorothy cocked her head to one side, but didn't pursue the comment. "So is there anything you want to share about your trip?"

"Other than I missed you every second I was away?"

She smiled and reached for his hand across the table. "Next time, we go away together."

"Count on it. Now as far as my trip went—yes, it accomplished what I needed, and I'm closer to some decisions than I was. With no distractions—" He grinned. "—I had a clearer focus."

"And what decisions are you making?"

"I only said I was closer, and you'll be the first to know when they're firmed up."

"If that's what you want, I can wait."

"I do, thanks. Now tell me, how are Max and Alanna?"

"You'd think they'd been together for years. I'm heading over there when I leave here." Her phone buzzed. "Figures. I had the ringer off and now I have two messages. HB," she mouthed, and then recapped. "Says the *Aye* is clear and secure after giving it a thorough stem to stern check. Sarcastic bugger says he's taken the liberty of upgrading my security systems!"

Paul chuckled and watched as she listened to the second message.

"You'll want to listen to this one," she said, replaying it in speaker mode.

Jim Addison's voice was next. "I just wanted to thank you again for your help in bringing down the Qus and Victor Lau. We've pretty much got an airtight case on the smuggling. I've also just left a message with Paul regarding more results on the cloth Henry Yamada was found in. Interesting stuff. Call back and maybe we can all meet for a recap."

Paul reached for his cell as the message ended and saw a message waiting. "Do you want me to call him back?" he asked, his hand hovering over the keypad.

"In a minute. There's something I want to say to you first.

"Shoot."

"While you were away, I realized that working with you made me think of the better days I had back on the force. And I want to thank you for that. Too often, I look back on those days with sadness and regret."

"And?"

"And as much as I appreciate and depend on my team, it's been refreshing to share the details of a case on a more intimate level."

"I think I understand, Dee." He was about to say more, but changed his mind. "Listen, you said you were going to see your dad. How about you do that, and I'll give Jim a call."

She glanced at her watch. "Good thinking. Dad will be wondering where I am. Call me after you've spoken with Jim."

They stood, kissed, and Paul watched her leave, determined that the next time they kissed it would be in more private quarters.

C∽C∽⌐

"Hi, Dad, it's me," Dorothy called, entering the apartment.

"Darlin', I thought I saw you arrive downstairs. Paul with you?"

"We had a drink downstairs, but he's got a call to make and then I think we're meeting with Jim a little later. Some updates on the case."

"That's grand."

"Anything new here?"

"Same old, same old. Although—" He hesitated briefly. "—I've been kicking off early the past couple of nights."

"Oh? You feeling all right?"

A small grin played at his lips. "Well, it's the only time, you see, that Alanna and I have to see each other. I'm working most of the evening hours and she's at work during the day. I've been thinking of taking a few days break from the bar and wondered if you recommend a good resort, with a spa."

"All by yourself?" Dorothy couldn't resist the tease. "Just kidding. I'm glad you two like each other. I'd not have predicted it, but if you're happy, then I am too. I know of one or two places and will send you the info. Somewhere I'm sure you'll *both* like."

The big man seemed at a loss for words, but the smile on his face spoke volumes. He coughed slightly. "Right, I'll be heading back downstairs then. I just wanted to catch up with you and ask about a getaway place."

She smiled and her thoughts turned to Paul and about getting away with him.

 espes

Returning Jim's phone call, Paul agreed that time together would be much in order. Jim left it with him to contact Dorothy and see what they could arrange.

Then Paul touched bases with Catherine, who brought him up to date on the office and was glad to report nothing out of the ordinary.

Drawing the conversation to a close, he said, "I'll be coming into the office tomorrow for a bit. There's paperwork that needs attention, and it'll give me a head start for Monday. So if you want to leave me all the particulars about Tuesday's event, I'll look things over. Oh, one more thing. Please see if you can book a meeting with Patricia for Wednesday."

Catherine assured him all would be in order for him. "I have to say you sound more relaxed, Paul. The time away has obviously done you some good. See you Monday, unless you want me to come in tomorrow as well?"

"No, you need to enjoy your weekend. I'll see you Monday. You've done a great job as always. I probably don't tell you enough how much you're appreciated."

"Glad to do it. Bye for now."

He made his way to the kitchen and put coffee on to brew. While waiting for it to finish, he began to wander from room to room in his house. As he did, his mind's eye saw Dorothy the first time she'd been in his home. He smiled, recalling how she'd been standing there in his living room, confident as all get out, after just breaking into his house. *And gorgeous to boot*, he thought.

He headed purposefully back to the kitchen and a hot cup of coffee. *Seems I've got to finalize those decisions.*

❧❧❧

The next morning, with the weekend underway, Paul busied himself in his study before heading downtown to his office, but found it hard to concentrate on any particular task. He thought back, over and over, to Dorothy's comments about being able to share details of a case with him. In his mind, they made a good couple and worked well together. If his newly evolved plan came to fruition, they could continue to work side by side.

Even before the merger plans and all that had happened with Victor Lau and company, Paul had been feeling a restless tug to start a completely new business venture. He wasn't confident that the newly merged company would fulfil his longing. The events of the past few days had made him feel more alive than he had in a long time. The excitement of being involved in an investigation, and its dangers, had turned the restlessness into a concrete idea. But one large question loomed over everything. How would Dorothy react to his brainchild?

You'll never know unless you ask her, he told himself.

Both he and Dorothy were anxious to meet with Jim and learn further details, but getting together would have to wait until after the merger event. There was also the anticipation of learning more details from the coroner's office and any further revelations from the continuing investigation into the activities of Victor Lau and the Qus.

Paul attempted to focus on those matters, as well as his own personal business ideas. He busied himself sorting mail and outlining his thoughts on paper.

Needing a break, he refilled his coffee cup and wandered outside, down to the waterfront path. He reflected on how his home, overlooking the water, had been his refuge from a broken marriage and daily business pressures. But not until that moment had he realized how lonely he'd become.

Brushing a few stray leaves from his bench, he sat, sipped at his coffee, and became aware of ducks squabbling nearby. They'd spotted his arrival and paddled eagerly toward him, hoping for a handout.

Puffs of cloud drifted across an azure blue sky. Trees had been brushed with an artist's palette in shades of green, and leaves stirred in a soft breeze. The peace and stillness of his garden helped Paul gather his thoughts and reach a decision.

He called Dorothy but got her voicemail. "Dorothy,

hi. Sorry, this can't keep until Monday. Can you call me right away? I'll be at my office within the hour if you want to meet me there. Miss you."

Hanging up the phone, Paul grabbed a quick shower and started to mentally prepare how he'd present his plan to Dorothy. His excitement at imagining her reaction became tinged with doubts.

She could say no. She could brush me off.

One minute he felt calm and confident, the next he was as jittery as a youngster on a first date. His mind raced a mile a minute as he entered his office building.

Being Saturday, he made mention to the security guard that he was expecting Ms. Dennehy.

"Please send her up when she arrives."

"Sure thing, Mr. Webster."

At his desk, he started in on paperwork Catherine had left regarding the merger. She'd left everything in order and also had set up the requested appointment with Patricia Barry for Wednesday. Paul knew that, if everything went as planned, he'd need the support of these two women.

And then Dorothy arrived, gently tapping against the glass entrance door to his business domain. "Your message had me a little concerned. Is everything okay?"

He took her by the hand and led her to the reception area, where they sat close. "Dorothy—Dee," he began hesitantly. "I'm having a hard time spitting this out, so here goes." He swallowed hard. "It's true we've only known each other for a short while, but I see no other way to live my life unless you're in it." He paused and searched her face. "I need you to share my life. I love you—and I can only hope you feel the same."

Silence.

Paul was sure she'd be able to feel his pounding heart while he waited on her to say something—anything.

He began to relax when he saw the faint beginnings of a smile forming on her lips. Even better, she spoke the words he'd been longing to hear. "I love you too. But—"

"But what?"

"What took you so long?"

"Oh, Dee!" He held her as if he'd never let go.

When they finally drew apart, he saw a look of relief on her face.

"I was afraid you were going to dump me," she confessed, stifling a laugh.

"And I was afraid you weren't going to feel the same way I do," he said with a big sigh.

She leaned in and gave him a kiss that forestalled any further discussion. "Where do we go from here?"

Paul hesitated. "Funny you should ask."

A raised eyebrow met his statement.

"I've been doing a lot of thinking the past few days. Business wise, I'm glad the merger is a done deal, and it'll be wonderful for the company to be partnered with Yashito. I'm just not sure that's where I want to be anymore."

"Really? Why not?"

"Let's just say that working with you and the FBI—being involved in the investigation and capture of Lau and friends—has whet my appetite once again for things a little more adventuresome."

"I can see that. You've got a good background for it. So?"

"So, I was wondering what you'd say to a new business partnership—for both of us."

Dorothy blinked then stared. "You'd leave your company after everything you've put into it?"

"Not exactly. I'd stay on as a silent partner. There are many capable hands I can leave the day to day running of this business with. But now, I want more than a desk job. I really admire the way you've built Dennehy Security and Investigations and think we could team up for a top notch investigative agency."

Dorothy took a moment to respond. "That's quite a lot of thinking you've been doing. Don't get me wrong. I've really enjoyed working with you as well, and certainly the skills you have would be a wonderful asset to any kind of investigation. But I'd need to think about this."

"I totally understand, Dee. In my mind, of course, I have everything already worked out. But this isn't a do or die proposition, and you need to think it through. Talk it over with your dad. I'll still love you, regardless."

She reached out to softly touch the side of his face. "Where have you been all my life?" she asked wistfully.

"I could say the same thing. But better late than never, right?"

c∞c∞

Once again, Monday rolled around. They had agreed to put any more talk about a future business partnership on hold until after the merger event. They turned their attention to the planned meeting with Jim and Ashley.

Answers were needed about the material composition of the dolls' dresses and Henry Yamada's shroud. They wanted to know why his body had been in apparently perfect condition when it was found in the storage cellar.

The relationship with Yashito and his company was strong, and Paul was still confident they'd make ideal business partners. Dorothy, on the other hand, was now officially off the clock with the Lau case. Any results from the FBI lab, or the coroner's office, would be icing on the cake.

Knowing that HB and Raymond were able to take care of things left her free to take time to consider Paul's suggestion. No wonder both were less talkative than usual as they sat enjoying a pre-work day breakfast at a diner near the waterside.

Dorothy laid her fork down as her cell phone rang. "Good morning, Dad." She smiled at Paul as she spoke, predicting her father's response, and putting the phone on speaker mode.

"How did you know it was me?"

"Call display, Dad, remember?"

"Oh, right, I keep forgetting. Can't quite get the hang of some of these things, you know?"

"As if, Dad. Anyway you didn't call me to discuss technology at this time of the day, did you? You and Alanna aren't going to cancel coming to Paul's media event tomorrow?"

"We wouldn't miss it for the world. Don't worry. That's not what I was calling about."

"Well, stop beating about the bush then." She laughed. "What's on your mind?"

"I looked into those resort places you told me about and have made a reservation, but would need you to cover for me at the bar if you could? We'd like to leave right after the celebration tomorrow."

"I don't mind helping, Dad. You think I can manage all by myself?"

"I have complete faith in you. Besides, the other staff, and no doubt some of the regulars, will help you out. What do you say?"

Paul gave Dorothy a thumbs up and feigned pulling a pint to let her know he'd help as well.

"I wouldn't normally impose, but Alanna and I seem to have grown quite close, and—"

"No need to explain. And I'm very happy for you and Alanna as well. Seems to be a theme these days," she said, glancing in Paul's direction.

"Isn't it, though?" Max agreed, without asking for details. "Would you and Paul like to meet us here for dinner about nine? We can go over some of the need-to-know things."

"I'll double check with Paul and let you know. Talk to you later."

"Thanks, darlin'. I owe you one."

As she closed her phone, she looked at Paul. "So, you want to help me barkeep for a few days, do you?"

Chapter 21

The much-anticipated merger day finally arrived. But Paul had other news for his management team before the media event began. The announcement that Patricia Barry would be their new boss was well received. All were assured that the principal players on the Yashito team were enthused about what they could accomplish.

Executives from both companies mingled at the post-press-conference reception. Excited chatter filled the room as media types vied for personal interviews. Patricia Barry had been promoted to Vice-President of Operations for the new firm.

The new company's focus meant a change in retirement plans for Archie James, who informed Paul in his unique way that, "Of course, laddie, no need to ask. I'll stay on for a wee while longer—with a raise, no doubt?"

Most exciting was the information about the participation in the upcoming Asian exhibit and the potential for a wider market.

As the event drew to a close, Akira Yashito and Paul introduced the new vice president of the merged company. The media were asked to direct any more inquiries to Patricia Barry's attention.

Dorothy, Max, and Alanna had kept their presence low key during the festivities and, as the last attendees disappeared, made their way over to Paul.

"Well done, my son." Max congratulated him with a hearty slap on the back. "Are you ready for round two?"

"Thanks, Max, yes, I think so. Hope you and Alanna have a great time away."

℘℘℘

Their first evening of bar duties had come to an end. Dorothy followed the last customer to the door and gratefully locked up.

Turning back to the bar with a bemused chuckle, she noticed Paul lounging against the bar, a well-used towel tossed over his shoulder. He crooked his finger at her, and she slowly walked toward him, a smile teasing her lips.

Within arm's length, Paul reached for her. "That was fun, my love, but I'm glad the evening's over."

"Oh, it's not over yet. Now we have to clean up." She grabbed the towel off his shoulder and flicked it at him. "The owner is a vile and mean barkeep who will have my head if all is not in order!"

"First things first," he countered. "Come and sit down for a minute."

Wondering what he had in mind, she took a seat beside him. "What's up?" When he didn't respond, she saw that he wore a very serious expression which caused her some concern. "Sweetheart, what's wrong? Have you heard bad news?"

Meeting her eyes, he shook his head. "No it's not bad news, but I do have something I need to talk to you about. And no, I'm not changing my mind about you, or us, but you might after you hear what I need to say."

The light hearted levity they'd shared, just moments ago, had now vanished, and she waited to hear what Paul had to say. She offered an encouraging smile. "I'm not going anywhere without very good reason, so let's hear it."

"Dee, I hope you know that you've come to mean the world to me and how much I want us to have a future."

She nodded but remained silent.

"And if we're to have a life together, then my past needs to be part of it, too. It's a part of who I am and I'd rather you hear it from me than learn about it elsewhere."

"I understand. Go on."

Encouraged, he continued. "It has to do with my military career. I haven't spoken much about it because it's a tarnished piece of my past, and I don't like to think about it. I risk you thinking less of me by sharing this with you. You were upfront with me about your past, so…" He rose from the table and wandered over to the bar for a glass of water and brought one for her. "I hadn't planned on a military career, but I was recruited by the navy as I was finishing university. Above average marks, and having been identified as a natural leader, got their attention. I did the basic boot camp but, apparently, I was never meant to see action. Once training was done, I began specialized training in the area of intelligence gathering and was soon given a small team to oversee. We worked well as a team, and I took a lot of pride in bringing them up to speed and helping them reach their full potential. Before long, I made the rank of captain, which brought more responsibility. We carried out missions, here and overseas. Our expertise grew and, as threats to National Security escalated, so did our work load."

"No wonder you were recruited. From what I've seen and know of you, I can understand that. How long were you in the service?"

"Almost ten years, and I'd probably still be there except for what happened. That's what I need to tell you about." He took a deep breath. "Most of the assignments we were given involved little personal risk, but we did have some that were dangerous. We had casualties along the way, on both sides." His eyes grew dark as memories came flooding back. Forcing them to retreat, he continued. "The last operation I was in charge of...well, that's the one that changed my military life forever. I had an exceptional team of five, and we were tracking intelligence chatter regarding possible terrorist attacks on the eastern seaboard. We geared up to follow and chase down any and all leads that came our way. During the course of our investigations, two of my best guys were apparently under suspicion and being watched by my superiors. I hadn't been advised of this and was completely blindsided when they were charged with treason."

"That's awful. Why weren't you told about it?"

"Get this. I hadn't been advised because I was also being investigated as working alongside them. I was eventually brought up on charges and faced a court martial. Not one of my finer memories."

Dorothy reached for his hand, her face ashen.

Paul squeezed her fingers gently in thanks. "That's where I met Rolin Montase. He was appointed as my defense lawyer. And a damn fine investigator, I might add. He admitted he had his doubts about my innocence with the facts first presented, but soon saw that things didn't add up.

"Anyway, while all the legal battles were taking place, the rest of my team became involved in a situation that got way out of control. Two of them were killed. I blame myself because, if I hadn't been suspended from duty, it never would have happened.

"I'd been set up, along with my other two supposed

co-conspirators. While all the focus was being diverted to the three of us and our expertise was out of action, an attack was being brought to fruition and came this close to being carried out."

"Unbelievable," Dorothy said. "But why do you feel this would make me think any less of you? Certainly, it's a tragedy when lives are lost, but it's not your fault."

Paul shook his head. "But that's just it. While I was under court martial, the additional charge came that I had ordered the executions of those two."

"*What*? I don't believe that for an instant!"

"Of course, it's not true—all part of the set up—but I blame myself for their deaths and always will. Their paying that price was all part of the plan to incriminate me. If I'd been more diligent, I might have found out enough information ahead of time to have prevented their deaths."

"What happened with your legal defense then?"

"To make a long story short, Rolin won my case, and I was given an Honorable Discharge. He uncovered the plot to discredit me, but due to National Security, it couldn't be made public. But the families involved still hold me accountable.

"They've been known to stir up old wounds from time to time. Letters, editorials in the press, and the Internet with its far-reaching exposure. Lots of potential damage could be caused. So there's always the potential for this to come back and bite me when I least expect it. Officially, there's only the Honorable Discharge on my service record, but it's all the rot underneath that haunts me.

"There's no way I ever want you to be unknowingly tainted with this if you're associated with me. And there's always the possibility it could affect any cases you might take on—if we were to be partners, that is."

"Paul, you listen to me. What's past is past, and now

that I know what might possibly crop up in the future...well, then we can *both* handle it. Deal?"

Visibly relieved, he brightened. "Does this mean you've come to a conclusion about my suggestion?"

She nodded affirmatively and nudged his shoulder. "I think we'll work well. After the ground rules are agreed upon, of course."

"You're really sure? You don't want to reconsider now, after what I've just told you?"

"I've no doubt in my mind at all."

"You've no idea how much better I feel. I should have told you a while ago, but there never seemed the right moment."

Dorothy just smiled.

Paul hugged her. "Enough chit chat then. Let's clean up so we can call it a night."

She stood up and waited for him to do the same, but he appeared to waver for a moment.

"One more thing Dee. Can you sit back down for just a minute, please."

Puzzled, she complied and watched as he stood and came to face her.

"I have something I'd like to give you."

Her eyes widened as she watched him reach into his pocket. "You're not going to go on bended knee now, are you?"

Momentarily confused, he didn't answer right away. But as it dawned on him, he grinned. "I don't think you need me on my knees for this, but I hope you'll like it, anyway." And, with that, he unclenched his hand to reveal a smooth brown-and-yellow stone bird.

Dorothy reached for the object. "Oh, it's beautiful," she exclaimed as she stroked the exquisite carving. "It's a quail, isn't it?"

"Very good, Sherlock. I picked it up a while ago

when wandering through Chinatown. It made me think of you."

"Really? Why?"

"It's jade, which is kind of appropriate, but I was told that a quail symbolizes courage and tenacity. Characteristics I most admire in you."

At a loss for words, she merely said, "Thank you."

"Let's invite Jim and Ashley here for dinner tomorrow to celebrate our decision to partner up, what do you think?"

"Sounds like a plan. I enjoy being with them, and it'll be a good way to tie up loose ends."

"Great, I'll call them tomorrow."

ତ⁄ନତ⁄ନ

Over a hearty breakfast the next morning, discussions centred on the changes to their lives and new business arrangements.

"I think we need a business name first don't you?" Dorothy asked as she sipped at her cafe latte,

"How about Webster and Dennehy?"

"No, no. I don't think so. No, that definitely won't work." The wounded expression on Paul's face sent Dorothy into stitches. "I was thinking more like 'Dennehy and Hired Help."

He chuckled. "Is that what you think of me? And you'd be willing to sleep with the help?"

"I'll accept that offer, but we need a good image and name for our business. Here's a question. Are we willing to accept assignments outside the country?"

"I don't see why not, so Webster International—and Help from Dennehy?"

A sausage flew across the table to land squarely in Paul's orange juice.

Laughing, he conceded defeat. "Okay, okay. Point taken."

A look of contemplation replaced the mischievous grin on her face. "Here's an idea. Quail International—Investigations and Security."

Paul sipped at his coffee as he considered the name. "Brilliant, I love it. And what if we use that little quail as our logo?"

"Perfect! Now I know why I love you—you think like me."

A Cheshire cat couldn't have grinned any wider.

ↄ৵ↄ৵ↄ

Dinner that evening found Paul and Dorothy taking a break from bar duties to enjoy a meal with Jim and Ashley. After learning about Quail International, Ashley offered her support on the international angle.

"I've lots of contacts and would be more than willing to keep you in mind if something comes up that could use your expertise. Your company's reputation and with Paul on board...well, after watching you two work together, I know you'll be an awesome team."

Jim raised his wine to clink glasses in a toast. "Let's have a toast to Quail International. Look out, bad guys, here they come."

Dorothy grinned. "Thanks, both of you. We appreciate what you did for us during the investigation," she said "Right now our fledgling business is still in the planning stages, and we have much to consider. It's a new beginning for both of us, and we've decided to go slow. Perhaps a long vacation and leave HB and Dad in charge of the domestic stuff."

"Oh, does that mean a wedding and honeymoon to plan," Ashley quipped. "I just love weddings."

"You can hold off buying the toaster, Ashley," Paul said, as he reached for Dorothy's hand. "Now that Dee and I have found each other, we have all the time in the world."

"He's right," Dorothy. agreed "For now, though, I'll be happy to close this case with all the details put to bed. Any news on the fabric, or pray tell, what's happening to my friend Victor?"

"Before we tell you about Lau and company and other details, we have something for you," Jim said.

Rummaging around in a large shopping bag at her feet, Ashley produced a flat box wrapped in fabric which resembled the kimonos Kimi and Yoko had been wearing.

Speechless, they silently took the offered box. Maxwell's was busy and music played lightly in the background, but it was as if they were all alone as they turned the package this way and that to inspect the material.

"A fitting reminder of recent events," Paul said.

"I think you should call your first two girls Kimi and Yoko and if you have boys—" Ashley had a reputation as a joker.

"No, no. Not Victor and Dominic. Please no," Dorothy begged, convulsing with laughter.

Amid the laughter, Jim cajoled them to unwrap the box.

"Oh, this is simply gorgeous!" Dorothy gazed in delight at the beautiful watercolor of two Japanese ladies wearing kimonos complete with fans and parasols.

The new business partners gave hugs all around.

Jim chuckled. "Just to set the record straight. This present's from Ashley and me to thank you for your help cracking this case, and your friendship. The FBI's not in the habit of handing out thank you gifts."

They settled down with dessert and coffee. Many patrons of Maxwell's had left for the evening, and only a few diehards sat at the bar. The foursome moved over to sit near the dying embers in the stone fireplace, where they were supplied with cognac and coffee.

"Okay, Jim, stop stalling. I know you said you had some more news for us," Dorothy prompted. "Spit it out, or I'll burst. Was there much more to learn, other than we already know?"

Jim took his time as he relayed what was happening to Victor Lau. "You have an impatient partner on your hands Paul," Jim teased. "It's no surprise that Victor has surrounded himself with some very powerful lawyers, who are working on his behalf to set him free. He claims he was duped by the Qus and wasn't party to what he's being charged with. The FBI is treading lightly at present because he's not an American citizen, and there may be diplomatic repercussions. They tell me he struts about his cell like a peacock. Must be a little cramped in there with the man and his ego. The Qus are another story. He'll definitely be going away for a long time—there's so much evidence against him—but Lily...well, she's been diagnosed with terminal cancer and won't be able to stand trial."

They were quiet for a few minutes contemplating Lily's fate.

"The cloth wrapping we gave you today isn't the same that was Henry Yamada's shroud, you'll be glad to know. Ashley hunted it down in Chinatown."

"Come on, Jim," Paul said, "you're driving me crazy. What did you find in the material that covered poor Henry?"

"Remember that Henry was slowly being poisoned. When he finally succumbed, they wrapped him in a bolt of the same counterfeit fabric Yashito knew about. Lab tests had already confirmed the manufacturing process

used a toxic dye, but they've now discovered a component not unlike formaldehyde was incorporated into it.
The combination would have made it a deadly garment
for anyone wearing it, especially if it got wet. So, apparently, that's what kept Henry's body in the state we found
him.

"No doubt the scientists working on this will find
out, sooner or later, exactly how this chemical stew was
incorporated. In the meantime, what evidence we have
will be used in the courts against Lau and Qu. Maybe
they'll find out before they even enter a courtroom. It's
always nice to tie up loose ends. Right, Dorothy?"

She raised her glass of cognac and smiled.

ᥱᢇᥱᢇᥱ

In the days following their stint as barkeeps for Max,
Dorothy and Paul cocooned at Paul's home. The cases
she'd taken on were minor and left in the capable hands
of HB. They spent their time learning more about each
other and planning their future. It was not without its ups
and downs, as both were independent and strong willed.

"Must be the Irish in her," Max commented, after
overhearing one of their heated conversations. "You
know, the red hair and all."

They'd been preparing a meal for Max and Alanna,
and lots of grumbling came from the kitchen.

"You're awfully restless this evening," Paul said, as
he carried a bowl of steaming clams into the dining room.

"Come on, eat up while it's still hot. This is my specialty," Dorothy said, ignoring the comment.

She added another bowl with pasta and a tray of
sliced Italian bread to mop up the sauce. As they tackled
the wonderful dinner, all were aware that she hadn't answered Paul's question.

Max placed his fork beside his plate and dabbed at his mouth. "I think I know why my little girl is so restless," he observed as he gazed at his beloved daughter. "She needs to get back to work. Am I right, darlin'?"

"Well, yes and no, Dad. Paul and I needed this time, but I have to admit I'm not used to being pampered and lazing around. However, I might have a remedy for that."

"Do you mean to say you don't like being taken care of?" Alanna asked.

"I'm just not the kind of person who likes lying around, and neither is Paul. Dad, you're quite right. We need to get going with the business, and I have the perfect venue to get us up and running."

"And what's that, Dee? More Victor Lau's on the horizon?"

"No, no case at the moment, but I had some correspondence today. It was from the International Federation of Private Investigators with details of their annual convention. I go every year, so what better way to introduce Quail International."

"That sounds great, Dorothy," Paul agreed. "We can network and find contacts to get the ball rolling. When is it?"

"In just a few weeks, so we'd better book our flights and register. I'll know a few people there and can't wait to introduce my new partner."

Max and Alanna smiled. "You didn't tell us where the conference is taking place, dear heart," Max complained. "Maybe Alanna and I can join you for a few days."

"Oh, didn't I tell you? It's in New York." She took a deep breath. "You know? My old stomping grounds."

About the Author

Jamie Tremain was "born" in the summer of 2007. A collaborative effort brought about by two fledgling authors Pam Blance and Liz Lindsay—work colleagues who happened to share a love of reading and writing—the natural next step was to try their hand at creating a story of their own.

Attending workshops and writing conferences, as well as blogging about their journey, has helped them along the way to hone their craft. As Jamie Tremain, they have worked hard to be a visible presence in the writing community, where encouragement and support are golden. It's been quite the adventure and the best is yet to come!